RECKLESS RULES

THE ELITES OF WEIS-JAMESON PREP ACADEMY

REBEL HART

Photo by Sara Eirew Photographer

Cover by Robin Harper of Wicked By Design

www.RebelHart.net

PROLOGUE

I wasn't here to fuck around at the Arcadia Invitational. I was seeded 17th in the Girls 300 Meter hurdles, and I was here to kick ass and take names.

I looked to my left. Carly Richardson was the girl I needed to beat to get to the finals. Our times were milliseconds from each other. Our lanes were four and five, and I was ready to ignite like fire out of the blocks. Coach had told me that I didn't have the acceleration to outrun her in the first 100 meters. I needed to outlast her in the last 100. I watched her jump, slap her thighs and sail through her pre-race routine. Her muscles rippled with effort.

Okay. Enough bullshitting.

I cracked my neck, did a couple jumps, high knees.

Adrenaline pumped through my veins, visceral and real, and my heart rate was elevated. I took a couple calming breaths.

Okay, Ophelia. I told myself. The official mounted. It was time to get into the blocks. I did another jump, feeling my legs quiver like jelly. I slapped them. *No.* Now was not the time for nerves to make me weak.

I was a fucking bull.

Just before I knelt to my knees on the track, I glanced at the sidelines. Coach was there, giving me a stern look. His look of determination fueled me with confidence. We'd worked on my kick for the last 100 so many times these past weeks. He'd pushed me to my very breaking point. My mouth tingled with the remnant tang of vomit – if I did this right, I'd beat Carly. I knew what I was supposed to do. My gaze drifted to my mother and my step-dad who were pressed against the railing, smiling.

And then, there *he* was.

My stomach dropped. He was looking at me like he was hungry.

Over the past two days, I kept seeing him. He wasn't a competitor, but his muscles strained against his shirt. Fit. Just how I liked them. His dark hair was artfully tousled. And his light-colored eyes kept finding mine across the crowd. It was as if everywhere I turned, my eyes found his form like a magnet. Behind me in the bleachers, waiting at the concession stand, drinking at the water fountain. Basically everywhere. Something about him told me there was something not *quite right* with him being here. But try telling that to my hormones and that fucking dream I had last night...

The guy smirked, and my body flooded with heat.

Fuck.

I couldn't be distracted.

I settled my feet into the blocks. A rush of familiarity calmed me. These were just like the blocks at my high school. Though Nike was branded across them, they served the same purpose.

I tensed, waiting for that gun shot. Waiting for my time to spring. A sense of calm soothed my whirring brain, and my body stilled, tensed, waiting. This was instinctual. This was mechanical. And I was waiting...waiting.

"You did great," came a voice from behind me.

I froze. My body, already weak and tired and achy and sweaty, clamped up. I whirled around, my bags swinging, and my eyes met *his.*

He was even more perfect in person. He had thick dark lashes that framed his stormy gray eyes. His lips were plump – totally kissable. And they were curled into a panty-dropping smirk. His face wasn't quite symmetrical, but the crooked nose and thicker bottom lip added to his edgy look.

"Thanks," I said, trying to keep the bitterness out of my voice. "I didn't make it to finals, but yeah."

Just thirty minutes ago, I had run my fucking heart out. I wanted to make it to finals so bad, I could fucking taste it. I'd had my eyes trained on Carly, and I passed her right at the 200-meter mark like Coach and I had planned out last night. But then, out of nowhere, some girl in lane 8 put on the blasters and passed both Carly and me right at the finish line.

She'd run a personal record of 41.55 seconds. Enough to slide her into the finals and boot Carly and me to the curb.

I'd exited the field, given my mom and stepdad a hug, talked to Coach about what went wrong, and then escaped to the girls room to avoid everyone. I'd sat in the last stall sullenly, listening to the flushes of toilets and the chatter of happy people.

I was so fucking disappointed. And angry.

I'd found a quiet corner against the back of the stadium. I just needed like ten minutes to myself to compose my face before I confronted my family and Coach again.

Until *he* had found me. Mr. Mysterious Good Looking.

"You're only a junior," he said. "You've got next year to make it up."

I jerked my chin up, narrowing my eyes at him. "Stalk much?"

"When I see a pretty girl? Nah, I just use the roster." He smiled as he pulled up a crumbled roster from his pocket. He offered it to me, but I declined. "Suit yourself."

I sighed. "Yeah, but who knows what will happen next year. I probably won't have enough money to go here again."

Bitterness soured my words. My body pulsed with irritation, disappointment and sadness. It crushed my soul to not be good enough. I clenched my jaw and let out an irritated growl.

"Ridiculous," I muttered to myself.

"Mmm," he said, nodding and pursing his bottom lip. For a moment, my eyes fixated on that lip. I wanted to bite it. Every nerve in me was short-circuited either from desire or anger, and I didn't know if I wanted to punch the wall or kiss him. "That makes sense. Kinda unfair though."

"Life's unfair," I ground out, shrugging my bag farther up my shoulder. "That's how it is."

"I'm Emmett, by the way" the guy said, extending his hand. I eyed the heavy veins that snaked down his arm to the back of his hand. I took it, delighting in the shivers creeping up my arm as his warm fingers enclosed around mine. "And you are?"

"You already know," I snapped, then realized I was being a dick. *I shouldn't take my disappointment out on him.* I smiled up at him. "But Ophelia. Ophelia Lopez."

"A pleasure," he said, bringing up my hand and brushing his lips against the backs of my knuckles. My stomach dropped. *Holy fuck.*

His gesture was old-fashioned. But holy fuck, it was sexy.

And it made the swirling knot of disappointment and anger in my chest dissipate with the press of his lips.

Our hands dropped but remained entwined by the fingers. Flickers of warmth skated across my chest, and I stared at Emmett. Why was I responding so strongly to him? This was insane. His eyes, I noticed, were dark, forbidding, like the Midwestern storms I was all too familiar with in the middle of buttfuck Oklahoma.

"So what are you doing here?" I asked, looking at him under my lashes. "You aren't a runner."

He stepped closer, and a delicious scent of expensive cologne filled my nostrils. Who was he? He gave off a different vibe than I was expecting. Something more...suspicious.

"I'm supporting my little brother," he said. His fingers left my hand and trailed up the inside of my wrist. I sucked in a sharp breath. With my response, he stepped closer, and an electrical current built between us. "But that's not important."

Suddenly, his elbows were positioned by my head, his face leaning close to mine. His masculine scent flooded my nostrils – heavenly. I pressed back against the stadium wall, shocked at how my body both wanted to be next to his and far away. His eyes raked my face, and I couldn't decipher the expressions in them. Curiosity, desire...and something else churned in the icy depths.

I jerked when warm fingers touched my cheek. His eyes heated. But my body was frozen, wanting more of his touch, craving it. His fingers trailed along the cut of my jaw, fiery tingles. I'd thought about this last night, dreamt of kissing the hot guy who kept popping up, but this was real. His body before me was real and warm and – my hand unstuck itself from the wall and trailed itself across his pectorals – hard.

"You're different and odd," I said, licking my dry lips. There was something just *off* about him. I couldn't pinpoint any outward sign or anything that told me this. But I felt it. "But I like it."

He made a small sound in the back of his throat. He grabbed my wandering hand and placed a soft kiss on the inside of my palm. The tender touch zapped me out of my stupor.

"Let me kiss you," he said, locking eyes with mine. He was demanding rather than asking. "Let me."

My mouth dropped in astonishment, drawing his heated gaze. He stared at my lips like an addict.

I should have said no.

But what was the harm?

My hormones were practically begging me to kiss him.

So I went up on my tiptoes and touched my lips to his. It was a small connection of flesh, but my senses went haywire, my body lighting up like a firecracker.

"Fuck," he murmured against my mouth. His hand wound into my hair, tilting my heated face toward his. His gray eyes were delirious with desire, and my breaths came in short pants at just his taste. "You taste fucking delicious."

His lips came down on mine again, and he deepened the kiss, opening my lips, sucking, nipping. Heat poured off him in waves. The kiss turned demanding, and I grabbed his soft shirt to press him against me. I whimpered into his mouth as his kiss sent me skyrocketing.

Emmett kissed like he was confused. His lips were soft, but as he grabbed for my body, his fingers dug into my sides. Almost punishing. Almost brutal. But I rolled with it, matching each sweep of his tongue with mine.

"Ophelia!" came my mother's voice.

I shoved Emmett away, finding my mother's shocked face over his shoulder. *Oh shit.* Coach, my stepdad Brendan and my mother were staring at me with a mixture of confusion, disappointment, and amusement.

"Sorry," I said to them, wiggling past Emmett's still form and walking up to the trio."I got distracted."

"I'll say," Coach said, fixing Emmett with a glare. "You look like a tomato."

I brushed my hot cheeks with the back of my hand. I decided to roll with it and dismiss their ogling. "Whatever. I just needed to get it out of my system."

But as I walked away from Emmett, I felt his heavy gaze on the nape of my neck. Shivers wracked my body and I ached to run back and finish what we had started. I couldn't help it – I sent a backward glance to where Emmett lounged against the stadium wall. When our eyes met, a flash of desire took hold of me.

Emmett was decidedly *not* out of my system. I shouldered my bag again, trying to brush off the sexual images burned in my brain.

Well, he needed to get out of my system. I was heading back to Oklahoma, and I wouldn't see him again.

1

CHAPTER ONE

I hate running.

I do.

It's painful. It's hard. It's monotonous.

But then again, there's always been some sort of thrill, some sense of accomplishment that I feel when I push myself to the brink of passing out. It makes my thoughts numb, everything focused on pulling my burning muscles forward, expanding my heaving chest, and feeling the sweat trickle down my back or off the bridge of my nose.

So maybe, yeah, I fucking *love* running.

I love the sweet satisfaction that comes from every cell in my body burning with this intense heat.

I love the pain.

I love the delirious effect of a good race.

I love the sound of my feet slapping concrete, track rubber, grass, dirt.

I love that however I do in a particular moment boils down to me. There is nobody responsible for my failures or successes other than *me.* I am the sole determinant of how good or bad I perform.

I'm damn good at running. Just not *that* good. I'm nationally ranked in the top 50 of the Girls 300 Meter Hurdles. Thoughts of the Arcadia Invitational sour my steps. Even though it was months ago, I still can't get it out of my head. Just how hard do I need to work to run those thoughts out of my head?

Too hard.

I shake off the tendrils of disappointment that threaten to falter my stride. I obviously wasn't ready to go to finals. Nameless Lane 9 had showed up to kick my ass in gear.

Today's a long day. Seven miles.

I usually don't mind the length. Back in Oklahoma, I switched between three different routes depending on what Coach ordered. However, I'm not in Oklahoma anymore. And the streets of Jameson, Massachusetts are unfamiliar and sometimes bricked. They are windy, confusing and different. But I like the change in scenery.

As I race through unfamiliar streets, the houses get

more impressive and old, and I think about the surprising turn of events following Arcadia.

Not a week after the meet, I'd received a phone call from the Headmaster of Weis-Jameson Preparatory Academy. He had an offer that made my jaw drop. A full-ride scholarship if I attended my senior year at WJ Prep. A little digging and I was hooked; their track and field program was nationally ranked, and they churned out an Olympic athlete every couple years. Their coach, David Granger, was legendary. A former Olympian hurdler himself, he'd gotten bronze back in his heyday.

Mom couldn't believe it. She'd grown up in Jameson when she was little – she hadn't been back for twenty years. She'd actually attended WJ Prep herself, where she'd met my bio-dad.

It didn't take a lot of convincing to move. Mom's ties to Jameson plus my scholarship and the opportunity to train under a former Olympian… Fuck, I could be set for life with just this one year stint at WJ prep.

And now I'm here. A week before the semester starts. In a strange town with the opportunity of my life. Pre-season workouts would start a couple weeks in, but David had emailed a 'suggested' workout. He wasn't technically able to supervise practice so early before the season starts in February.

Jameson is hilly, and I'm not used to hills. I push

myself, feeling the remnants of my strength ebb as I struggle to put one leg in front of the other. With another right, I face an ornate gate: Crescent Hills, it reads. And holy *fuck* do these bitches have money.

I slow my pace, entering the community. The homes I pass get bigger and bigger as I go along. Immaculately landscaped yards feature fountains, perfect grass, trimmed hedges and sparkling driveways. Each one is breathtaking – clearly, this is the Mansion District. Many have gates across their drives, which lead up to columned porches framing massive wood or glass doors. Large stone potted plants decorate the porches, and I wonder what else these luxurious homes could be hiding behind their large windows and rooftop terraces.

As I run, each house rises into the backs of the mountain, and the road winds higher and higher. The steep elevation crucifies my legs. Jesus. My breath is painful, ripping an agonizing tear through my chest each time I inhale. What if I stopped here? I'm close enough to halfway.

I pause at a bend in the road. It overlooks the city before winding behind me, to further houses buried into the hills. Excuse me. *Mansions.*

Jameson sprawls below me. It is lit by the waning late summer light. I take a moment to bounce on my toes, feeling sweat dry on my calves as a cool breeze hit me. It's a gorgeous place, that I can admit. My town back in Oklahoma was flat, with concrete buildings and concrete roads and concrete fences. It was a concrete jungle, with little style and no beauty points. Only in the spring months did the flowers contrast the gray.

Time to go.

I start down the hill, letting gravity doing most of the work. Ahead, the first car that I've seen emerges, slowly driving toward me. It's a fucking fancy car. I stare at it. It glimmers a fire engine red, and as I get closer I notice the Lamborghini logo.

Fuck, these people are hella rich.

Suddenly, the car revs. It beelines toward me. A rush of red. The engine roars. A loud engine. It barrels down. Its lights aren't on, I notice. I can barely register what's happening before I dive out of the way. My foot dings the headlight as the car swerves just at the last second.

I land in the ditch. My feet are instantly soaked from the days-old water. Tremors shake my legs as I inch myself down to the sweet, sweet ground.

They just tried to run me over!

Cold adrenaline shocks my system.

I could have died.

"Oh my fucking gawd," screams a high-pitched voice.

A wafer-thin girl appears above me. Her manicured nails are gripping her sharp hipbones, and she looks *pissed.* Her honey-blonde hair falls in heavy curls, and her face is Instagram-beautiful. Her pouty lips are curled into a sneer.

"You fucking dinged my car, bitch," she says.

I frown. She's wearing a pencil skirt and pink blouse. But she looks my age, around seventeen.

"Your car?" I ask. The red sports car is pulled over, idling. There's another girl lounging on the trunk. Her red hair is pulled back into a severely high bun, her lips as red as blood. She's also beautiful, but in a kinder, softer way. "The one that tried to run me over?"

"Don't get smart with me, bitch."

I start to stand up, but before I can even register movement, her platformed heel hits my shoulder. Hard. I tumble down, my butt landing in the water. A sharp pain radiates up my arm. A breath stills in my throat as I pull my hand up, cradling my wrist.

Great. Now I'm soaking wet and my wrist is sprained.

"What the fuck, bitch?" I snarl, pulling myself out of the ditch. She's shorter than me by a couple inches, and I've got at least twenty pounds of muscle on her. She doesn't look as intimidating now. Her blue eyes, still haughty, flash with momentary fear. "What's your problem?"

"Vivian and I are just needing to clean up the white trash in the street," she snaps. "So next time you go running, make sure to watch where you're going."

She turns on a heel, stalking back to her car.

"Who the fuck do you think you are?" I call after her. My wrist throbs. Goddammit. I'd just gotten over a thigh strain, and I was looking forward to running without pain for once. "Hey, you!"

"I'm sorry," said the red-haired one. Vivian. Yeah, the name suits her. She purred with disgust. "We don't acknowledge dripping garbage."

They pile into the car. Then reverse. I jump out of the way, glaring daggers at them. The girl who shoved me rolls down the window.

"What is your fucking problem?" I ask. "Who are you?"

"Oh, you'll learn about us pretty soon," says the girl named Vivian. She leans across the console, giving me a patronizing wink. Her eyelashes are so heavily layered in mascara, it's a wonder she can even keep her eyelids open. "Very soon."

"Look, new girl. I know *all* about you," says the girl in the driver's seat. "And you're going to wish you'd never even heard of WJ Prep."

"Why do you care?" I ask.

"You're scholarship scum. And if I ever see you running through *my* neighborhood again... " She breaks off with a laugh then fixes me with a glare that turns my insides cold. She smiles, her tone now hauntingly playful. "I won't miss you next time. Ta-Ta!"

With a peal of tires, she spins out, the red lambo taking off down the street with a scream. The smell of exhaust lingers in the air.

I stand there for a few moments, letting the waning sun bake my feverish skin. My heart rate calms its erratic pounding. I close my eyes and tilt my head up to the sky. What the heck just happened? Suddenly, all the beautiful houses I had been passing look ominous. It could be a combination of the darkening sky or the recent interaction I'd just had, but I notice that the windows are dark. Of nearly all the beautiful houses, only a few have their lights on.

The need to leave strikes me. I start running again. My wrist has recovered somewhat, but each jarring step reminds me that I'll need to ice it tonight.

Who was that girl? And how did she know who I was?

My step-dad, Brendan, is cooking dinner when I arrive home. It smells heavenly, and my stomach is growling.

"Hey, Dad," I say, giving him a kiss on his gruff cheek. "Whatcha making?"

"Hey, Ophelia. Spaghetti and meatballs," he says, looking at the timer on the oven."Just a little over ten minutes on the meatballs. Sauce is simmering. Hand me that packet of pasta by your left hand. Please."

I do as he asks. "Here. I need to shower."

"Yeah ya' do," he says, not looking at me. He's a focused cook, and I can't help but smile when he says, "You absolutely *reek.*"

"Thanks," I call out sarcastically. Brendan has been my dad since I was ten, though he's been with my mom much longer than that. He's more of my dad than my bio-dad, who I've never met and who I never really want to meet. He skipped out on my mom just months after I was born.

Brendan is a large teddy bear. His physically imposing form throws some people off – not to mention his tattoo sleeves and scruffy beard. But in my entire life, I've never once considered him anything other than my dad, and he's loved me as he would a daughter.

The duplex we are renting has two bedrooms and one bath, but it's cozy and recently renovated. I grab my shower stuff and a change of clothes before hitting the shower. The hot water works out all my knots. But the strange, uneasy feeling that's twisted in my gut doesn't go away. As I towel off, the blonde girl's cruel smile flashes in my mind.

Next time I won't miss.

Jesus, what kind of girl goes around threatening to run people over?

Apparently rich and entitled assholes.

My wrist aches a little, so I pop a couple aspirin from the cabinet. After I change, I join Brendan in the kitchen.

"When's Mom getting off?" I ask.

"Her shift ends at 8:30, so pretty soon."

As a Registered Nurse, Mom sometimes works odd hours. But she was able to get a job lined up at Golden Hills Community Medical Center even before we left Oklahoma. For the past week, she's been in training. Brendan has a couple of interviews lined up this week. There was always a demand for an Electrical Power-Line guy, but I can tell he is getting antsy playing domestic.

I play with my phone as Brendan finishes up cooking. He hands me a plate and I fill up. The first thing we did when we moved in was to finish unpacking the kitchen. Mom doesn't like eating off plastic plates.

"How was your run?" he asks around a mouthful of meatball.

"Horrible," I say before I can catch myself.

He frowns, concerned. I've never been super negative about my workouts before. "How so?"

"Some asshole teenagers tried to run me over," I say. "Fucking teenage little shits."

"You are a teenager."

I roll my eyes. "Are you missing the larger point, here?"

"Did you get the license plate?"

"No, I was too shocked to do anything. She also got out of her car and shoved me into a fucking ditch and I sprained my wrist." I stab a meatball viciously. "And now I'm going to have to work out around a fucking sprained wrist and I was *just* getting over my strained hamstring."

"Where were you?"

"Crescent Hills. Apparently the place for rich people."

"You know who it was?"

"Nooope," I say, extending the word with irritation. I stab another meatball and fit the whole thing in my mouth. "Ah, ah, hot hot hot!" I chew with an open mouth and swallow the meat when I can. I take a gulp of milk. "But if it helps, she drove a flaming hot red Lamborghini."

Brendan snorts around his beer. "A kid? Jesus, no kid needs such an expensive car. That insurance must be through the roof!"

Practical Brendan. Thinking about things in terms of money. "Like how much?"

"An insane amount. I know we spend 450 a year for you with your Good Student Discount. I can't imagine adding a teenager to an insurance policy with a Lambo on it."

There's a rustling at the door, and Mom enters, carrying several grocery bags.

"Ophelia," she says, stumbling over to the counter. "There's several more bags in the back."

I grumble but oblige, heading outside in my stockinged feet. I grab the rest and let the door slam behind me.

"Ooh, meatballs," I hear my mother say. "What's the special occasion?"

"I figured Ophelia's first day at school is celebration enough," says Brendan. I enter right as they kiss, and hide my smile.

Brendan is huge. My mother is decidedly *not.* She's full on Mexican-American – thick black hair, tanned skin and short. She passed on her light-brown eyes to me, though I inherited my height and athleticism from my wayward bio-dad. When my parents kiss, Brendan has to hunch to reach her lips.

I have always found it comical. With my mom barely reaching five foot and Brendan well over six-four, they're quite a pair.

"Okay, okay," I say, "Let's eat. I almost got ran over today and I'm not feeling very in tune with the world right now and just want to eat my spaghetti."

"What?" Mom rounds on me, her eyes widening in surprise. She's still in her blue scrubs, and she rushes up to me. "Are you hurt?"

"Nope," I say. She hugs me like I'm the last life-saver in the ocean. "It's fine. It was a one-time incident."

It takes some time to convince Mom that yes, I'm unhurt, and yes, I'm not going to run through Crescent Hills again. She finally calms down enough so we can finish eating. I have to reheat my food in the microwave, piling on seconds. As I wait, my phone buzzes on the counter.

I look at the number.

Unknown. (617)-722-0000.

I watch it ring until it stops. It's not from Massachusetts, but something nags me in the back of my brain. I frown.

"Something wrong, Ophelia?" asks Mom.

My phone buzzes with a Missed Call Notification. I watch it to see if a message will pop up. "No," I answer. I take my plate out of the microwave. "Motherfucker!"

"Ophelia!"

"Sorry," I say, waving my hand in the air. My fingers burn. "The plate was hot."

As I join my parents at the table again, I stick my phone in my pocket. It vibrates against my thigh. I sneak a peek.

The Unknown Number has texted me: "Ophelia."

A cold chill spreads through my chest. No way. It has to be that fucking bitch who tried to run me over. I'm almost certain of it.

"Sorry," I say, pulling my phone onto the table. My mother has a strict no-phone policy when we're eating together. I see her eyebrows dip in disapproval, but I'm too busy deleting the text message and blocking the number to care.

Whoever that girl was – and her stupid friend Vivian – I'm not going to let them get to me. Never mind how they got my number or know who I am.

"So, Mom," I say, putting my phone back into my pocket. "Tell me about your day."

As Mom talks about her first full day of work, my mind runs at a million miles an hour. Tomorrow is my first day at WJ Prep, and for some reason, these two rich girls hate me. It wasn't getting off to a great start, but I was sure they would forget me by tomorrow. Don't rich girls have attention spans like goldfish? I'm sure I read that somewhere. Besides, I'm only here to run and get good grades. I don't want to make a stir, and if I stay out of their way, they'll stay out of mine.

My fingers play along the screen of my phone. My unease returns. How did they find my number so quickly? A chilling feeling settles over my skin. Suddenly, I'm not excited to attend school tomorrow.

2

CHAPTER TWO

Weis-Jameson Preparatory Academy is a private Catholic school.

The tuition? It'll replace the cost of a nice new Honda Accord with *all* the nice finishings.

The endowment? In the millions.

It's not surprising that given the cost of attendance is so high, only around five-hundred students 9th-12th grade attend. From what I read on their website, tuition-waiver scholarships are rare.

I've never worn a uniform in my life. A couple days ago, a large box with my name on it appeared on the front door. Inside it was the most uncomfortable apparel I've ever seen. I live and breathe athletic and comfortable. When I opened the box, I was greeted with five sets of pants and skirts, two "spirit" tees, three different types of jackets and cardigans and four uniform polo shirts. Each top had a monogramed WJ logo on it.

They were a surprisingly good fit. Clearly they'd taken my size from the publicity photos at the meets. But still uncomfortable.

I sit in my car in the parking lot – the lady at the front desk instructed me to park in the visitors' lot until I got assigned a space. This morning was hot, and I put on the khaki skirt and blue polo shirt.

I regret choosing something that exposes so much skin. I should have bundled up. The students... They are intimidating at first glance. The ones streaming by my car to enter the cavernous front of WJ Prep somehow look cooler than I do.

I watch them, fingering the hem of my skirt. What makes them different? Is it the stylized bags the girls have draped over their forearm? Is it the one-hundred-dollar hair-cuts the boys are sporting?

It's like I've entered a different universe where everyone is gorgeous and perfect and look cut out from a magazine. At my old school in Oklahoma, the dress-code was whatever you could get away with. Miniskirts, crop tops, see-through leggings, fishnets, baggy pants, wife-beaters, baseball caps – anything went so long as you avoided the stricter teachers in the hall.

I steel my nerves. Okay, so I'm uncomfortable. The

tag of my polo itches my neck. My beat-up sneakers are a far cry from those expensive-looking ballet flats that girl is sporting.

But so what. I'm here to run.

I open my car door and step into the throng, making my way to the front office. When they'd offered me the scholarship, I'd done a campus visit. I'm not as in awe this time as I walk through the sparkling glass doors and enter the office.

There's a slew of students hanging around the front desk, so I join a line.

"Ophelia Lopez," I say to the secretary. Her manicured nails type my name into the system.

"Your liaison is Jason," she says, handing me a freshly printed schedule. "He'll take you around to all your classes today."

"Jason?" I echo.

"That's me," comes a masculine voice behind me.

I turn around. Jason is tall, intimidating and *angry.* A flicker of unease builds in my belly. Who spat on his cornflakes? His eyes flick up and down my figure before landing on mine with disgust. He's got a shock of blonde hair that's shorn on the sides, and his face is thin, pinched.

He almost reminds me of Draco Malfoy. I want to see his sneer to confirm.

He snatches my schedule out of my hands. "What's

your first class?" He groans, then shoots me a look of contempt. "Fucking Calculus. Way on the opposite side of where my class is."

Jason's bitter attitude sours my expression. "What is your deal?" I demand, grabbing my schedule back. He takes off, presumably to direct me to the Math wing, and doesn't answer.

"I'm Ophelia," I say to his back.

"I don't care," he growls. Suddenly, he whirls around, his hand finding my chest and shoving me back. I stumble into a girl, who glares at me.

What is wrong with the people at this school?

Jason steps close, but I stand my ground. I can't let these people see that I'm weak. This is obviously some sort of first day harassment.

"Look, New Girl-"

"Ophelia," I remind him.

"Tragic," he sneers flippantly. Boom. Draco Malfoy look-alike contest won. And I don't know if he's referring to the fact that my name is old and out-of-date or of the horrible, tragic fate of my namesake, Ophelia from *Hamlet.* "You'd best start to understand some rules around here."

"What's your policy on bullying?" I quip. "No-tolerance?"

His hand comes up again, but this time I dodge his shove. Fast reflexes thanks to track. But he cooly places it on the locker, leaning and bringing up his other hand to pick at his fingernails. Almost as if planned. *Smooth,* I think.

I glare at him. "Clearly not."

"There's a few things you need to learn," Jason says, ignoring my jab. His haughty look makes me roll my eyes. Where does he get off? "There's a hierarchy here. Older than you will ever understand. And we follow it to the 'T', just like our parents did, just like our grandparents did. And bumfucks like you, rednecks like you…." He leans in, but I jut my chin out. Even though I'm starting to feel ill about the absolute *loathing* in his eyes, I try to channel confidence. "Are at the very bottom."

"I don't care," I say. And part of me doesn't. But when his eyes flash darkly, I wonder if I said the right thing. "If *you* don't like me. I don't know what your fucking problem is, but you better check the attitude."

He barks a laugh, and its cruel edge lodges a sense of suspicion in my chest. "Oh, baby," he says, leaning in close. He smells delicious – a woodsy scent – and it's deceptive. "It's not me you need to worry about not liking you." His voice lowers, almost as if confiding a dark secret. "It's *them.* And if *they* don't like you, then nobody does."

Jason dropped me off at Calculus like it was a court-ordered community service act.

His sinister smile as he said, "Enjoy" made me feel like he wasn't talking to me but the bunch of wide-eyed rich kids I'd just stumbled on. When I walk through the desks to the back, each of them bends their head furiously over their phones. An eerie sixth sense tells me they were texting about *me.*

Lucky me, I think sardonically.

"Hey," I say, sitting down in the second to last row. The girl sitting next to me is pretty in a girlish type of way – round face, freckles and big green eyes. "I'm Ophelia."

"Hey," she says softly. She doesn't look at me though. Nor does she introduce herself. She looks at her desk like it's the most interesting desk in the world, that it will soon transform into a shuttle and blast her off into the moon.

That's how interested she is in that desk.

Okay, what the fuck. I've been the new kid in school before – before Oklahoma, Mom and I had lived in Kansas. But maybe fourth-graders are different than seniors, because clearly nobody is interested in being my friend.

Jason, those two girls last night... What vipers' nest have I stumbled into?

"What's wrong with this place?" I ask, pulling my backpack out and readying my supplies.

Her hazel-green eyes meet mine for the barest of seconds. "It's just how it is."

"Well, it's weird."

"You have no idea," she says, and she suddenly comes to life, twisting in her seat and motioning me closer. "It's basically hell."

"How so?"

She seems to war within herself, looking up to the class to see if anyone else was paying attention. "You know how this town was founded?"

"No."

"Well, okay." She pulls out a notebook and starts scribbling. In a few seconds, a diagram appears with lines and names.

The teacher walks in, and the girl's eyes glaze over. Something about him sets her off. She starts rapidly firing information so quickly and so quietly that I nearly cut myself in half leaning over the desk to hear her.

"Look, so the town is called Jameson. Basically they're the founders. The Jamesons, you know, back in the 1800s. And then, one of the Jameson sons got together with a bunch of other sons of these families" – she points to the words written: *Weis, Blackwater, Whitworth, Nikelson* – "And they created the Jameson Automobile Corporation. You know, luxury cars. Like, for the ultra-rich. Now, though, only these three"– she points to Blackwater, Whitworth and Jameson– "are still in town. And they've founded this school, and their children think they're God's Gift to Humanity."

"You're tripping."

She rips the piece of paper and hands it to me. "*Don't* get on their bad side."

She's circled many names and called them "The Elites". I almost want to snort – this is absurd! – but the serious look on her face makes me pause. I scan the list.

Emmett and Bernadette Jameson.

Vivian Blackwater.

Trey and Vincent Whitworth.

Understanding lights up inside me. Vivian Blackwater. No wonder she had such an ego complex last night – she's got a fancy little name and a fancy little history. But my bet is on Bernadette being the skinny bitch who almost run me over.

Things start to piece together.

"And where is Jason in all of this?" I ask.

The girl frowns. "Jason?"

"The guy with his stick up his ass."

Her lips wiggle wildly, as if she wants to smile but physically can't. What is up with this girl? She grabs my paper and scribbles some more words on it, just as the teacher starts talking to the class. I hadn't realized the tardy bell had rung.

"Satellite Elites – think of them as wingmen," she says, then turns in her seat and ignores me.

I inspect the paper. More words. More names. My head is spinning. The girl next to me – I still don't know her name – ignores me for the rest of class. I'm uneasy and on edge, and I can barely remember what the teacher has said. When the bell rings, I find Jason lounging outside the door, picking at his fingernails.

"That's a bad habit," I say, because I want to rile him. He's one of those Satellite Elites, and while I don't know what it means, I'm betting it means he's easily riled up.

"Shut your whore mouth," he says, "and follow me."

"Wow, good one," I say sarcastically.

But instead of getting angry, he smiles at me. And his smile is *sinister*, ominously spreading across his face.

Suddenly, understanding knocks me on the head. The weird phone call last night. Obviously these people have money at their disposal. Finding out my name and identity and contact information is probably easy when you have a tech army at your side.

The more I think on this, the more I realize I should probably delete my Facebook and Twitter accounts. I don't use them, but if they can easily find out who I am, then they can probably hack into my accounts. Safety first... But my Instagram account – I can't delete that. Probably should just change my password often.

"You're a good little whore," Jason says, dropping me off at my next class. "You kept quiet the whole way."

I throw him the bird and stalk into my class. Jason is the least of my worries now. I need to think of ways to protect myself.

I bury my head in my hands, and a little chuckle escapes my lips. What was I thinking? This is ridiculous. I was all wound up from that girl talking about a stupid hierarchy. The Elites. I chuckle again. What a fucking pretentious name. It wouldn't even work as a band name.

The morning passes quickly, and by the time it's lunch, I've pushed out all thoughts of The Elites from my mind. This was probably just first-day harassing. Nothing more. And Jason can suck my dick for all I care.

I stop by the girls' bathroom, taking a quick look in the mirror. I tried to style my chocolate brown hair nicely this morning, but the waves are now poofy in reminiscent eighties style. I redo my hair into a bun, applying chapstick and wiping away smudges from my mascara.

There's a piercing scream. "No, no, I'm sorry!"

My feet rush me into the hallway, and I'm met with a confusing scene. The girl from the morning is on the ground, covered in trash. One guy finishes dumping the trash-can over her, and I watch, horrified, and some nameless black sludge drips onto her head.

"I'm sorry, I'm sorry," she blubbers. "I was just trying to help her."

There are three boys. More like men than boys, as each one of them is tall and muscular from what I can tell of their backs. The one who throws the trash-can across the hall, he's the tallest, with dark blonde hair and a cruel glint to his eyes. Another one – a thick-shouldered guy, built like a footballer – grinds some sort of horrible concoction of trash, sludge and food into the girl's thigh with his foot. The girl doesn't do anything, whimpers escaping her mouth as she keeps her eyes closed.

"Please, I was just trying to let her know."

My shock dissipates, and I feel my limbs slowly thaw to life. Rage flows through me like lava, and I nearly sprint to the group, shoving away a guy and standing in front of the girl. I am nearly quivering with fury, and I feel loose, like a cannonball.

"What the fuck do you think you're doing?" I demand, giving them each a hard gaze.

Until. . .

Until I meet *his* eyes.

"*Emmett*-Emmett?" I stutter, looking into his beautiful gray eyes. They're as reckless and dangerous as a tornado storm. "Like Emmett from Arcadia?"

"I'm glad you remember, Ophelia," he says as his eyes rake over my body. Goosebumps pepper my skin as a hot coil of desire reaches low into my stomach. *Fuck.* "You haven't changed one bit."

"Arcadia was a couple months ago," I say, almost lost.

How can *Emmett* be here? My thoughts are beating against my brain, and a firestorm of emotions fight for dominance.

Emmett Jameson was one of these "Elites."

I'd tried to fuck him out of my system, but my hand didn't do the intense *need* that thrummed through my body justice. Each time my fingers ventured down there, his face popped into my mind. And I was left wanting the real thing.

And I hadn't remembered him clearly. He's as every bit as handsome, but his hair is now shorn on the sides and flipped to the right. I can feel my hormones taking over, quickening my blood at just the sight of his lips, wanting to tousle his hair with my fingers, feel him groan against me.

No, Ophelia.

There's a small sound behind me, and I look at the

girl struggling to stand up. I extend a hand, but she waves it off. I'm kinda glad – her hands look sticky and wet.

"Lily," says Emmett, his eyes never leaving mine. "You're free to go."

I open my mouth, but before I say anything, Emmett glares at me.

"You say one word and you'll end up like her." He whips his head to the sodden, trash-riddled Lily. Her mousey brown hair has a gum wrapper in it. "Come with me."

Okay, so Emmett is a hot fucking jerk.

"What the actual fuck," I say quietly, looking at the two guys who've now circled around me. Emmett pauses about ten feet away. "You're all fucking insane."

One of the guys, the footballer-built guy, cracks his neck. "You clearly don't know what's going on."

"Clearly," I say sarcastically. "I do. You're fucking bullies."

"Ophelia," says Emmett loftily. "You'll *follow* me, or Trey and Vincent will help you."

"I'm not going anywhere," I growl, and when I say this, something glints happily in Emmett's eyes. It is almost as if he was wanting me to deny him. "So fuck off."

Rough hands grab my shoulders, wrists, and suddenly I'm being pulled. My hurt wrist screams with pain. My feet dig into the tile but the two guys are too strong for me. With a yank, I'm jolted forward and only avoid falling on my face thanks to their death grip on my arms.

"Fucking hell, stop!" I scream. Panic bubbles into my chest. I seriously cannot get out of their hold. I struggle, trying to bend my arms this way and that. They're dragging me to a door, and a fresh burst of fear fuels me. I try to trip the one to my left, but he just laughs, grabbing my leg so I'm hopping on one. My skirt bunches against my hips and I'm certain I'm flashing Emmett, who waits inside with a smarmy grin.

"Stop stop stop, what the fuck?" My voice is breathless and panicked. Teeth! Why didn't I think of it before!

As I struggle, I bite down on a forearm. There's a yowl of pain, and suddenly I'm flying, weightless. Pain cracks my skull, and for a moment I'm dazed, feeling my body being dragged. Everything is fuzzy, and the dull click of a lock barely registers.

"Oh fuck," I say, touching my head gingerly. Before I can move, arms scoop under my armpits and haul my limp body up. My butt lands on papers and pens, but it's nothing compared to the headache I have. "Ow."

Warm hands press down on my thighs. Emmett appears in front of my face.

"Knock it off," he says harshly. "You didn't hit your head that hard."

"Fuck you," I growl through the haze.

I'm unprepared for the hand that grips my hair and yanks. Sharp pain radiates from my skull and I gasp as Emmett's lips touch the shell of my ear.

"We can do that, baby," he murmurs darkly. "You just need to be a good little pet and do as you're told."

"Get off!" I yell, placing my two hands on his chest and shoving. It's enough to get him off me, stepping away. His two cronies watch with beady eyes and salivating mouths. I realize my skirt is up, my blue lace panties being shown off to these creeps. I tug it down, glaring daggers at them.

"Who the *fuck* are you?" I say.

"You know who I am," Emmett says, sitting on a desk in front of me.

"Who are your cronies?" I jerk my thumb to the idiots who dragged me into this room. My body aches from their manhandling.

Emmett whistles softly. "You don't know much about us, do you?"

"I'm Vincent," says the football-looking guy.

"Trey," the blonde guy adds.

"They're fraternal twins," Emmett offers, carefully watching my face. I don't know what he expects from me, but he's disappointed I don't react more. He sighs.

"My, my Ophelia. What are we going to do with you?"

"Let me go?" I grind out. I play with my hands like an idiot, struggling to maintain my composure. I can't let them know they've got to me. Bullies thrive off fear. "Like, obviously?"

"Oh, we can't do that." The ominous tone in his words... It's down-right chilling. My heart rate spikes as he slowly stands up. "You've gone too far."

"I don't see how," I say.

"Oh, you don't, do you?" says Vincent, crowding in on my personal space. His legs brush my knees, and it's all I can do to not wither into a ball. "I think you know *exactly* why you're here."

We look at each other. He towers over me, and the sheer *strength* he exudes reminds me of Brendan's. But far, far more menacing. Trey's eyes are black, and they suck me in like a vortex. I have a feeling he hides many secrets behind them.

He seems to be waiting for a response. "Uh." My voice is tight. My tongue is dry, and I tumble around the words. "Lily?"

Vincent and Emmett look at each other. Trey has taken up residence on a desk, looking bored.

"Come on, you guys," he says, "Let's move on with it."

"You don't belong here," Emmett says slowly, as if

he's explaining something important to me. "You are a fucking *cunt* who doesn't deserve to lick the bottoms of our shoes. But you're here. And we need to make sure you understand just how things are around here."

His words don't hurt. They fall upon deaf ears, because all I can hear, feel and see is a raging tidal wave of anger.

I fucking hate him. I barely know anyone in this school, and they're trying to make me miserable.

"You interrupted our assertion of power. Lily was under strict orders not to talk to you. And you bust in, upsetting the balance of things. You don't *do* that around here without expecting to pay."

"Pay what, an exorbitant tuition fee?"

"You've got a fucking smart mouth for a charity case," Trey sneers.

"Your school *wanted* me," I snap back. My temper is flaring, and I struggle to rein it back in. "I didn't go seeking you guys out – you did *me.* A lowly, poorer than shit girl from buttfuck nowhere. And *I'm* who your preppy little entitled fucking school wants." I pop off the desk, landing me chest to chest with Emmett. "So remember *that* when you jerk off to the mirror tonight."

I ram my shoulder into his, wanting to run for the door but not wanting to seem scared. I can feel knives being dug into my back, but I'm almost to the door, I've almost made it when-

WHAM!

The knob is jerked out of my hand. I feel a body press against mine, locking me against the wood. Emmett's scent floods my nostrils as his hands grip my wrists and pull them above my head. I yelp in pain, but that causes him to grip harder, digging in a way that I know will leave a mark.

"All it takes is one word from me," he whispers in my ear. His breath tickles. "And you're gone. You'll walk these hallways alone, invisible. Your grades here will tank that precious GPA of yours. Your coach will turn a blind eye to the bruises you wear. The colleges you think you can go to? They'll be warned away. Your life will become *nothing* if you displease me."

"Get off me," I bite out, but he presses against me, securing me tight.

"I can make your life hell, baby," he murmurs, dragging his lips up my neck. His touch makes my skin crawl.

"I won't let you." I try to move again, but it's like he's a boulder. I'm strong, but Emmett makes me feel helpless. "You can go ahead and fucking try."

A dark laugh curls out from his chest. "Oh, I'd love to, baby girl."

I stay silent, closing my eyes. *Just wait it out.*

Emmett's face nuzzles next to the sensitive hollow of my ear. A warm breath cascades down my throat, and suddenly his body softens against mine, pressing against me gently, bringing my wrists down, though still clasping them in his hands.

"It seems she likes you," remarks Vincent, and his tone is amused.

"Maybe," Emmett says, and his nose trails along the side of my face.

Stay still. I must stay still. I cannot move. Maybe he'll lose interest if I stop responding. Maybe he'll just let me go. I squeeze my eyes and fiercely pray he'll just move on.

I can play dead like a fucking opossum.

I won't give them the satisfaction of a response. I'm done. Even though I feel violated and assaulted, I can still leave with the high ground.

"Let me kiss you again," he demands, and memories of that day flash back to me. Of the hot press of his lips, the warmth of his invading tongue, the press of his chest against mine. "Let me."

I can feel his hard length pressed against me, growing larger and harder. It scares me. How helpless I could be if he decided to... But he doesn't grind into me. Thank god for small miracles.

Ophelia, sit through it. Document it. I go into my head, taking stock of the situation, remembering all that has happened up until this point. Then I'll report it.

He reads my tense, still body as a no. I almost want to sag with relief when he lets go of my wrists.

"Do you promise to be a good little pet?" he murmurs in my ear.

I want to lash out at him, claw his eyes out, rake my nails through his skin, yank his dick off. A fresh swell of rage courses through me.

I want to hurt him like I have never hurt someone before.

He waits for an answer. I can feel his breath against my neck. Elevated. Quicker. The longer I wait, the more aroused he becomes. His dick is now full-on hard, and because of our position, it's pressing into my back.

What kind of fucking monster gets off on this?

But I wait, tense, and ready to fight when he tries to pull something. I just want to leave. I almost cry out – *please just let me go.* I'm scared and I'm done with this fucking game.

He bends his face and presses a kiss on my shoulder. I flinch, terror shooting me straight in the chest. What if I was wrong? What if this whole situation turned south? What if he and Trey and Vincent pinned me down and raped me?

"You know, Ophelia," Emmett says into my ear.

His voice sounds tired. "You'll be a good little pet." He kisses my ear, and I try to think of anything, anything but the absolute *need* to turn around and punch him. "And I always treat my pets very, very nicely. I give them what their body wants. I *never ever* take."

His next words send a true shock of fear through my spine.

"And soon, pet, you'll be begging for me."

3

CHAPTER THREE

David Granger must delight in his athletes' pain.

I can't remember the last time I've been so exhausted. Sprint drills push me to the brink. 300 meters at 95% effort. 100 meters at 100%. Rinse and repeat, until I'm dripping with sweat and the lactic acid build-up in my legs is killing me.

David Granger isn't present – he stopped by for a quick hello at the beginning of the session. He reiterated that these pre-season workouts were on our honor. He'd open up the track for us every day after school ended at 3:15 pm and expected us to be done by 5pm. We could only log so many hours.

I'm by far the best in-shape of the girls – even the girls who were nationally ranked last season took a couple months off. I didn't. But, nearing the end of workout, the assistant extends our rest period by a minute, and I find myself greedily sucking in lungfuls of air.

Sweat slicks my skin when the assistant walks away, signaling the end of our group session. The assistant really isn't an assistant but a fellow WJ Prep student, "suggested" by David to hold a timer and stand in the field. A couple of the long jumpers and high jumpers meander to their pits – they'll practice their form.

The track is fabulous. State-of-the-art, actually. Almost as good as Arcadia. And much better than the weather-beaten, warped track at my old high school.

I grab my bag and chuck my spikes into it. I haven't really gotten to know my teammates yet, but I figure that as we suffer together, we'll bond. It always happens. Pain does that to groups.

I don't dally – I'm hungry and tired, and I want to shower. I head to the parking lot, but my eyes pick out three figures hanging around a car parked next to mine. Anxiety knots my stomach – it's *them.*

I won't talk to them. I want to run to my car, but my legs are too exhausted to even walk. I can barely hold myself upright as I beeline straight to the driver's door. I see Emmett move smoothly out of the corner of my eye.

He slides in front of the door just before I get there. My jaw ticks with irritation. *I just want to go home.*

"What do you want?" I grind out, staring at his chest. I will not give him the satisfaction of my gaze – I don't want him to see the fear in my eyes.

He must've been working out while I was training. He's changed into a tight muscle shirt that strains against his chest, and I can faintly smell his sweat. There's a leftover droplet clinging to his Adam's apple. My fingers itch to wipe it away.

"You're taking a ride with us," he says.

"No, I'm not. Please move."

"Seems like she's not cooperating," comes Trey's voice, winding around the side of my car.

"Ah, I do like the struggles of a woman," Vincent muses, sliding around the other. "So...appetizing."

The two guys stand on either side of me, too close for comfort, but I know I can't outrun them now.

"You're a sick fuck," I tell Vincent.

He smiles. "Aren't we all?"

"So, are you coming?" Emmett asks like I have a choice.

"I'm not getting into a fucking car with you three psychos." If only my phone wasn't in my bag, then I could call the police. But I don't want to alert them. "Never."

He shrugs, and my blood both chills and heats – it's a weird combination. I'm both full of fear and hatred, and I don't know which one will win out.

"Suit yourself."

Vincent and Trey pounce, and my body gives a half-hearted dodge backward. Steel-like hands grip my arms, and for the second time today I feel my feet leave the ground. I hiss in pain and I know I'll have bruises tomorrow.

"What the fuck!? Stop!" I scream as they rough me up to the car. I'm completely useless. "This is fucking kidnapping!"

"Stop screaming," Emmett says almost patronizingly, like scolding a child. He opens the back door. "No one from the track will help you."

His words send tendrils of deep fear into my chest. I'm shoved into the backseat, and my wrist stings from breaking my fall. Fuck, this thing will never heal.

Emmett gets in behind me, and I scramble for the other door, furiously pulling the handle.

"Child-locked," he says.

Of *course* it is, I think grimly to myself.

He moves to the middle, and I squish myself against the soft leather interior. Thoughts torpedo through my mind. What the fuck am I doing here? What do they want with me? I can't get out of the car, which is now backing out and pulling out of the parking lot.

"So, what do you want?" I demand. I'm trying to keep my fear locked tight – I don't know what they can do to me, but in my weakened state I know I can't put up much of a fight. I can't escape them either.

"Oh, nothing," says Vincent, twisting around and giving me a sick grin. "Just a little Jameson hospitality."

I don't want to know what their definition of "hospitality" is.

My track bag is shoved between my legs. My phone is in the side pocket, but it's pointed toward Emmett. *If I could just call 911 without them noticing...*

Emmett is on his phone, seemingly oblivious. I move my fingers to my thigh. No indication he notices. I move them to the zipper, trying to fiddle with it inconspicuously. His eyes flicker over, but when he notices I haven't done anything, he goes back to scrolling through Instagram. I casually try to gather my bag into my chest, but his fingers whip out and wrap around my forearm.

"Drop it," he says, still looking at his phone. A painful squeeze. "Now."

I do several things at once, one singular thought in my mind: 911. I reach over and knock his phone out of his hand. It bounces on the seat next to him. I put my back against his shoulder, and use my body as a shield, rummaging around in the side pocket. My fingers brush the cool glass of my phone before suddenly I can't breathe.

I choke. Emmett's fingers tighten around my neck.

Panic stops my heart – I cannot *breathe.* The feeling is all-consuming and terrifying, and I grasp for purchase on his fingers, clawing at them. I need air. His fingers *dig* and I cannot make a sound. The air is muted around us. There's a rushing sound in my head.

Is he going to kill me?

"Phone, baby," he says in a low voice.

I'm seeing spots. My limbs are heavy. Somehow, I manage to pull my phone out and hand it to him.

Blessed air surges into my lungs. My vision returns and tears rush to my eyes. I bend at the waist, chest heaving and burning, and what just happened shoots through me with frigid awareness.

He could have killed me.

I rub my neck, feeling heat rise from the indentations his fingers left. I choke again, then suck in air like a fucking vacuum.

"You okay now?" Emmett's voice is distant, far away. Briefly, I'm aware of a hand on my back, rubbing soothing circles. I wrench myself away, pushing back against the door.

"Are you fucking insane?" I rasp – I sound like a smoker.

He reaches out, gaze fixed on the hot tears rolling down my cheeks. His eyes are a dark gray, but they're filled with a soft emotion. If I didn't know better, I would call it concern. I smack his hand away.

"Don't touch me," I say weakly. My throat is still fucked. "Ever."

Emmett stares at me. His gaze sends a bad taste in my mouth.Then he turns to Trey, who is driving, and says, "This is good enough."

I look outside – I hadn't realized we'd traveled outside of the city. The forests of Massachusetts rose up on both sides of the road. I don't recognize the road at all. I curse myself for not paying attention.

"Out," Emmett says. I look at him like he's crazy. Deliberately, I pull the handle.

"The child lock, genius," I snap at him.

A flicker of anger crosses his handsome features. Then he scoots to his side, opens the door, and steps out, motioning me to follow.

I grab my bag and exit into the cool evening air. It's quiet. The road is one of those roads that needs some tender loving care, with black tar patches crisscrossing everywhere.

If they try something, I'm sure I could outrun them now. But Vincent and Trey stay seated in the car, and Emmett closes the door behind me.

"So, what now?" I say. I tense, ready to run, ready to fight for my life. I don't know what he's got hidden under his clothes, what his diabolical plan for me entails. But I won't go out easily. "What the *fuck* do you want with me?"

My voice breaks ever so slightly, and he hears it, eyes roving curiously over my face. I grit my teeth – I wish I could incinerate people with lasers. Emmett Jameson would be the first to go.

I wait and see if he moves closer, but instead he rakes a hand through his dark hair, meeting my eyes again. They're impassive, blank. Again, I'm reminded of how fucking handsome he is – his gray eyes are stormy clouds, framed by thick black lashes I would kill for.

I instantly clamp down on a flicker of desire. He's choked me, manhandled me, and hurt me. I don't want to even entertain a *positive* thought about the bastard.

"Not anything right now, Ophelia." Emmett looks into the trees. "When we do want something from you, you'll know. For now, we ask your total and complete subservience."

I don't respond. There's nothing to respond to. His words hammer the final nail into my coffin. I wonder if it is too late to move – surely other schools haven't started yet.

"But it doesn't have to be a bad thing," he says.

I give him a withering look, raising my eyebrows. "You're kidding."

"It can actually be quite okay," he insists.

"In what world is you kidnapping me and bringing me to the middle of the woods 'okay?'" I cut harsh quotation marks in the air. "Or trying to choke me out? Because in my book, that's assault."

"We're just giving you a little insight to what will happen if you don't comply."

"Comply with what?" I snap. I'm tired and irritated, and this whole situation doesn't make sense. "What the *fuck* am I supposed to comply with?"

He gives me a hard look. It's like he doesn't believe I don't know.

"The whole hierarchy code?" I suggest. It sounds ridiculous when I say it. It's like I've stepped into some sort of weird drama series.

"My family built this town," Emmett says slowly. He's still got that curious look to his eyes. "And there's a certain expectation surrounding that. A certain sort of-"

"Hierarchy?" I suggest, but I can't stop my voice from lilting with humor.

"Respect," he finishes, grey eyes narrowing. "That comes with it."

"Like what?" I challenge. My hands find my hips, and I try to send him a contemptible smirk. "What more respect could you *possibly want* other than me staying out of your way?"

"You can't just escape, Ophelia," he says, and his warning gives me shivers. "You can't just try and avoid this."

"What is *this?* Look, I said I won't bother you. Great. That's what I was doing all along." Lily's face flashes in my mind and I wince. I realize I'd given these guys fodder to mess with me. "And I won't interfere."

"You're not the type to sit by idly."

He's right, but I'm not going to tell him that.

"Please," I say, lowering my voice. Great, I sound like I'm begging, "I just came here to run. That's all I want to do. Run and then leave."

"And that's all you're here for," Emmett says, but his tone seems more like he's trying to convince himself than me.

"I'm just here to run," I reiterate. I want him to get that into his pea-sized brain. "I just want to run."

We eye each other, sizing each other up. I notice he has the faintest of freckles speckling the bridge of his nose. It's cute, in a sort of devilishly innocent way. Like the rabbit from the Holy Grail.

But something in his gaze… It's the smallest speck of confusion.

Why would Emmett be confused?

"Back in Arcadia," I say, and the moment I do, his gaze locks on my mouth like a heat-seeking missile. "What was your brother competing in again?"

And there it is – his smile twists knowingly, and I suddenly understand. A breeze picks up, and suddenly I'm cold all over.

"You have no brother," I whisper, and it's like a knife has cut my sense of safety. My sense of understanding this world. "You were there for me, weren't you?"

He doesn't answer, but he's given me enough proof already: Emmett had been watching me. For *months* now.

"Why?" I ask.

I need to know why. I need to know why he was there, watching me, scouting me.

He finally opens his mouth as he shrugs. "I picked you. The school sent me there."

I don't buy it one fucking bit, but I keep my mouth shut.

"Yo, Emmett," says Trey, sticking his head out the window. "We need to go."

"Bye, Ophelia," he says, stepping into the car. For the first time, I notice that it's fancy. Sleek. And dangerous looking. I don't recognize the logo, and realize with a jolt it must be a car from the Jameson Automobile Co. "Have fun on your walk back."

With the snap of a door and the rev of an engine, the car does a U-turn and heads back into civilization. I feel an urge to stomp out their taillight, flip them the bird – do *something* to them – but I'm completely out of my league.

A chilly breeze hits me right now. The sweat has

dried on my body, and goosebumps light up my skin. I shiver.

There's a reason for all of this, I think dully. There's a reason for Emmett showing up at Arcadia, for the scholarship offer. Emmett has some sort of ulterior motive for me. And I don't like it one bit.

And there was a reason they brought me out on this road, I think as I start walking.

Nobody ever fucking drives it.

4

CHAPTER FOUR

I sit in my assigned car spot – the very last spot at the very back of the lot. Yards away from anyone else. Figures. Even though there were plenty of open spaces before me that I could have, they assigned me the last one.

I can't help but think Emmett and the others are behind this. Clearly, it's some sort of status thing.

Last night, I did my research on Jameson, Massachusetts.

What Lily had given me proved accurate.

The Jameson, Blackwater and Whitworth families were the remaining founders, and their kids, Emmett and Bernadette, Vivian, Vincent and Trey went to WJ Prep. The Whitworths had another son still in middle school.

There was no record of a Jameson from Jameson, Massachusetts in the Arcadia track attendance.

Emmett was a lying sack of shit.

But yeah, a Forbes article last week had done an exclusive interview with Thomas Jameson. I promised myself I would read it, but I was so exhausted after coming home that I just went to bed instead.

Mom and Brendan had bought my "going out to dinner with the team after practice" bit. I wanted so badly to tell them everything, but I didn't want them to worry. They have enough on their plates as it is. Though they had been disappointed I hadn't told them about dinner. I tried to bite my tongue, and the hole in my pocket where my phone normally occupied... I knew they were doing shitty things on it. That phone has sensitive information.

I'd done my makeup that morning. An extra application of mascara, a dash of highlighter and a fresh coat of cherry chapstick. There were deep bruises on my arm, starting to turn dark purple, as well as marks on my neck. A hardened part of my heart told me not to cover them up. To bear what they had done to my body loud and proud, to stick it to them that I wasn't afraid of their bully tactics and assault.

So I rushed out the door that morning, my neck red and my throat swollen, to avoid Brendan's offering of cereal and eggs.

I flip down the car mirror and gingerly touch the marks. The ghost of Emmett's fingers are swollen and perfect indentations. The more I look at them, the more they distort and twist, and my mind flashes back to silent suffocation, the primal desire for air, the sinking feeling that I was at his mercy. I hadn't been able to move or make a sound, my breath lodged in my throat, Emmett's fingers stopping it.

Fuck them.

Fuck this place.

Fuck this weird sort of world I've entered.

I want nothing more than to scuttle back to Oklahoma. At least there I have friends, and I have Coach.

But for now, I need to show they haven't gotten to me. Honestly, how hard could it be to get through a school day?

Lily looks up when I enter, but then she quickly looks down at her desk. She's cleaned up, and she smells fine. I wonder how many showers it took to get rid of the smell.

I open my mouth to say something, but then close it. Lily got in trouble for talking to me. I look around at my classmates. They're talking to each other, writing things in their notebooks, but they keep glancing back at me.

What little snitches. They probably tattled on Lily yesterday.

So throughout Calculus, I ignore Lily. She does the same. Not even a glance in my direction. It stings a bit – it's not like I'm expecting a thank you, but it seems like we're caught in the crosshairs of the Elites.

When the bell rings, Lily jumps up and nearly sprints away. All heads swivel back to me – even Mr. Brayburn stares. There's a feeling building up inside me – *What!* I want to shout. But instead, I slowly gather my things and exit, refusing to give them the satisfaction of a backward glance.

I keep my head high throughout the morning. I get strange looks. Pitying looks. And I hear my name in whispers. I don't see any of the three guys, nor do I see the two girls. I do pass by Jason, though, and he breaks up laughing. My senses are on high alert – something has happened, and I don't know what.

During a bathroom break after third period, two girls fall silent when I enter. The sneers on their faces are mixed with contempt and pity. My cheeks redden– I know they're talking about me.

When I enter the stall, I hear one of them whisper to her friend. "Do you think she knows?"

My pants are halfway down my ass. I pause, hoping they'll say something else. But they titter out into the hallway, leaving me with my heart in my mouth.

Do I know what?

They have my phone. Maybe they unlocked it, maybe they discovered how to access my data without it. The sinking feeling grows. I try to think of the things I have stored on my phone, but I'm running a blank.

And then the door opens, and I hear the distinct sound of a *click*. Someone's locked it. My heart races, and I look underneath the stall, but it's just a pair of nice girl loafers.

"Ophelia?" comes Lily's voice. "Ophelia, I know you're in here."

I open my stall door. Lily's hazel-green eyes fall upon my neck, and she winces, giving a small sound of sympathy.

"Do you want makeup to cover it up?" she asks, nodding to my injuries.

I shake my head. Her sudden gesture of affection and sympathy unsettles me. "No. I won't show them I'm afraid."

Her eyes meet mine. "Good," she says. "You're much stronger than I was."

"They did this to you too?" I ask, intrigued. I wonder how Lily got mixed up in all this mess.

She winces. "Not exactly. It's hard to explain, really."

"I'm all ears," I say, walking to the mirrors. The bruises are becoming darker, and I feel a sick sort of satisfaction wearing them. I will not cover them up. Lily joins me, and our eyes find each other in the mirror. "I've literally got nothing else to lose."

Lily winces again, and she bites her lip. "It's complicated."

"Do you want to tell me or not?" I try not to sound irritated, but it comes off harsher than I expected. I sigh. "Sorry, I'm just very... I'm in a weird spot right now."

She nods like she understands, and again, I try and think of what she's gone through."The Elites don't exactly like my family."

"Okaaaay."

She looks at me. "That's it. The Elites don't like my family." She sighs at my raised eyebrows. "More specifically, my dad. When we first moved here, he rejected an offer to work with the Jameson Co. And the rest was history."

"What do you mean?" I ask slowly. "Because he didn't accept a job offer, they hate him now?"

Lily runs a hand through her hair, frustrated. "I

know it sounds weird, but in this town, either you work for the Elites, suck dick for the Elites, or are valuable to them in some other way."

"And if you're not?"

"If you're not and you're poor, fine. If you're successful...like my dad, then you're basically Blacklisted."

"Are you going to get another trash-can dumped on you for talking to me?"

Her eyes meet mine, and for the first time I see a flicker of worry. "Perhaps. But I'm hoping not."

"What a fucked up town," I mutter.

"It's going to get a lot worse before it gets better," she says, comforting me with a hand on my shoulder. "But if you make it through, you'll be okay."

"How old were you?"

"It was just freshman year. The Elites train their children well."

"Train?" I bark a laugh. "Like dogs?"

She looks serious, her hazel-green eyes unblinking and steady. "If they want to inherit the shitload of money their parents have, then yeah, they do whatever their parents want."

Jesus. What sort of cult have I stumbled into? Where beautiful, frightening and dangerous teenagers walk around, doling out violence and at the mercy of the will of their parents. Where money is their only love in life, and they don't care who gets crushed under their giant egos so long as they inherit the millions their parents possess.

"What did they do to you?" I ask suddenly.

Lily's face transforms into a blank mask. It was so quick that I almost didn't see it – one moment, she was wearing her emotions on her sleeve, the next she was an impenetrable wall.

"So, do you know?"

I face her. "Do I know what?"

She rummages in her bag and pulls out a gold-cased phone – it's the latest Iphone, I notice. In fact – I scour Lily – she's got the look of a rich kid. While not flashy, her uniform is ironed, her shoes are undoubtedly expensive, and the earrings in her ears... I lean closer... are diamonds.

Lily is rich.

But why is she not with those idiots?

She pulls up an app. "The school... We have an app. Basically, the Elites run it. It sort of serves as a blackmail list – if the Elites have dirt on you and you displease them, this app sends a text to everyone in school." She bites her lip again, and she offers me a pleading expression. "Please, Ophelia, don't get mad-"

"What did they send?" I ask, and the cold, hard truth blankets my body.

She closes her eyes and then hands over her phone.

The color leaves my face. I stare at the picture. My hands begin to vibrate. I can't feel, can't think. All I feel is dead.

One of my nudes.

They sent one of my nudes.

I'm laying back across my bed, looking up seductively at the camera which my ex, Mark, is holding. My eyes are hooded and you can tell I've just had sex. Mark's hickey claims my neck, just above my collarbone. My breasts are pushed up in my hands and my bush peeks out from between my crossed legs. I remember this picture – it was the first, and only time, I've taken nude photos.

I want to die.

I want to disappear.

And then I scroll through the chat. Disgusting comments about my body, boys declaring what they'd do to a girl like me, girls slandering my small boobs. The more I scroll, the more I feel heat burn my face.

Everybody has seen this intimate moment of mine.

This *thing* has been downloaded fifty-seven times. I feel my breath start to accelerate. Fifty-seven boys are going to jerk off to my picture and distribute it amongst my friends.

I want to cry.

"Ophelia, I am so sorry," Lily says. And she sounds

sincere, she really does. But she also just spent an hour in Calculus with me and didn't say *shit.*

"Please leave me alone," I hear myself say. I realize, vaguely, that my voice is weak, breathless.

She looks like she wants to stay, but she nods and leaves. When she does, I hear her whisper, "oh, no".

I take a look in the mirror, but all I see is that fucking seductive, cringey as fuck photo of me. So that's why they took my phone. I close my eyes, rest my hands on the sink. I consider going home. My body sags with the weight of too much shit.

What kind of monsters are these people?

I've done *nothing* to them!

Hot tears prick my eyes, threatening to expose my weakness. I tilt my head up, willing them to go back in, willing myself to not give a shit.

I will not be broken.

I am strong enough to face this. *The sun will rise in the east and set in the west, and I will be okay. I will be okay. I will be okay.*

When I open my eyes, they're red with unshed tears. But it's better than nothing. I straighten my shoulders and smooth out my polo shirt and skirt.

I will fucking *end* The Elites.

The door swings open and a girl says, "*Oh. . .*"

I look at her. She's young, probably a freshman, but my eyes are drawn to the *things* littering the hallway behind her. She looks downcast and she starts to back away.

"Move, please," I say, maneuvering beside her.

It can't possibly be. . .

I look up and down the hallway. Thousands upon *thousands* of my nudes have been printed out and scattered upon the floor. Curiously, I realize that on these photos my face has been blacked out. Why? At the very end of the west wing, I can see a janitor start to sweep them up. My cheeks burn – he probably has a family.

Just then, the bell rings. I want to scream at it – *make them go back inside!* Time slows. My classmates stream out of their classes. Some boys whoop, grabbing pictures left and right. Most of them get trampled. I watch as my dignity and my respect crumble before my very eyes.

Emmett and Vivian appear in the throng. Her red hair is in curls this time, and when he wraps an arm around her tiny shoulders, he twirls one with his finger. His eyes catch mine, and the smile he sends me is positively *vile.*

I school my face into a mask, but inside I can feel my composure shattering. I race back into the bathroom and lock myself in the farthest stall. It takes every reserve of strength to not break down. The commotion of the hallway settles down, and when the tardy bell rings, I inch back out after the last girl leaves the bathroom. I want to make a break for my car. Screw school today. I just want to go home and have a good cry under my blankets and never see anyone ever again. But when I peek out, there are several lingering groups.

I shut it, sweeping the manual lock into place.

I will not cry. I will not cry. I will not cry.

There's a jiggle on the handle. A polite knock.

"You can't have the door locked, dearie," says the female on the other side. "It's a fire hazard."

I don't respond. I can hear the woman waiting for my response. But I can't trust my voice or I might start crying.

I open it, and it's a nice little lady. Probably from the front desk.

"You got a hall pass, sweetie?"

My throat is mute. Before I can form a remark, my feet are sweeping past her and I'm speed-walking down the hallway. I keep my eyes to the ground. *Walk. Walk. Walk.*

"Oh my god, did you see her *face?*" comes a high-pitched squeal.

Nope nope nope.

I pivot on my heel and race back to the bathroom. I slide in, almost startling the sweet lady as she exits. Taking refuge in my stall, I pray that I mistook the voice.

"-but like seriously, it was like beet-red and totally fucking hilarious," says Vivian.

My soul crashes to the tiled floor. Just my fucking luck.

I can't hold my tears back any longer. Unbidden and vicious, they pour down my cheeks. My face's screwed up, and I try to hold back my sobs.

"Good, she's like, super ugly." Bernadette has a distinctly higher voice, more nasally. "And such a slut. Like, seriously, what fucking blowjob lips."

There's some ruffling around, and then Vivian takes the stall next to me. They continue talking. My feet are pulled up onto the toilet seat, and I hug my knees. I feel small, contained. Trapped. Tears continue to well and fall, and I wish I could make them stop.

"And like, did you see her try and make her boobs bigger? Like pushing them up would make *any* guy fall for that trick?"

"Right? They're like fucking tiny grapes."

"And, like, also, her bush. Like, a bush is so gross. It smells, it's nasty. No respectable guy would ever want to bury his face into that bear of a pussy."

"I bet she smells horrible."

"Ugh, totally, right. She runs all the time so it must reek."

"Do you think she went home?"

"Probably." There's a smack of lips popping. I

imagine them doing their makeup in the mirror, but I'm too terrified to move. "I hope she's embarassed and ashamed as fuck."

"She looked pretty mortified," Vivian chuckles, flushing the toilet. She doesn't wash her hands. "Like, completely horrified."

"Good." There's some more ruffling, a spray of liquid, and the scent of coconut and vanilla fills the air. "Maybe now she'll be a good little pet and stop fucking this up."

Pet. There is that word again. It has such sinister connotations, and I shudder to think of what the word means to them.

"Emmett says she has no clue," Vivian says. At the mention of Emmett's name, my heart stutters a bit.

"Emmett's got his dick in a twist," Bernadette says. Almost flippantly, like she's mentioning some sort of mild affliction. *Oh, he's just got a cold.* "My brother can't be trusted with her. She's gotten under his skin already."

"She's such a fucking bitch!" Vivian's tone becomes enraged, and I wince. Clearly, I'm some sort of threat to her. Well, she can fucking have Emmett – they're made for each other. "I hate her."

Right back at you, Vivian. Less than seventy-two hours and you really can learn to hate someone.

"Calm down, he'll be right back in your lap when

this whole thing is over," Bernadette soothes. "He won't lose sight just because she's a talking pussy with legs."

"But you just said-"

"Look, I know my brother. Once he fucks her, he'll toss her aside." She pauses, and then adds in a thoughtful tone: "Actually, it'd probably be good to just mess with her that way. Toy with her feelings, you know?"

"I don't want that bitch near him," Vivian snaps. "She'll probably give him a disease."

"Ooh, that's good for the next rumor," Bernadette says, almost like she's excited. "What should she have, like herpes?"

"Genital herpes." The snideness in Vivian's tone makes me sick to my stomach. "Like, that's a permanent one, right?"

"Yes, Viv." Her tone is exasperated. "It's fucking gross. Here, look at this picture."

A pause. "Oh fuck, gross!"

"Yeah." Bernadette moves a couple things around on the counter, almost like she's arranging her makeup. "Like, total fucking gross. Some of them even ooze I bet."

"Ugh, fuck, that gives me such anxiety!"

"Yeah, so let's go tell the boys we've got the next

rumor down pat. I'm tired of Emmett just controlling all of this."

My ears perk up. Emmett was the one in charge? I cast my thoughts back... Now that Bernadette mentions it, it did seem like he was the one who was directing Trey and Vincent. I bet he was the one who found my nudes and decided to leak them.

Resentment and anger coil in my chest. I want to burst out of the stall and drag them around by the hair, but something stops me. Whispers that maybe, instead of rushing into things, I should instead observe.

Clearly, this is their version of some fun game. Fuck with the new girl, destroy her reputation and self-esteem – it's all fun and games and cocktails and something to do in their free time. Almost like a hobby – *Let's crush Ophelia, how can we ruin her today!?*

I have never, in my entire life, been so mortified and humiliated before.

But I cannot let them get to me.

If they get to me, they win. They've shown who is better, who controls who. They've shown me my place, which is exactly what they want. Emmett's soft words whisper in my ear: *your total and complete subservience.*

Suddenly, Bernadette's phone rings. It's some gawdy classical music song, and I cringe as she answers it with a chipper, "Hello, Daddy!"

My tears have dried. Listening to Bernadette and

Vivian slash me apart is enough to show me that clearly these girls have no shred of empathy or kind emotion in their bones. They shit on compassion and tear apart kindness – all in a day's work for two rich shitheads.

"Oh yes, Daddy, it's all going very well," Bernadette simpers, her voice like poisoned honey. "We're all just having a blast." A pause. "Oh, he isn't? Well I'll tell him then! Bye, Daddy!"

"Bye, Mr. Jameson," Vivian chimes in.

Mr. Thomas Jameson, their father. I cringe to think of ever responding to Brendan like that. He would laugh his ass off at the fake, honey-dripped sweetness and demand I speak to him like a normal human. Not to mention calling him *Daddy.* I shudder – what gross perverted relationship they must have.

Either that, or Bernadette is *actually* the living embodiment and stereotype of a rich Daddy's Little Girl.

She probably is. Her shoes, which I can see from under the stall door, are that sort of causal rich. The ones you *know* cost thousands of dollars.

She probably gets an allowance larger than Mom and Brendan's mortgage. She probably spends the kind of money someone earns in a *year* in a week. Her "Daddy" probably bought her that red Lamborghini for her sixteenth birthday. She's probably never had macaroni and cheese with cut-up hotdogs in them.

The sound of Vivian and Bernadette fade away – the door opens and closes, and I'm left in silence. Alone. Finally. But I don't feel like crying any more. I don't feel like hiding.

Suddenly, I'm bitter. I feel the bitterness and anger eat away at my humiliation, hardening my skin. People like me are just ants for her to squish. For her to hold a magnifying glass and say "oh, how cute" as she burns us to death.

A cold, dead sort of anger hardens my heart. I will not be intimidated. I will not back down. And I certainly won't let them show that they've cracked me. So what, the whole school has seen me naked? So what, they think I'm a slut?

I'm *not* going to bow down.

I grit my teeth and wipe the sticky tracks of mascara from under my eyes.

I'm going to fight back.

5

CHAPTER FIVE

"Hey, little whore," a slimy voice whispers too close to my ear, and I feel the heavy presence of a boy beside me. My elbow connects with the soft tissue of his stomach, and he gasps.

I step aside, slamming my locker and watch the sophomore clutch his stomach. He groans. He's on the larger side, with a gut spilling over his khakis. He wears glasses, and when he recovers, he squints his beady little eyes at me through dorky rims.

"You were saying?" I prompt sweetly.

His eyes zero in on my boobs, and the disgusting lust in them almost makes me gag.

"I'll pay you twenty bucks to let me fondle them," he salivates.

"My rate is too expensive for you, sweetie," I grind out. "You couldn't even afford me."

With a twist of my heel, I walk away. It's lunch period, and many students are gathering in the cafeteria. That's where the Elites will be. I know if I show up, relatively unfazed, I'll have one notch up on them. They may think it's humiliating to walk in front of my peers, but if I do it with enough of a *fuck you* attitude, perhaps it'll come off differently.

At least I hope.

The cafeteria at WJ Prep is ridiculous. There are several buffet options available and one grill station that produces hamburgers, hot dogs and even fucking steaks on demand. The meals are all inclusive in the tuition fee – when I looked over their menu, I noticed they even have a sushi chef come in twice a month, and their in-house pastry chef provides at least five different desserts. They boast vegan, gluten-free, lactose-free and sugar-free options for the girls who like to calorie count or who've adopted a serious allergen diet as a "lifestyle choice".

There's a minor disturbance when I walk in, but the cafeteria quickly resumes normal activity as I walk around and select my food. I'm starving, unsurprisingly. I need to eat a minimum requirement of calories in order to maintain my figure, and I've forgone breakfast because I didn't want Brendan to see the marks.

Okay, I think as nobody is throwing things at me. *This is fine.*

The Elites occupy the center table. I can see them laughing and enjoying themselves. Their artfully styled hair, perfect teeth, immaculate uniforms – it's like they were born to be the center of attention. Either that or made to be. My mind casts back to Lily's comment – *trained.* Trained probably since birth to be in the spotlight, to gather attention effortlessly and to find ways to keep the spotlight on them at all costs.

I select mashed potatoes, green beans and two salmon fillets, grab two cookies and wade through the sea of tables to get to theirs. They see me coming, and Bernadette and I make eye contact. But it's like she sees through me – I'm beneath her, I realize, to even acknowledge. Suddenly, Vivian stands up and slides around to where Emmett sits, curling her body around his.

"Hey, baby," she says into his ear. Her eyes meet mine in show of dominance.

It's laughable, how she thinks I want him. I smile sweetly at her – he's all hers.

Yet, some part of me notices that Emmett, while he still lets her cling to him, doesn't react in any way. He's deep in conversation with Vincent when I arrive.

"Is this seat taken?" I ask, pointing to the empty one next to Bernadette.

Her eyes find the seat, then flick up to mine. She cocks her head. "Obviously."

"Well, I can't stay," I say, " So I'll get right to it. Where's my fucking phone?"

"Don't have it," Trey says, shrugging nonchalantly. He's seated next to Bernadette, who is rolling her eyes. "Don't know where it is."

"Unlawful possession of pornography of a minor, tsk, tsk," I say sweetly, loudly, placing my tray at the edge of their table. "What will the authorities say?"

Trey laughs."Oh, you think we'd be as stupid as to download your nudes onto our phones?"

"What are you, stupid *and* a whore?" Bernadette sniggers.

Trey holds a french fry between his fingers, twirling it like a pencil. "We didn't upload the photos from *our phones.* You did."

"I did no such thing."

"Try proving that," Bernadette says haughtily. "It's all from *your* phone."

I want to punch her. They made it look like I committed social suicide. Though we all know who was responsible, there's no way to prove that I didn't upload the photo myself. Or printed the hundreds of thousands of printouts.

"What you guys are doing is harassment," I point out. I jerk my fingers to my neck, and then pull up my sleeves, exposing the angry bruises. "And you think that they don't have camera footage of you dragging me into a room against my will?"

Trey's smile is almost pitying. "And who's going to go look at it?"

"The police."

I was hoping that the mention of the police would cause them to pause. But Bernadette's pealing laughter upsets me. Clearly, I had said the wrong thing.

"You think you can go to the police?" Trey says in between barks of laughter. His face turns red from the effort. "Oh my god, that's rich."

"We basically own the police, honey," Bernadette says with an irritating, condescending smile. "So that's cute."

"I love self-admitted extortion rings," I mutter to myself. But for some reason, I believe her. I'm starting to realize there's much more influence behind their names.

"Now you're learning," Trey says with a wink.

"Where's my phone?" I snap, voice rising.

Emmett, as if he's just noticed my presence, procurs my phone from his pocket. He dangles it in front of him, his long fingers playing with it. Vivian watches it like it's some sort of magic trick.

"Ooh," she says, "Look, it's her phone."

I almost expect her to start clapping.

"Give it back to me."

Emmett's cool gray eyes follow my outstretched hand up to my boobs. Heat rises in me – he knows what they look like, thanks to that fucking photo. When he finally finds my eyes, I feel violated.

"My," he says with disapproval, "were you raised in a crackhouse back in Oklahoma? Where are your manners?"

"Where are yours?" I fire back. I extend my hand again. "Phone, please."

"Not even a full sentence?" Vivian laughs. "Did your crackwhore mama teach you that?"

She's trying to bait me, and just a couple hours ago it would've worked. But this is a new Ophelia. They might try to go for my Mom, but I know she would want me to take care of myself first.

"'Your Mom' jabs? Wow, what are we in, sixth grade?" I laugh, and I think I nailed the whole patronizing tone of it because Vivian scowls fiercely. Emmett, on the other hand, gives a small twist of his lips. Almost like approval. "I didn't realize that's the level we're playing at."

"You're sassy today," Emmett remarks.

"Having a very private photo of me leaked to the entire school will do that to you." I flash him a blinding smile, and I wonder if he can see the cracks in my facade. "But no harm no foul. Give me my phone please."

"Emmett, don't give it to her," Vivian snaps.

It dawns on me that they are under no obligation to give my phone back. They don't care – phones are like rocks to them: they probably have the latest models. They don't play by normal rules, but they might recognize that they can use it as a weapon against me.

I certainly don't have anything as humiliating and degrading as more nude photos.

But I'm sure they could find a way to twist the information on my phone to their advantage.

"Beg him for it," Vincent says. It's the first time he's spoken, but the sinister expression on my face causes my stomach to drop. "Beg him for it like a good pet."

The moment the words are out of his mouth, my heart pauses. Like a dog. They want me to beg him like a fucking dog.

"I'm not opposed to the idea," Emmett muses, and his eyes rove over my body.

"She'll look good on her knees," Bernadette intervenes, smirking at my open mouth. "I'm sure she's used to it."

Heat colors my cheeks. She can't be serious.

"I'm not getting on my knees," I say, and I look at

Emmett. His handsome face tilts to the side, almost as if studying me and he finds my reaction curious. For once, I just want a speck of decency to shine through him. For once, I want him to do the right thing. "Emmett, please just give me my phone back."

He licks his lips, and the heat in his eyes warms me in all the wrong places. "On your knees, Ophelia."

"I'd rather die," I say ruthlessly. And it's true. I would rather die than show them that they have one iota of power over me. I will not bow to them. I scoop up my tray and give them a sour smile, and their expressions are hard to decipher. "See you around."

I walk away from them.

"Let me handle this," I hear Emmett say, and I increase my pace. He's following me.

My fingers grip my tray – should I whip around and hit him with it? But I'm hungry, I want to eat. I want to be left alone. My feet carry me toward the exit, and I can feel hundreds of eyes on my back, at the girl that Emmett is following to teach a lesson.

I'm just about at the double doors when a hand grips my elbow. I'm yanked back, my food flying, and suddenly my back is pushed against the milk dispenser. The cold of the metal is nothing compared to the absolute ice in his gray eyes.

I gasp at the sudden change. Emmett looks *murderous*. His jaw is clenched, sharpening the hollows of his cheeks, and his nostrils flare. His expression accentuates just how handsome he is, and I'm at the brunt end of his fury.

"Kiss me," he whispers harshly, just centimeters above my mouth. His breath is hot and smells like the hamburger he was eating. "Kiss me and you can have it back."

"What?" I gasp at the sudden warmth and pressure of his body against mine. He leans closer, and amidst the fury I can see it.

How much he wants me.

It burns within him, is eating him from the inside out.

Emmett Jameson wants me. And he's angry.

And I don't know anymore. Is his anger from my defiance? From my refusal to bow, from my refusal to let him intimidate me? Or is he angry at how he wants me? The fire in his eyes, the parted kissable lips – he wants me. I search his face, dumbfounded, wanting to know.

"What if I begged you," he murmurs, softer this time. "I just want another taste."

His words are for me and me alone, though our audience is the entire cafeteria. They don't know what he is saying to me, or know what he wants – they think he is putting me in my place.

"You know you want to," he teases, and his tongue

darts up to wet his bottom lip. "You feel this too. You want this too."

I'm drawn to the movement, and my pulse quickens, desire pooling in my stomach. I hate how he makes me feel – both wanton and helpless, both filled with desire and repulsed by him. He's handsome and he scares me. He's done nothing but make me miserable.

And yet, I'd fuck him in a heartbeat if I had no control.

I want to pull him down to me and forget how angry he has made me feel.

"In your dreams," I finally rasp, and his eyebrow quirks at my quivering voice. "I will *never* kiss you."

His fingers come up and when I don't flinch, he presses his palm along the side of my face. His touch is tender, though I know inside hides a cruel monster.

"You will," he says with certainty. Again, the tip of his tongue wets his lip. The action sends a thrilling response to my core. "You want this just as much as I do."

His hand comes to my stomach, and I frown. A hard rectangular object is between us. My fingers come up and grasp my phone. As I take it from him, his thumb presses into my bottom lip. A dizzying rush of desire clouds my thoughts – *I want more.*

"Remember who this is from," he says, before breaking the spell by stepping away.

I don't want to remember. I'm tingling and dizzy and my core is throbbing. Emmett knows how much his presence affects me. As he gives me a wink before loping away, I realize that Emmett will always remind me.

I do want him. And I shouldn't. It's all sorts of wrong. There's nothing normal about this situation. There's nothing normal about Emmett Jameson.

That one sophomore kid is back at my locker. I almost groan with frustration, but I bite my tongue and walk up to him. I need my books for next period.

"Hey, little whore," he says, eyes glued to my boobs.

"Get lost, perv." I'm not in the mood to deal with him. He and hundreds of other horny male teenagers have seen my boobs, and I don't want word to go around that I can be harassed.

That role, it seems, is exclusively for The Elites.

And I will not tolerate this shit from anyone else..

"I thought you'd say that," he says, and I notice he has a slight speech impediment. There's Cheetos dust on his fingers and around the collar of his polo. Gross.

"So I propose a proposition. I mean, we all saw what just happened in the cafeteria."

"I said get lost. Or are you just braindead?"

His hand reaches out, and in a flash I've got my elbow on his neck and his back up against the locker. My movement surprises me. His fleshy neck bends under my pressure, and his eyes bulge.

"What the *fuck* do you want, you twisted fuck?"

It actually feels good to take back some control.

"Let him go," comes Vincent's voice from over my shoulder. I freeze. "You hear what I said or are you just braindead?"

My words come spitting back out to me, but this time they drip with malice and promise. Vincent will hurt me if I don't do as he asks.

I drop my elbow and step away, but Vincent grabs me. My wrists are behind my back before I know it.

"Let me go," I growl, trying to struggle out of his hold. "Ouch, fuck."

"Shut up," Vincent says, and I stop, chest heaving and my wrist reminding me that it's still fucked up. "Go on, Nico, what was your proposition?"

The kid suddenly looks greedy, and he's looking at my chest like I'm the last cheeto in the world. "Boobs, under the bra, thirty dollars."

"Nah, I think he can touch them for free," Vincent

whispers in my ear like we're conspiratory partners. "What do you think, Ophelia?"

"Over my dead fucking body," I snap.

I struggle violently, putting all my weight and strength into freeing myself. One of my wrists gets free, and I twist around. I will fight until my very last breath. I must have surprised Vincent though, because his dull eyes are widened. My foot comes up, connecting with his crotch, and he hisses in pain. He lets go of my other wrist, and I take off running down the hallway.

My feet slap the tile as I pick up speed – I race past doors and lockers and dodge other people. When I look back, Vincent is nowhere to be seen. My breaths are sharp and frantic – Vincent was going to help that kid assault me.

What a sick fuck.

The rest of the day, I'm propositioned by at least two other weird kids. I brush them off, but I don't touch them. In the hallways, Vincent passes by and wiggles his eyebrows at me. He thinks this is hilarious. I'm just some sort of object he can toy with.

I desperately want the day to be done already.

I just want to go home and sleep.

In seventh period, I debate whether to go to practice or not. It's what's expected of me. It's what Coach Granger wants. But my body is bruised and tired and achy. I'm mentally strung out, from being on high alert each moment, waiting for the next thing the Elites throw at me. The teachers are looking at me different – that is to say, they won't meet my eyes.

I'm betting the teachers are under the Elites' thumb just like the police. Figures why I haven't been called into the principal's office to talk about the blatent nudity and minor pornography littering the hallway. The trash-cans are full of the pictures – I see them everywhere I walk.

Screw practice. I need a nap.

There's a small form waiting for me at my car after school. I almost turn around and call a cab before I recognize Lily.

She has a hood over her head, and when she sees me, her eyes light up.

"Come on," she says, nodding impatiently to my vehicle. "Get in."

"Lily, I can't talk," I say, and my voice cracks with strain. "I'm exhausted."

"I-I-I know," she says. She looks at her loafers. "I just wanted to say that I'm sorry. And that I can't imagine how rough it's been. And that I'm glad you're staying strong."

Her kind words touch me, and unshed tears burn

my eyes. I want so desperately for things to stop, for everyone to just leave me alone. Lily doesn't understand just how much her words mean to me.

A tear spills over and slips down my cheek. I hastily wipe it away.

"Thanks, Lily," I say, struggling to keep my composure. For some reason, just knowing that Lily is rooting for me makes me inconsolable. "I just want to go home and nap. Besides, for whatever reason, you're still talking to me and I don't want you to get dragged into this again."

She nods, like that makes sense. "I was going to offer to let me cover that up for you. You know, since I'm sure your parents don't know."

It's a cruel sort of world when Lily looks at me like she knows. They've done this to her too, long ago. I nod feebly, and we clamber into my car. She pulls out some heavy concealer. The color is lighter than my skin tone, but it'll have to do.

I close my eyes as Lily gingerly covers up my mark. Her touch is kind and gentle, and again I feel the onslaught of emotion nearly overcome me. I've been nothing but trouble for her, but she's still willing to help me when she can.

"There," she says after a couple minutes. "All done."

I flip down the mirror. It looks as good as it can get. “Great job, Lily.”

“Thanks, I just figured you would need it.”

Her small act of kindness means more to me than she’ll ever know. I swallow the lump in my throat and just nod wordlessly. We stare out the windshield silently for a couple seconds before Lily shifts uncomfortably.

“What did Emmett tell you at lunch today?” she asks.

I look at her sharply. “He’s just trying to bully me.”

“Oh,” she says.

I realize that I’m being unduly harsh, and I try to soften my words. It’s not her fault I’m hurt and angry and sad. “I’m just tired, Lily. I’m sorry.”

“It’s fine. I should probably get going here pretty soon, but do you mind if I wait until we see The Elites leave?”

I nod. “If you want, you can get into the back – it’ll be harder for them to see you there.”

After a minute of shuffling and scooching around, Lily is settled into the back seat. I touch the freshly applied makeup with my fingers. “Thanks again, Lily.”

She nods curtly. “No problem.”

“Oh, there they are,” I say, twisting over the back of my seat to see out the back window. Lily and I watch the Elites mosey out of the school. Emmett’s arm is slung over Vivian's shoulder, and Bernadette is nestled into...

"Are Trey and Bernadette a thing?" I ask, watching him jostle her against his side as she laughs, tilting her head.

Lily's nose crinkles. "Sort of. They've had an on-and-off thing for a while."

It's just one huge Elite Orgy. Maybe they're all inbred. But they're all ridiculously gorgeous, so probably not.

We watch as Emmett's black car and Bernadette's red Lamborghini speed out into the main road. Vivian, it turns out, drives another one of those black cars with the Jameson logo on it. A flickering steam of jealousy heats my face. She probably got gifted one of those cars. Maybe for fucking Emmett. The Whitworth twins drive away in a sleek sports car – yellow and indistinguishable from this far away.

"Okay," Lily says, opening the car door. "Thanks for letting me hide out."

"It was the least I could do," I say, and when I reflect on what those words mean, I wish that I wasn't so sincere. What kind of world do we live in where she needs to thank me for hiding out in my car? "Honestly."

When I arrive home, it's silent. Mom won't be back until 8:30, and I take Brendan's absence as a sign that he's occupied with an interview. I hope he gets it.

Exhausted, I slip into a pair of comfortable panties and an old track meet shirt. I turn off the lights and flip over onto my back. My room is still bare, and the only things out of their boxes are my clothes and sheets. The rest of my nicknacks – photos, memorabilia, posters and track medals – are still packed away. I know I should at least hang my golden and purple tapestry I found at the flea market back in one of the cities I had a meet in. But the effort seems trivial.

What's the point in trying to make my room feel homey when clearly nobody wants me in this town?

For the first time, I take a look at my phone. It's fully charged – they must've plugged it in for me. The thought of them going through the effort of keeping my phone charged strikes me as odd. Why would they care if it died?

I put in my password and the home screen is just how I left it. I view my recent google history – nothing. But since my phone is linked to my computer, they clearly saw my efforts to research them last night. Of all things, the idea makes my cheeks heat with the barest hint of shame.

Emmett Jameson had added himself as a contact.

He even had the audacity to put a little heart at the end of his info.

Suddenly, I receive a text from Emmett. My phone dings just a second too late, and my heart leaps. The good thing about this phone is that I can read the messages from the notification alert.

Check your notes, pet ;)

Like a zombie, I go to my note sections. There's only one note there – I don't make a habit of leaving notes in my phone. It was created yesterday at 1:12 am. The title is: To Ophelia, From Emmett.

You're going to give in, pet.

You want me to fuck you. I can see it in your eyes. I can feel it in your body every time I touch you. You shiver when I come close, and you can't stop staring at my lips.

I'm going to bury my cock in your sweet pussy. I'm going to pound in you until you come, screaming my name. You're going to want me to do it. You're going to beg me. And I'm going to enjoy it so much. I'll eat you out like you've never been eaten out before.

Arcadia was just a taste. I want more of you. All of you. Writhing and screaming beneath me, milking my cock because I feel so good inside you.

You want more of me. I know it. We both do.

I'll see you tomorrow, pet. ;)

My breaths come in quick pants. There's a liquid lava heating my core, and I feel like I can't think straight. Emmett's face flashes in my mind, and a strike of desire lights me on fire as I think of his tongue wetting his lip.

No no no no no.

This cannot be.

I cannot let this happen.

I quickly – even though I want to read it again, even though I want to memorize the words, even though I want to feel how hot and bothered they make me – delete his note. But the damage is done. Just thinking of us together is sending me off the rails. Just knowing that he also feels the same way makes me want to think that it's okay.

But it's not okay.

This is ridiculous. I cannot be having these thoughts and feelings about him. He's perverted and disgusting and hurtful and cruel and everything I don't want in a partner.

He'll do nothing but use me and abuse me.

I need to seriously get Emmett Jameson out of my head.

6

CHAPTER SIX

They're planning something.

I just don't know what yet.

The rest of the week passes by uneventfully. I eat my lunch in my car. Whenever I passed by one of The Elites, they didn't look at me. Whispers followed wherever I went, but it seemed the horny fuckfaces had backed off on the propositions. I gave the sophmore the middle finger a couple times, but he didn't react.

My teachers, it seems, are oblivious. Either that or too scared to do anything. To them, the first two days of school were completely normal. Absolutely nothing happened.

Coach Granger doesn't say anything when he sees the faint marks around my neck. Instead, he runs me into the ground every day. Or, the assistant does. But I know he watched me kick ass. When he left after the start of practice, I watched him go and sit in his car. It was strategically placed on the Visitor's parking lot, an elevated lot right behind the main office. He stayed there for the entire practice, every practice, and I couldn't help but smile.

Sometimes, coaches are as obsessed with the sport as the athletes.

Practice is going generally well. I'm performing at top-notch, and my body feels strong and capable. But school still nettles me.

But what bothers me is the absolute absence of anything. No acknowledgement. No side glances. No pointed glares. No shoving. No sexual touching. No nothing.

The Elites are ignoring me. Hard. And I can't help but think this is part of their diabolical plan. Their "ruin Ophelia for life as no one clearly gives a fuck" plan.

They don't seem like the kind of people to just back off. No. There is a reason behind everything they do.

The last bell on Friday rings. I'm free.

"There's a party at the Whitworth Mansion tomorrow night," comes a small voice. "They'll be distracted."

I know it's Lily, but she's trailing behind me. Her

voice is lost amongst the hundreds of others excited about finishing the first week of school.

"And?" I say, staring straight ahead.

I feel like I'm in a movie. Lily shadows me close, but not close enough to be suspicious, and the hairs on the back of my neck rise.

"They'll be there. We should hang out somewhere else."

"Ah," I say.

I still don't understand Lily. She's taken a trash-can over the head for talking to me. Yet she still keeps coming back.

My curiosity burns. I want to know more about her.

"Come on," I say, scanning the hall for The Elites. "Let's go to the bathroom."

We slip into the nearest bathroom, and Lily takes off her hood. Her mousy brown hair goes to her mid-back, and as she shakes it out I laugh. She then goes to check under the stalls, then marches right back to the door and latches it.

"You had your hood on?" I can't help but chuckle.

Her eyes narrow at me, daring me to deny the obvious. "Clearly – it's just easier to keep under their radar."

I search her face. She's dead serious. "You're serious."

"More serious than a heart attack," she says, watching the remnants of my smile fade. "You still think this is a joke." Her voice turns dark, her eyes hard. "The Elites don't fuck around. They are ruthless and they are cruel, and they *will* hurt me and you if they see us together again."

"So why are you still talking to me?" I ask. "I don't understand."

"That's what we should talk about," Lily insists, extending her hand. "Give me your phone number and we'll meet up this weekend, away from all of this."

She heads to my messages, then pauses. Her eyebrows shoot up. "He got your phone number?"

Emmett had been the last one to text me, aside from Mom and Brendan. I run an anxious hand through my long dark hair, trying to push the note out of my mind. "Yeah."

Before I can say anything, she clicks on it. "Check your notes, pet," she repeats, then looks at me, expecting an answer.

"I deleted the note." Is it warm in here? I feel hot.

"But not his contact information or his text?"

I rub a hand down my face. "What would be the point? I'm sure if I block him he'll just find another way around it."

"True." She nods. "True, yeah."

She quickly types out a message with her contact

info, then sends it. A few moments later, her phone buzzes in her pocket. It's one of those high-pitched dog sounding buzzes that teachers apparently can't hear.

"Why?" I ask, nodding pointedly.

Lily's eyes meet mine. "You'll soon understand that if The Elites don't like you, neither do the teachers. And I've had enough stupid fucking detentions for texting in class."

"Ah," I say.

"Anyway," she says, adding my contact information. "Do you have a fake?"

Her question throws me off. "A fake ID?"

"Yeah," she says, waving her hand in the air. "A fake ID. You know, a driver's license that says you're of age to drink."

"No need to sound patronizing, jeez," I tease her, but then turn serious. "No, I don't."

"Oh." Her frown is momentary. I wonder what sort of activities Lily gets up to in her spare time. Something tells me she isn't having tea parties to drown out the stress. "That's fine. We'll just go to a place I know."

"What do you mean?" I ask.

She looks at me, and her hazel-green eyes are insistent, almost like she wants me to understand. Her demeanor changes, and she's stiff. Her hand comes up and rests on my shoulder, though it feels weird since I'm several inches taller.

"There's only a few places in town that you can still go to where The Elites don't have eyes," she says slowly. "And I can't bring you to my place, and I'm sure you want to keep where you live quiet. At least until they figure it out. They probably have figured out where you live, now that I think about it." She shakes her head, refocuses. "Never mind. My point is, you need to be careful of where you go. And we need to be careful of where we meet. The Elites like to keep tabs on the people they hate."

"You're kidding," I say, a bone-chilling coldness settling deep into my body. I thought I'd left them every day once I was off school grounds.

Of course not.

The Elites are everywhere. They are like fucking God, and they sure play the part.

"Unfortunately, I'm not," Lily says, watching the information take hold, her hand squeezing my shoulder sympathetically. "You'll need to leave your phone at home. They've probably installed a tracking device on it."

The place Lily gives me directions to is a renovated warehouse. As the sun goes down, I drive through the shadily lit streets until I land on number 127.

It looks decent enough. Light streams out of the bottom floor windows, and a couple people mill about the uncut grass and weeds out front. Cars are parked haphazardly on the gravel lot, so I pick one far away.

The sign across the open double doors says: *The Rooster Cafe.* Below it is a sign: "Jameson's Number One Growler Fill Station and Family Restaurant."

I step in to see the place is literally split in two, a low half-wall extending through the back, zigzagging here and there. From the ceiling, heavy curtains of beads fall, reflecting the disco lights and pulsing purple lasers. It stops halfway at a railed balcony with even more seating.

It's a weird concoction of family restaurant and club, but with the dim lights and low-playing EDM, it somehow works. It's heavily packed when I go inside, but to my surprise, I find children lurking about the stools, cuddled up against their parents. Their parents are young – clearly this speaks to a certain crowd.

I find Lily to the left, nestled into a deep booth, picking at a plate of fries. She's dressed in a nice t-shirt but nothing fancy. I slide in across from her.

"Hey," I say, looking around. I spot the large neon blue sign that says *The Rooster Cafe.* "Weird place."

"It's got a certain quirk," Lily says, munching on a fry. "You know they don't cut the grass deliberately?" She shoves the basket in front of me. "Want some?"

I take a few and dip them in ketchup. I feel like a fish out of water, and when I strain my head up over the half-wall, I'm greeted with a group of twenty-somethings ordering craft beer.

"So, how's it going?" Lily asks.

"Oh, fine," I say. I'd spent the day lounging around in sweats and a dirty t-shirt, and I showered just before I came to meet her. "Literally did nothing."

"How are you holding up?"

I blow out a long breath, grab more fries, and stuff them into my mouth. When I swallow, I admit, "I'm okay. Not the best, but it's whatever."

"Has he tried to text you?"

"Nope," I say. "Thank god for small miracles, huh."

Lily gives a sad smile, like she agrees but doesn't want to. "Yeah. You want something to drink?"

"Sure," I say, and now that I think of it, my throat is a little parched.

Lily stands up, and her eyes land on someone behind me. Her face breaks into a genuine smile, and she beckons whoever it is with a dainty hand.

The waiter comes over, dressed in all black with a neon glow stick necklace around his neck. His face is sour, and he glares at Lily. "What can I get you?"

"Hey, Luke," Lily says, smiling up at him. "I'd like

some more fries." She then looks at me critically, a sneaky smile on her lips. "You want a beer?"

"Uh, sure?" I say. I try to look at Lily. Surely they wouldn't serve alcohol to minors? She doesn't look at me, but her smile is still blindingly happy.

"Two Pilsners and fries please," Lily says to Luke, waving him off with a dismissive hand.

Instead of answering, Luke huffs and stalks away. My eyes widen – what was up his butt? She clearly knows him. Lily sees my expression and gives a chuckle.

"Luke's my brother," she explains. She gestures to the place around her. "And this is our weird restaurant."

"Oh shit," I breathe out. I cover my face with my hands briefly. "Sorry, I didn't mean to-"

But Lily is grinning, more amused than offended. "I know, I didn't design it. My mom did. Apparently this style is all the rage in New York."

"She's an architect?" I ask.

"Yeah, she designs buildings and stuff."

"What does your dad do?"

"He's a stock-broker."

"I don't know what that means."

"Neither do I," Lily admits, and we grin at each other. "What do your parents do?"

"Mom's a Registered Nurse, and my Dad is like a technical electrical guy."

"Nice," she says, and the genuine warmth in her tone makes me feel happy.

"So how exactly do you guys own a restaurant?"

Lily shakes her head. "Sorry, I should've been more clear. Dad buys properties and rents them out. He normally does like duplexes and things like that. This is one of his first commercial buildings, and Mom cut them a deal on the designing. And basically we eat here for free, and Luke gets me drinks." Her eyes cut past me, and she grins. "Don't you, Luke?"

Luke appears with our drinks and another basket of fries. He sets them down before me and sends his sister an acidic glare. She simpers and blows him a kiss. It's all I can do to refrain from laughing, and I hide my smile into my shoulder.

"If you guys basically own this place, why are you working?" I ask Luke.

He looks like his sister – he's got mousy brown hair that's shorn close to his head. There's several tattoos on his arms, and the tail end of one on his neck, and he looks like a rich kid trying to be gangster. Both of them are delicate, with thin wrists and narrow chests.

"Work ethic," he says. "Dad says it's good for us."

"Luke also skipped out on college when he graduated last year, so Dad says he needs to work until he goes to Yale."

The casual mention of Yale sends dollar figures before my eyes. Luke doesn't look like the kind of person who wants to go to an Ivy League college. But hell, I know that attending a place like Yale means legacies are first priority.

"So you went to WJ Prep?" I wonder what his experience was with The Elites.

He wrinkles his nose. "Unfortunately. I take it you do now?"

"Yeah," I say, but then fall silent. I want him to offer up his own interactions with The Elites, but the way he's holding himself – cornered, with his arms crossed and his body leaning away from me – tells me that he's not going to divulge his story freely.

"Thanks, Luke," Lily says. "Ophelia and I are gonna chat now."

He nods curtly. "Good to meet you, Ophelia."

"You too."

Luke walks away and heads to another table, and I direct my attention back to Lily, raising my eyebrows.

"What's his story?" I ask.

Her face darkens, and her eyebrows lower into a frown. "That's for him to tell."

I back off. "Sorry, I just was-"

"Don't say you're sorry," Lily says, but her eyes are

thousands of miles away. "It's just...it's just something he should say on his own time."

A blanket of seriousness drapes over us, and I twiddle a warm fry between my fingers. The air is heavy, and even though there are people talking and laughing and enjoying themselves around us, it's like a switch has been flipped and we're left alone.

"So my dad is a stock-broker, right?" She looks for confirmation, and I nod. "Well, apparently there's this thing called day-trading in the stock market. My dad's pretty good at it." She makes a face. "Well, he's actually super good at it."

"That's nice," I murmur. "But where are you going with this?"

"The Jamesons, Whitworths and Blackwaters approached him. They wanted him to day trade some of their companies' money. You know, the Jameson Automobile Co money. I don't know how much, but it was a ridiculous amount. My dad refused."

"Why?"

She shrugs. "Part of the reason we left New York when I was younger was to have a slower lifestyle. Dad's got enough reserves to keep us going. He wants to retire here soon. He just didn't want to take on such huge clients...and be responsible for their money."

"So now they hate him."

"Hate is a strong word when it comes to The Elites," Lily says.

"What else could it be?" I bite back too harshly. "Sorry, I'm just angry."

"It'll dull over time," she says, swirling a fry in ketchup. When she pulls it up, the fry sags from the condiment weight. "Trust me, eventually it'll just feel like a dull ache."

"So what happened to you?"

She goes silent. A dark shadow crosses her face, and she sips her beer. I have yet to touch the beer. Lily's hazel eyes snap to mine, and the fury in them surprises me.

"What didn't they do?" she says bitterly. "It wasn't like they had any morals or human decency."

I stay silent. I don't feel like this is the time to interrupt.

"In the beginning, they toyed with my feelings. They brought me into their inner circle, and I was treated like a friend. Vivan and I actually became super close. Or so I thought. And then Emmett turned his attention on me."

I watch her quietly, and her fingers start racing up and down the beer glass, wiping away the condensation. She stares at it intensely, like she's trying to unlock the secrets of the universe.

"I had a crush on him, big time," she confesses,

and there's color on her cheeks, spreading down her neck. "Like huge. And he knew it. And...he used it against me in the worst possible way."

Thoughts flash through my head, none of them good. Most of them are worse than the last, and Emmett's cruelly handsome face mixes among them.

I don't want to hear what happened. But I do.

"And so, basically Emmett invites me to the homecoming dance. I'm like, so excited and happy and I can't believe it. Vivian and I like, even go dress shopping together. And then the night of the dance, everything just...shatters."

"What happened?" I ask.

She gives a curt laugh. "What didn't happen? Emmett and Trey and Vincent start screaming at me. Vivian and Bernadette tear my dress and steal my shoes. Emmett starts kissing Vivian in front of the whole school. When I try and run away, Bernadette grabbed my hair and dragged me to the punch bowl and dunked me in it. But that was only the beginning."

"Why didn't the chaperones do anything?" I'm incensed on her behalf – cruel, heartless monsters don't deserve shit, and The Elites clearly aren't human. "Why the fuck did anyone let them do that?"

"The school is *funded* and *ran* by their families. *No one* has the balls to go against them. They have ways of ostracizing people and running them out of town. Sometimes, overnight."

"What the fuck?" I say. "What the actual fuck is wrong with them?"

"Money does shitty things to shitty people." Lily leans back, and gives a strained chuckle. "But that wasn't the end of it."

"What else happened?"

"Vivian and Bernadette started sending me hateful texts. Telling me to go kill myself, to just do the world a favor. Every morning, they'd try and douse me with water or slushies or coffee or whatever they could get their hands on. Emmett started spreading rumors about me being easy, as if that's why he broke it off with me. And then..."

"And then what?"

"Then they planted a joint in my locker second semester of high school. Told a teacher. I was suspended, and thankfully my dad was able to convince them that this was a setup, otherwise I would have been expelled."

We fall silent. Lily's experience – no, torture – hangs between us, a giant reminder of who not to fuck with.

"They will remind me every so often to stay out of their way," she says quietly. "They like to, you know, resort to public humiliation or rumors or physical intimidation. Really just what they're feeling like that day."

"That's fucked up," I say. Lily's experience juxtaposes against mine – she's had four years of constant harassment and bullying, and I've only had two whole days. I dread what might come next. "How'd you get through it?"

"Therapy," she says. "But I had to go to a therapist in Boston. Anyone else is connected to them, and they would've found out. Also, lots of chocolate. I gained a lot of weight my freshman and sophomore years. That certainly didn't ward them off."

My heart hurts. I feel like I'm confined in a box, trapped on all sides, and The Elites just keep pushing and pushing and waiting until I break down. Until I beg to be let out.

My eyes find Lily's. She's pensive, looking at me with concern, wondering how I'll react. I want to tell her that there must be some way to retaliate against them, some way to get them to stop.

"That's hella fucked, Lily," I say, shaking my head.

"Yeah, but what are you going to do?" she says. "This town has been built around them. This place is *theirs.* It has been theirs for centuries, and it's not like it's going to change any time soon."

Unfortunately, I'm worried Lily is right. I rub the

condensation on my glass – is this just what I'll have to deal with?

"Okay," she says, "enough about this. Let's go have some fun. Chug, girl!"

I laugh – Lily is a little crazy. Sure, I've had my fair share of drinks before, but it's always been in a controlled setting. At someone's house, at home – never in public, where we could get in trouble for being minors.

"How about we just sip and talk?" I ask. "I'm not really feeling up for getting drunk."

Lily rolls her eyes, but she smiles at me. "You'll stop being bummed by them soon. You'll soon realize that it's just a stupid fucking game and that it doesn't matter, even if it hurts all the time."

"That's morbid," I tell her, taking my first sip of the Pilsner. It goes down nice and easy. I don't like the taste of beer, but this is tolerable. "I don't think, you know, that's okay."

"It's not okay," she says. "It's the farthest thing from okay. But what can we do about it? We've got one year left, and then we can get the hell out of here."

She's using "we" even though I met her six days ago. But I like that she's included me in her statement, and I realize that Lily is on her way to becoming a friend. A friend of circumstance and coincidence, perhaps, but a friend nonetheless.

"Hell yeah," I say, cheering her. I lift my glass and we clink to celebrate. "One more year."

"Less than three-hundred days, actually," she says. She pulls out her phone.

"Hey," I say, eyeing her. "How come you could bring your phone?"

"This is a burner phone," she says, wiggling her eyebrows at me. "I just bring it when I go out – nobody except my family and now you know I have it."

"What the fuck," I mutter, more in awe of the fact that she's had to use a burner phone, and her family most likely put her up to it. "And your family knows all about The Elites and stuff?"

"Yeah, they do." She's busy pulling up an application on her phone. "Luke and I are very close with our parents. Anyway, here, this is what I wanted to show you."

I grab her phone and eye the countdown box. It's surrounded with glitter and fun little animations that look like stringers and confetti. *Days Until June 5th: 279*.

"Graduation," she points at the phone. "That's when we graduate and we're done. We just have two-hundred-and-seventy-nine days left."

I groan. All I see is two-hundred-and-seventy-nine days of potential pain and torture. But the happiness and glee that Lily has when she sees that number... I don't have the heart to tell her that none of this is normal. We should be counting down the days happily, in anticipation of our next step in our journey.

Instead, we're counting down the days until we escape *them.*

By the time I get home, it's almost midnight. Mom and Brendan are sitting in the living room, watching Office reruns. Mom's holding a glass of red wine in her hand, and when she turns at my arrival it nearly spills over Brendan.

"Honey!" she says, excited. "You're home!"

"Eh, watch it woman!" Brendan says, taking away her glass and gingerly placing it on the side table. "You almost spilled on me!"

I roll my eyes and walk over to give them a hug from behind. "The Office? Haven't you guys watched that like seven times through already?"

Brendan gestures to Mom, who is quietly giggling. "It's her show! And I just let her do what she wants."

"Clearly," I tease, giving them both a kiss on their cheeks. "Okay, I'm going to bed. Love you."

"Love you too," they chime in, my mother's a little slurred. She breaks into a fit of laughter at some joke, and it follows me into my bedroom.

I'm half-naked, only in my running shorts, when

my phone rings on top of my bed. I glance at it – Emmett is calling. Just seeing his name pop up gives my heart a little jump. A flicker under my stomach. Why would he be calling? What could he possibly want from me? I press my hand on the green phone icon before I come to my senses. What did I think I was doing?

I quickly swipe the red phone icon. Ha. Take that you pretentious prick.

He's quick. A text pops up: **I want you now.**

He probably wants a ton of people, I think to myself. My stomach constricts. He's probably drunk and horny – Lily did say the Whitworths were having a party today. The urge to text back almost takes over, but then he shatters the lusty build-up in my stomach.

I guess we'll see what happens Monday.

Nope. Not going to give in. Anger starts to build in my chest, eradicating any sort of sick lust I had. My fingers vibrate with frustration and anger, and I want to text him a paragraph that he'll never forget. But I resist.

I do what I should've done earlier: I delete his contact info. I know it's a short term solution, but I don't care.

As I curl up under the covers, I try and think what will happen on Monday. Lily's shown me their scope of cruelty is limitless, and it takes me forever to fall asleep.

7

CHAPTER SEVEN

School goes by slowly.

Like, if a snail was drunk and stuck on a glue mouse trap.

That kind of slow.

The slow that burns and aches and makes you want to tear out your hair from boredom. The slow that whispers *this isn't supposed to be happening*. The slow that is cloaked in tension so thick a circle saw wouldn't cut through it.

The slow that said: Ophelia, just you wait.

I caught Emmett's eyes two times in the hallway. Once, when I was exiting Calculus. He'd lounged against the lockers across the door, his hair ruffled, his gray eyes piercing. He wore his polo shirt half-untucked, and his collar was half-flipped, and he was making me half want to fix him up and half want to kick him.

He'd smiled at me, waggling his eyebrows suggestively. I gave him the middle finger, but his musical laugh followed me down the hall. My back broke into a sweat and my body tensed – for what? I didn't know. To be tackled, to be squished against the wall, to be hauled up against his warm body...but nothing happened, and soon a headache pounded at my temples.

The other time had been when the bell dismissed us for lunch. The Elites normally join up at the end of the hall and sweep toward the lunchroom together. Like some weird show of power. All walking in a straight row, forcing everyone to move out of the way. I didn't exit the building to my car fast enough, and I got caught walking toward them on my way out.

Emmett and Vivian, in another gross display of couply romance, were walking side by side. His arm was slung over her shoulder, and she had her hand looped into the back pocket of his pants. I noticed they didn't hold hands – perhaps too gushy? Too romantic? Too much softness for them?

I pressed to the side, like all the other good peasants did, but they'd already noticed me. It was like some attitude had been switched on – one moment they were laughing and joking with each other, the next I was at the full-front of their attention. I felt my skin, hair, outfit be torn apart by Bernadette, whose cutthroat gaze sliced me raw.

But then, I couldn't help it.

Emmett's face was blank. Clinical. And he studied me like I was some sort of object under a microscope. No hostility, no desire. Just...curious apathy.

It sent shivers down my spine.

My headache developed throughout the rest of the day, and by the time I'm at practice the pain is nearly unbearable. I try to stretch out my shoulders and neck, and while it helps, the throbbing comes back in full force.

I pinch the bridge of my nose, trying not to grimace.

"You okay, Lopez?" comes Granger's voice.

I open my eyes. Coach Granger is looking down at me. The big black watch on his hands shows 3:33 pm. We're waiting for the assistant to arrive.

"Yeah," I say, trying to add some pep to my voice. "I'm great."

"Come over here, Ophelia," he says, gesturing me over to the stands. He climbs up to the second row and pats the metal beside him. "Sit, sit."

I do as I'm asked, bouncing my toes a little. The pounding matches the beat in my head, and when I look at him, I'm surprised to find deep concern in Coach's eyes.

"Look," Coach starts off with a low voice. He clasps his hands between his knees. He always sports a ball-cap – either Nike or WJ prep – and it hides the graying sides of his head. "I know we haven't known each other for a long time, but I think we both know that something is going on."

I stay silent – what is he talking about? I don't want to give anything away. If he knows something, he'll have to be the first one to say it.

"And I don't like the looks of my athletes getting hurt," he says. "It's not right, and it isn't good for your performance."

"If I've been slacking- "

He holds up a gnarled hand to stop me. "You haven't been slacking. You've been kicking ass. As far as I'm concerned, you're the best athlete on this field. My concern is that this whole thing – whoever has hurt you, and whoever is probably giving you that migraine right now-"

"How do you know I have a-"

He smiles, his teeth a bit yellowed but straight. "Kid, I know a thing or two about migraines. And looking like you're going to throw up is one of those things."

"I'm hoping it'll go away during practice."

"My point is, kid, is that I want you to know that I'm here for you. I'm your coach. I'm here to support you."

I nod, looking at my Nikes, hoping he doesn't see just how touched I am by his comments. "Thanks, Granger," I say. "That means a lot."

He pauses, almost like he's waiting for me to say something else, but when I don't, he slaps his hands on his thighs. "All righty then, Lopez," he says. "Time to get on back out there. Short practice today."

When Coach Granger says short practice, what he really means is that it's your own tempo. The faster you can get through it, the faster you can go home.

The moment I see a darkened figure at my car is the moment I realize that Monday has twenty-four hours in it.

"Ophelia," Emmett says, his grin spreading as his arms open up wide. He looks sinful, his lips pillowy and his cheekbones high. When he smiles like he means it, it sends a zip to my core. "How was practice?"

I check around us – my teammates are slowly driving away, their windows down and looking at us. But I don't see any of the other Elites.

Emmett is alone.

Which is unusual.

And bad.

For me. Very bad.

I stop about five feet from him. He's parked his black car next to mine, on the drivers side. I can't help but think that's not a coincidence. Sweat has cooled my skin, and my need to brush away my wayward hairs is stemmed by my desire to not look like I'm primping in front of him. I'm wearing my sports tank that's a razorback, exposing my collarbones, shoulders and shoulder blades. My shorts are high-thigh and tight, and I know my legs and butt look good in them.

I wish I'd brought sweats and a sweater. His eyes flick down to my toes, meandering up my body, and settle on my lips. He stares at them a little too long.

"What do you want, Emmett?" I demand. I don't want to walk closer to him or to my car, so I stay put. "I'm not in the mood."

He unhitches himself from the car, and I contemplate making a break for it. But instead I'm rooted to the concrete, a tiny voice in my ear saying *bad move, Ophelia.*

"You know," he says, "I've been trying to think of how to punish you for hanging up on me on Saturday night. And then blocking me."

"Oh great," I say sarcastically, but inwardly a twinge of fear strikes a chord. "You know how I just love to be punished."

His lips twitch. "You've been a bad girl."

"That's relative. I'm great, actually." He's getting closer, but it's like he's approaching a wild deer, and his movements are slow, coordinated. I step back. "Why are you walking toward me? Please stop."

"Then don't back away," he says, stepping forward again. "Come on, I just want you to take a ride with me."

The normality of his voice chills me. Almost like the blank stare he gave me earlier in the day, with Vivian draped around him. None of the lust from our first encounter. And none of the sadism of every encounter after that.

"What the hell makes you think I would willingly go anywhere with you?" I snap. My voice cracks from the uneasiness. I had gotten used to the cruelty, but this strange, calculated, yet distant, eerie deadness in his eyes is shooting straight to my gut. Everything in me is telling me to run, but I know that will only make it worse.

And then…there is the other part of me that feels sucked in like a moth to a flame. His gaze is locked on to mine as he steps closer and closer, too slowly. I can almost hear the Jaws theme playing through my migraine, but that's too comedic for a moment this dangerous.

He freezes, inches from my face. A disturbingly cold breeze hits the strands of my loose hair ever so slightly…seemingly freezing time right along with his body. Everything slows.

His hand reaches for my face, and for the first time since I arrived, I don't feel the urge to flinch or bolt. It's like I'm suspended in some magnetic hold.

"You can try to ignore me, block me or whatever else you like," he says softly, his fingers brushing along my jaw. "But we both know what's going to happen. It has to. Sooner or later."

I give my best sarcastic laugh, but it's too thinly veiled. I know he sees straight through me. My defenses are officially tattered.

"And just what is that?" I tilt my head, trying to sound as harsh and uninterested as possible. But the seriousness in my face is giving me away.

"When two bodies are drawn to each other like ours," he whispers in his low, grumbling voice that ripples straight through me, "we have no choice but to act on it eventually. Why torture ourselves like this?"

He is close. Too close. His lips so close to my neck I can feel his hot and heavy breath burning into my skin. I swear I hear a growling snarl between each inhale and exhale.

I hate myself for it, but I want to give in. I want to believe he's right…That however fucked up it may be, our bodies are meant to meld together, in violence or in sex. And obviously I'd prefer the sex, if he'd actually behave like a decent person.

"I could never be with someone like you," I snarl against his neck. "Not after the things you've done to me."

"Oh no?" he smirks, completely unfazed. "So, you're telling me when you read that note…and my texts…you didn't linger on them? Think about it all… even just a minute longer than you meant to?"

His fingers trail through the back of my hair. I want to turn into him more, push my body against his. Break through all of this sick tension that has been building.

But memories of the cruel and vicious side I'd seen of him stop me. I can't move.

I wish I could run, or that he couldn't read my mind so well. It sickens me that for all he has put me through, he knows that some part of me deep down still can't deny this primal attraction to him.

"You know, no answer is an answer," he murmurs

with a cocky smile.

I am paralyzed. I have no energy to fight back, to deny him. And I don't hate myself enough to surrender to him.

He finally takes several steps backward, leaving the places along my face and neck that he just touched cold. A loud and trembling exhale escapes my lungs, just for the simple relief from the pressure of saying or doing anything. For a brief moment, I'm free.

His hands go up in a surrendering motion as he continues stepping back. It's not like him to give up. To show any sign of caring for my comfort. It only unhinges me even more.

What the fuck is he up to?

His eyes dart down to specks of gravel scattered across the pavement as he kicks them around with his shoes. "Look…I know we've made it hard on you. *I've* made it hard on you. The way things work here…the hierarchy…the system… It's not easy to adjust to."

He has to read minds. Has to. Or maybe just mine. He knows when I'm at my breaking point. And when to back off just enough to make me think I could maybe…maybe not be filled with rage and an intense desire to knee him in the balls. Or worse.

"I want to make it up to you," he says, still not looking up from the rocks he is fiddling with across the black tar. "Give you a chance to…I don't know." He looks up and away, almost bashfully. "Get to know me. The real me." For once, his smile almost looks like one a normal teenage guy would flash when he's talking to a girl he likes.

I can't stop myself from laughing out loud…until my laughter almost turns to tears of frustration. Then I stop real quick.

"That's rich." I look away, trying not to cry.

"Just take a ride with me," he insists again. "I promise I won't hurt you. I mean, it's a beautiful afternoon." His hand flails toward the almost ready to set sun.

It is a beautiful afternoon. The air is perfect – not too hot or too cold. A breeze rushes through every few minutes, urging you to do something to keep up with the fleeting warmth. It's my favorite running weather.

It would also be a wonderful afternoon for a girl's crush to take her for a drive. If my life was still anything close to normal. The realization of just how far from normal I've been since arriving hits my gut like a knife.

Memories of my life before coming here start flashing before my eyes. How simple everything was. And moving here… That plays like a cheesy movie montage. One where I am blissfully naïve and optimistic. I had no idea how wrong things were about to go. I want to walk straight up to my former self and shake her. Warn her that this wasn't some dream come true. It was going to be a nightmare.

To my horror, the tears don't hold back with the thought. My eyes burn as they begin to pool.

I quickly shoot my fingertips up, pushing the drops away too roughly. Enough to tug the skin in pain and poke into my eyes. I deserve it. I'm angry with myself for letting any weakness show.

He's getting to me, and he knows it now.

His hand is suspended in midair, beckoning me to follow him. Get into his car. Surrender my safety and freedom. Trust him.

And like an idiot, I do. I know it's the wrong call. Everything in me screams to stop stepping forward. Stop following him. Don't slide into the passenger seat as he opens the door.

But my body follows him like a zombie. A dumb zombie.

I resentfully note the cleanliness of his car. Psh. Probably pays someone to detail it for him at least once a week. These people's cars are perfect, clinging to that new car smell for dear life.

Nothing like my beat-up old car, littered with empty water bottles and protein bar wrappers.

A blur of something in the back seat catches my eye. Something that makes me feel foolish for thinking about petty things like paid help or clean cars. It is a passing nothing at first, but quickly turns into a blaring alarm. A siren going off in my brain telling me to run. My pulse pushes to an impossible speed as my muscles tense and my jaw slacks. I'm unable to move, frozen with bulging eyes through my quickening breath.

Rope. Gloves. Other random things I can't make out…but whatever they are, it can't be good. Not with our history. And the fact that I am so completely alone out here.

By the time my mind absorbs the warning signals, he's plopping into the driver's seat as I tuck into myself and lean toward the door, as far away from him as I can manage. I know I only have mere seconds before he's going to lock the doors. My head shakes reactively with my mouth frozen in a panicked circle as my hand smashes against the door handle, blindly fumbling for a grip to fling it open. My shaking body prevents me from being able to pull the handle fast enough.

Just as the tiniest light seeps back through the door as it swings to open, a sharp blaring pain sears into the back of my head, causing me to cry out in pain. His fingers are digging into my scalp, catching a big enough handful of my hair to yank me backward. The door, and any hope I have at escape, slams shut. I beat mercilessly at it anyway, thrashing wildly against it with my hands and feet to no avail.

My heart started racing the moment I made that

lunge for the door, and now it only quickens, the sound thrashing in my ears, as his tires screech across the parking lot, pealing away from everyone and everything that can help me.

I know the roads around here are long, winding and empty. Once he starts driving down them, I am completely at his mercy. And given everything I've seen so far, I can't convince myself he wouldn't kill me… after putting me through unspeakable torture for who knows how long.

My head hangs low and my teeth gnaw into the side of my mouth as I keep a side-eyed glare glued onto him with a need to see any other lunge for attack before it happens. I can't let him out of my sight for a single second, but my mind races for some kind of solution. An escape. I fight through the voice in my head telling me I deserve whatever happens for getting in the car in the first place.

The only thing I know to do is move and fight and try to escape this in any way I can.

The car. He's in control of the car. If I take back that control, even if only for a second, maybe I can find a way to escape.

My hand juts out to the steering wheel, mindlessly jolting it in any direction opposite from where he thinks he's taking me. My scream is the only thing I can hear when the streetlight post appears in front of the windshield. It sounds foreign and far away, as if it's not even coming from my mouth. But I feel it ripping through my throat all the same before there is a terrible, deafening crunch of metal and everything goes dark.

8

CHAPTER EIGHT:

You're being punished. Just like he promised.

That's all I can think as I come to. My head wobbles around as my line of sight fills with indistinct blurs of harsh light and red spots. I feel like I've been punched in the chest and my head is throbbing. There's a hiss of smoke and dying car parts croaking in the background.

I look over to Emmett's foggy silhouette. His head is hanging limp and heavy from his neck. He's still out. I want to think over my options for killing him… making it look like it was from the accident.

But an urgent need to get out of the car takes over. The seatbelt buckle sticks at first, causing me to panic. I don't want to be stuck in here…with him. But my frenzied jiggle of the contraption finally sets the buckle free. My chest burns as the belt loosens. I can imagine a big red and purple strip across my skin from being flung against it so hard. I begin pushing on the car door which sticks at first – the same as the seatbelt. But once again I am able to pry it open. Some sort of adrenaline-powered strength, I figure.

I realize all of this is being made more difficult by the giant white balloon pressing against me. It whistles as I awkwardly maneuver around, not deflating fast enough to make this any easier.

By the time my feet finally touch the ground again, I nearly fall over. Everything aches and hurts. But not with the rewarding swell I am used to feeling from running. These pains are blunt and sharp. Unnatural.

I manage to find my footing as my eyesight slowly readjusts. That's when I realize my ears are ringing. The sound takes me back to what I saw just before the crash.

What was this fucker going to do with that rope? Just how was he going to punish me?

But then my heart begins to beg a different question… What if he wouldn't have hurt me at all? For once. What if he really did only mean to take me for a nice, innocent drive.

I remind myself of how he yanked me back into the seat as I tried to run. *Don't be stupid, Ophelia. There was nothing sweet and innocent about this.*

This is punishment, I think again.

For letting my guard down. I *willingly* got into that car. I let him know that all he had to do to get me where he wants me was pretend to be nice for a few minutes. Looking back, it wasn't even that convincing of an act. I only made him put forth the bare minimum effort of a show.

How could I be so easy and stupid?

I tell myself it's only because I was exhausted. But that's not good enough. No excuses. I don't get to run slower or cut the miles short…no matter how tired I am. I don't get to cave into these Elite fuckers just because they're wearing me down.

Toughen up. I clench my fists and repeat it to myself over and over.

I hear Emmett rustling out of his door. My feet immediately begin to bounce, needing to run far away from him. But the sight of blue and red lights stops me.

There's blood dripping from his forehead as he shoots his eyes straight to me. They're filled with rage and confusion, but I can tell he's blaming this all on me. Taking in the sight of his car and his banged-up body, he has the nerve to look to me with a *What did you do!?* victimhood.

I shake my head, snarling at him through my own bloody lip. How dare he look at me as if this was my fault. *Don't stalk girls, trick them into getting into your car, and then hold them by the hair when they try to run. Then your car won't get smashed up.*

Thankfully before he can say or do anything, he has the police to answer to.

"Are you two okay!?" One of the officers yells out as their doors swing open.

Oddly though, they both run up to Emmett and immediately begin giving him all of their attention. Wrapping him in a blanket, propping him up on their arms to help him over to their car to sit down.

I am left standing with the sickening reminder that everyone in this town is shoved up the Elites' asses. Even the cops. They did warn me but standing here now…just as bloody and beaten as my perpetrator… while the two cops that should be helping me are fawning all over the town's golden child. It reminds me just how alone I am in all of this.

"What happened?" they ask him, willing to get his side of the story before they even so much as acknowledge my existence.

I wait for him to blame this on me. Find some way to twist it all around to make this completely my fault.

"It's my fault," he confesses. "I feel so stupid… I guess I was showing off doing donuts and dumb shit like that…But I was distracted having a beautiful woman in my car. You know how it goes."

One of the cops laughs, "Oh, son. Believe me, I do. No sweat. Just be glad you're okay."

The other cop finally comes over to me and helps me over to lean against their car…too close to Emmett. I guess they can acknowledge me now that I'm not considered to be a problem or an enemy. I wonder if he had told them he was just getting ready to rape me if they would have helped him finish me off or dumped me somewhere.

More flashing lights emerge from the nearby winding roads. This time an ambulance. Each new arrival makes me feel safer, no matter how entrenched they all are in the game of the Elites. Safety in numbers. The more people who are here, the more likely it is that someone will make sure I'm okay.

I lean into the back seat of the cop car, their door wide open. Emmett is in their passenger seat. Our bruised and cut legs are perched out the side of the car on the pavement. I try not to notice his eyes burning into me every chance he gets. But I can feel the weight behind them.

I can practically hear his voice warning me telepathically…*You just wait. You're really in for it now.*

The EMTs get to work on us like busy bees – patching this, sanitizing that. Just enough to get us ready for a trip to the hospital. The reality swirls around my swaying head, my vision unable to focus.

But my mind intact enough to piece together what's about to happen. There's only one ambulance. They're going to make us ride together.

The thought of being crammed into that tiny space with Emmett makes my stomach churn too quickly for me to hold anything back.

Chunks of whatever I managed to eat that day crash into the back of my throat as I thrash forward, puking onto the ground right there in between my legs.

I'm instantly plagued with embarrassment...that I puked in front of Emmett, which only makes me sick again.

I want to ask the doctors what is wrong with me. I must have a brain tumor. Why the hell do I still care what he thinks? How I look in front of him?

They barely let my stomach settle before piling us both into the back of the ambulance. I want to feel comforted by the additional presence of the EMT guys but knowing they're probably just as much on Emmett's side as the cops lessens my hope.

No one asks my side of the story.

It only gets worse at the hospital. We're both treated in the same room, our beds side by side which I'm sure Emmett is getting off on. I fight off any positive feelings I have about getting to stay close to him.

This is Stockholm Syndrome. Has to be. I wonder if that sort of thing shows up on a brain scan.

I'm treated for a concussion and a sprained wrist. I want to scream at the doctors that my wrist wasn't from the car accident, but I know better. I bite my tongue. Emmett is treated for whiplash which brings me a sick joy. It's about time he got hurt for once.

Once we're all bandaged up and our hands are stuffed full of printed papers for aftercare instructions, we're left alone while the doctor draws up our discharge papers.

"You fucking bitch," he grumbles the first chance he gets, with no one around to hear.

"Oh yeah…" I scoff. "This is my fault, right?"

"You grabbed the steering wheel."

"Why didn't you just let me go!?" I cried, my voice cracking from frustration.

He slowly stands to his feet and makes his way over to my bed, taking a seat right next to me. His arms wrap around me, squeezing too tight. He envelops me, towering around me with a threatening eeriness.

I keep my eyes glued to the passing nurses and doctors in the hall, hoping one of them will barge in and stop him, but of course to them he looks like a caring guy, merely comforting me.

His lips sink down to my ear. "But the fucked up part is…you're wondering what I planned on doing to you. And not just in a terrified way…but in a curious way, huh?"

I struggle to push him away, "Fuck off!" But his grip is too tight. I barely move a muscle.

"You're dying to know how I would have hurt you in all the right ways… How I would have had my way with you, not giving you a choice…then you wouldn't have had to feel guilty about wanting it. You wouldn't have had to blame yourself for not trying hard enough to get away."

"Obviously," I retort sarcastically, barely able to get the words out as he tightens around me like a boa constrictor. "That's why I was willing to risk our lives and slam us into that telephone pole before you could get away with me. Because I was *so* excited about whatever sick shit you had planned."

I crash my foot down onto his, brutally pinning his toes beneath my sneaker. He winces and accidentally loosens his arms, giving me the chance to run to the other side of the room.

We're both panting like wild animals by the time he stands up and starts to close in on me. His eyes and nostrils flare with rage with each slow scary step he takes. Like a lion about to pounce.

And he does pounce. Too quickly for me to react. But just as soon as his arms are around me again, his lips are against mine. I tense up, refusing to melt into his kiss. I turn my head away as much as his grip will allow and crash my hand into the side of his face.

The slap only encourages him. He glares into me, burning on nothing but fumes of adrenaline, anger and lust. I take in the sight of those gorgeous plump lips, sickened by the fact that I only find them to be more enticing with the giant gash from the accident.

An urge to fight back surges through me, but it's coupled with longing. Before I know it, our mouths collide once more.

The doctor barges in, ignoring our teenage horniness, rattling off directions for leaving the building and filling prescriptions.

I can't stop thinking about the kiss as we walk through the halls and ride on the elevator. I shudder to think what I would have let him do to me if we had been alone on that elevator. I wonder what will happen when we leave. Will we run away together?

But just outside the elevator doors, we're met in the parking garage by his stupid posse.

Vivian races to Emmett's side, pummeling him as far away from me as she can get him.

"Oh, you poor thing!" she squeals in an alarming display of concern.

I was beginning to think the two of them didn't know how to feel and express genuine emotions like concern for others. Even each other.

"Are you okay?" she asks softly, her hands gripped

tight into his face, shoving her tongue down his throat before he can even answer.

My heart pangs. I want him to shove her away, but instead, he kisses back even harder, flashing his eyes to mine to make sure I was watching. I did it again. I keep forgetting who I'm dealing with.

Vivian's humanity quickly shatters as she whips around to me like a viper. "What did you do to him, you stupid fucking bitch!?"

"Why don't you ask him?" I quip back, hoping she tasted me on his lips just then.

She's unbothered, stomping toward me, venom practically spewing from her clenched teeth.

"Listen here, you little cunt," she sprays, getting so close to me I catch the spit of her rage on my cheek. "You stay the fuck away from him. I've had about enough of your skanky white trash ass always getting in the way."

Before I can respond or expect Emmett to defend me in any way at all, another car pulls up. My mom and Brendan, thank god.

My mom races toward me, sending Vivian recoiling into the sweetest body language she could muster – her shoulders drawn up, her hands clasped to her side like a precious little doll. It was so over the top. She didn't even know how to *pretend* to be decent.

Mom and Brendan fawn over me incessantly, asking a million questions.

Emmett watches me closely, waiting to see if I'll corroborate with the bullshit he fed to the police. I do for fear of what will happen if I don't, and because some demented part of me wants to please him. Wants to leave myself in his good graces enough to see what could come after that kiss.

"Emmett was just picking me up from practice," I lie. "We were goofing off. His car hit a light post."

"Well, I hope you learned your lesson," she scolds. "And at least you're okay."

I am filled with joy to see Brendan's eyes dart over to Emmett's. He'll let him have it. He's about to tear him a new one, and then maybe, just maybe, the only thing Emmett will have left for me will be any remnants of sweetness he may have buried within him. Enough to make me feel okay doing all of the things I want to do with him.

But Brendan's papa bear rage is cut off before it can even erupt past a dirty look.

"Trey!? Vincent!?" my mother's voice squeaks in surprise, stopping my heart cold.

They both smile and nod to her like schoolboys sucking up to their teacher.

"Oh my gosh! Your mom and I were friends in high school!" she squeals. "How is Cheryl!?"

"Mom, you know these people?" I ask, half terrified, half heartbroken. It feels like a betrayal.

She completely ignores me, making her way over to them to chit chat. Vivian hangs on every word, inserting her own bullshit fake niceties when she can. I am forced to stand there and watch as my worst enemies win over my mother.

My concussed head tries to work harder than it should to process what this all means. If this twisted hierarchy system has been around for ages, and my own mother was best friends with someone at the very core of its roots, does that mean she once played these games too? Was she one of them?

I try to stick close to Brendan, who now feels like the only person left on my side. I am still hoping he's going to pounce across the parking lot and tackle Emmett.

But, to my horror, Emmett marches confidently over to him and extends his hand.

"Sir, you must be Ophelia's step-dad. I'm Emmett," he offers politely.

"You can call me Mr. Lopez," he replies sternly, tightening my stomach as he graciously shakes his hand.

My eyes dart from my mom playing pals with the twins and Vivian back to Brendan treating Emmett so respectfully. I want to transfer images directly into their brains, showing them flashes of all the things these assholes have done to me.

"Just goofing around?" Brendan finally presses Emmett.

I want to believe this is it. This is the moment he puts him in his place. Scares the shit out of him.

"I feel terrible," Emmett lies. "I should have never been so careless with your daughter's safety. I care for her a great deal, and this was a poor example of that."

He's laying it on thick. I feel like I might puke again.

Brendan nods in acceptance, but before one word of reprimanding can begin, we're all interrupted by our doctor coming out from the elevator.

"Mr. and Mrs. Lopez!" he yells as he scuffles across the pavement. "I'm glad I caught you. My nurse just gave me your message about the questions you had. She said you were on your way here so I thought I'd talk with you in person."

"Yes! So glad you found us!" My mother exclaims, rushing over to shake his hand. "As I said in the message, Ophelia is a runner. She's on scholarship and on a pretty strict practice schedule. Just wanted to review how it might need to be adjusted."

My mom and Brendan get swept to the side with the doctor. I try to avoid eye contact with the Elite gang who are circling around like sharks. I stick close to my mom, clinging to safety, but they begin flipping me off so that only I can see.

I want to fly across the parking lot and pummel them. Their faces and attitudes are nauseating on a good day. But watching them go from sweet talking my parents straight back to their heartless little antics in the blink of an eye takes things to a whole new level of despicability.

They go right back into their fake polite smiles and manners the minute my mom and Brendan turn to say goodbye. But as soon as their backs turn again, the Elites are frantically shooting me every crude gesture they can think of.

My mom and Brendan lecture and fuss over my wellbeing the whole way home. But their words melt into distant buzz. I just stare out the window at the passing houses, which get notably smaller the closer we are to home.

I realize just how many times Emmett has made me fear for my life and I feel like I am drowning. This is too much for me to handle on my own. Even with Lily's support…I feel like I am completely alone. After all, she never found any relief from their wrath when they were torturing her. She simply had to wait it out. And I'm beginning to wonder if I'm strong enough to do that.

Every few seconds I inhale sharply as if I'm about

to start speaking. The entire story is so close to spilling right out of my mouth, but as I review it all in my head…I wonder if they would even believe me. And then what? They go to the police? I am already terrified that any action they might try to take would prompt the Elites to bring our whole family down. The way they tried to with Lily.

More than spilling everything to them, I begin to think I need a therapist. Amidst all of this there is still my lingering attraction to Emmett, which I hate myself for. And somehow the accident and the kiss in the hospital has only intensified my sickening desire for him. That's not the kind of thing I could explain to my mom. Only a professional could psychoanalyze me through that one.

9

CHAPTER NINE

I head straight for the stairs the moment we get home, refusing to eat dinner. My stomach is in so many knots I can't even seem to get down a glass of water. My duffle bag flies from my careless hands, landing across the large chest that sits at the foot of my bed as I collapse down onto the mattress.

I feel like I'm coming down with the flu. My body is still sore from the crash but coupled with a relentless nausea. There is a pain in the back of my throat that swells every time I remember kissing Emmett in the hospital room or how things felt for just a few brief moments when I first followed him into his car. Before I saw his torture tools in the backseat.

I squeeze my favorite blanket against my body, clinging to it for some sense of safety and security, as I rock gently on the edge of my narrow, unmade bed. I feel the conflicting pull of wanting to be far away and out of reach while also close and protected all at once.

The brush of it against my skin sends a shiver of memories washing over me. Emmett's crushing grip followed by his kiss. My body releases, wishing I could have melted into his lips, but even the stinging recollection of my hand across his face turns me on in ways I wish it wouldn't.

That look in his eyes, fueled by so much pent up rage and lust, struggling in an all-out internal brawl against one another. Creating tornadoes that tunneled up behind our eyes, before our lids flickered and we kissed once more.

I shake my head and turn to the Bluetooth speakers on my nightstand. With a flick of my wrist, I turn the volume knob to blast over the rage that is rapidly bubbling up inside. Underneath the shroud of blaring music, I clutch my pillow and scream into it at the top of my lungs, wishing the feeling of release was enough to fix the actual problems at hand.

"Ophelia!?" My mom's voice breaks through my refuge with a light tap at the door, interrupting the muffled scream ripping through my lungs. I should have known turning my music up that loud would bring her to my door. My hands clench at the sound of her voice. All I can hear from her mouth now are the ghost tones of her speaking to Vincent and Trey.

"I want to be alone, mom!" I reply through grinding teeth as my jaw tightens.

"We saved you some leftovers from dinner," she persists gently. "They're in the fridge, but I could get them back out and heat them up if you like?"

"I'm not hungry right now! Please, I just want to get some rest!" I try to yell over the emotional cracks in my voice, fighting against the giant lump in my throat. I just want to be alone.

She carries on from the other side of the door with explanations of logistics for the week. Which practices I could and could not go to. A reminder that the doctor says I shouldn't run for a couple of days. Follow up doctors' appointments, pharmacy trips and her work schedule. Boring logistics that could all be just as easily reviewed in the morning, but she's worried and desperate to find some way to stay near me.

I answer her in one-word responses, knowing anything more than that will give me away. If I engage or let on to how upset I am, she'll barge right in and never leave until she's convinced I'm okay.

I do want to run to her. To lay my head in her lap and cry as she strokes my hair like a child. But it would only comfort me if I could tell her everything that was going on. And I can't find a way to play that scenario out in my head that ends in actually helping me or effecting any real change at all.

So instead I stay alone and silent, wishing she would just go.

Once she says goodnight and I finally hear the gentle click of her bedroom door down the hall, I sit up on the bed and cradle my legs in my arms, gently rocking back and forth. Her interaction with the Elites in the hospital parking garage is all I can think about now. Which quite honestly is a relief in the midst of my unrelenting sexual attraction to Emmett.

Even after luring me to his car with a backseat full of evidence that he was up to no good. The yank of my hair jerking me back into the seat, unable to escape. Leaving me feeling safer slamming the car into a telephone pole than to be carted off alone with him. All of that and I still buckled under his kiss.

Shaking it all away once again, I return to my unanswered questions about my mom. I know she keeps a box of her old yearbooks and high school photos in the attic. I don't know why I hadn't thought to dig into it all sooner. Really I should have the moment I was invited to WJ Prep, but for some reason none of it seemed relevant until I saw her talking to them in the hospital parking garage.

When the house has been quiet and still for a while,

I creep slowly toward my bedroom door, overstepping dirty clothes strewn across the floor.

On my way out, I catch sight of myself in my tall bedroom mirror hanging against the wall. Turning side to side, I can see the effects of WJ Prep on my body. My muscles are still firm, but the rest of me is gaunt. As if I'm wasting away. My skin is ashen with dark circles under my eyes, the skin around them is red and bunched up into a pained stare.

The sight only motivates me more as I head for the attic door, taking care to step as quietly as possible around my mom's bedroom. I'm not going to let these assholes waste me away to nothing. I will not lose everything I have worked for so far on account of their sick and twisted games.

Ignoring their rules and social structures and chain of command hasn't worked. So now I have to find something that gives me the upper hand in their game long enough to find a way out of it. Suddenly, my mom's mysterious connection to them seems like a potential light at the end of the tunnel.

I pull down the rectangular hatch door and fold-down staircase of the attic and make my way up, my hand reaching blindly in the dark for the pull string to bring some light. The bare lightbulb buzzes as it clicks on, revealing dusty floorboards that creak as I step across. Pipes and wiring twist up above me in between exposed wooden beams.

The moonlight is filtered through a grimy windowsill littered with dead bugs, casting an eerie glow on the room as I search through the faded boxes labeled with marker until I spot the one I had in mind. My mom's high school relics, yearbooks included. I push past the smell of insulation and stale air filling my throat as I pull the box down from its stack.

Clouds of dust shoot out from the sides of the box as I shove it with my foot to the light in the middle of the room, causing me to cough into the sleeve of my hoodie from the tickle it creates in my throat. I crouch down to open the box, the masking tape squealing as I peel it from the dusty and bent cardboard.

I pull out the glossy hardcover book and begin carefully flipping through the pages that catch on the stomach of my hoodie as I go. Briefly, I freeze at the muffled footsteps of my mom and Brendan echoing through the air vents, and I hope they can't hear me in return.

I need to be alone right now. I have no energy for putting on a face for anyone. Not even them. Especially not while I have this rush of persistence to fight back. I need to ride this wave of energy for as long as it lasts and find out everything I can.

I almost flip right past a photo of my mom and

have to go back several pages to look at it more closely. There she is in a puffy eighties-style prom dress, complete with permed hair. Standing next to her is a man captioned as Theodore Nickelson.

I race to my feet, shaking the grime from my jeans as I run over to another box of photos. One I haven't looked at in years. Old baby photos, some that feature my father still lingering behind, though my mom had thrown most of them out.

I find one of him by my mother's bedside in the hospital, her cradling me in a receiving blanket with him looking down from above, flipping it over to see the handwritten names…Lala and Theo with baby Ophelia.

Theo. Theodore. It couldn't be.

My body stiffens at the sight of it. It never occurred to me that my mom could have met my biological father at WJ Prep. All she had ever told me about him was that he was complete scum who wasn't worth her breath to speak about. Anything about him always brings on an uneasy feeling in the pit of my stomach, which only worsens now that I know he also went to WJPrep.

More than that, there is the haunting missing piece of the puzzle. Theo's full name. I feel like I know it, but I have to see it. My eyes dart between the yearbook and the baby photo of me featuring my dad. I can't deny the resemblance, but I won't accept what I fear to be true until I see evidence.

I remember Lily's run down of everything. Weis, Blackwater, Whitworth, and…Nickelson. The founders of the Jameson Automobile Corporation and the cornerstones of the Elites.

Now my trembling hands hold two photos… One of the man I know to be my father. The other of a man with the same first name…Theodore Nickelson standing next to my mother at prom. Nickelson being the only name Lily mentioned no longer being around town.

I turn back to the yearbooks, needing to find every photo of Theodore Nickelson that I can. A few pages later, I really feel sick. First there is just one, but then a flood of photos quickly follows after. This man who looks like my father cozied up with Thomas Jameson and Walter Whitworth. The three of them with an arrogant lean against lockers or the side of the school. Football games, swim meets and even in the background of other people's pictures.

They were obviously a clique, doing everything together. Meaning, if Theo was in fact Theodore Nickelson… My father…was an Elite.

Visions of my mom play on repeat through my brain. I analyze anything and everything I can remember for some kind of sign that tells me what this means. Was she with them too? How could she be so closely entangled with this sick society of games and hierarchy?

Her kind, smiling, caring face now seems like a mask, but even that conclusion is clouded in doubt. If I could get sucked up into this mess, surely she could have been tricked or forced just as easily.

I try to move through my baffled state well enough to clutch a couple of the most relevant books and photo boxes close to my chest and make my way back to the safety of my room.

I quietly race back into my retreat, locking the door behind me and collapsing across my rug with everything I collected. I open up the yearbooks again, spreading everything across my bedroom floor and staring for a long time. Scouring the pages for each and every mention of my mom or Theodore.

Soon the black and white images are running swirling circles around my head, pulling my hands to my temples. I can't believe it. I throw the book across the room, wanting to be far away from it. It flies across the top of my dresser, sending makeup and hair products raining down in a clatter.

The sound is like the crumbling of whatever I thought I knew about my mom and her past. How I came into this world. It's my own fault for not asking more. But she never seemed to want to talk about it, so I took her silence as all I needed to know.

My face melts in shock, my eyebrows drawing together in an inward stare. A forceful breath escapes my mouth, and suddenly my thoughts are a jumbled swirl. I can't make out a single coherently clear one amidst the scattered and muddled pieces. I need more information.

I place my fingers in a pinch across the bridge of my nose, pushing out slow, deep breaths to try and calm down enough to think of my next move. I need the library, but it's too late and I'll never make it out of the house without being caught. Brendan and my mom would assume I was trying to sneak in a forbidden run and send me right back to bed.

All I have at my disposal is the internet. I scramble to clear the stacks of school papers, pens, pencils and phone accessories from my desk so I can get into my laptop, nearly knocking my lamp over as I move in a frenzy.

My music stopped playing long ago, leaving only the taps of the keyboard to fill my silent room. My fingers restlessly tap against the mouse in between clicks, as I dig for any confirmation I can find of my mother and father's attendance at WJ Prep.

The sound of a flushing toilet from down the hall causes me to jump, as if I know I am uncovering dangerous top-secret information. Things that someone would want to protect and could jump out at any moment to punish me for even trying to uncover it all. A thought that seems absurd in the comfort and safety of my own home, but nothing feels safe right now. It hasn't since my first day at that damned school.

Digging through every free record available to me on the internet, I am finally able to locate several that both relieve and terrify me. I find the original certificates of my mother's marriage and my birth. Both featuring my mother's name as…Lala Nickelson.

My eyes narrow at the name on the screen, the glow of it burning into my pupils until they start to water. The laptop slams shut and then open again. I can't decide if I need to look straight at it for two more hours before I believe it, or if I'll throw up from staring a second longer.

I fly into a manic pace around the room, muttering names and dates as I rub against the back of my neck. I feel stupid. Why had I never asked what my father's last name was? A name that surely would have been both mine and hers at some point in time.

But then I wonder…even if I did have the name Nickelson floating around in my brain, would I have even thought of it when Lily told me about the Jameson Automobile founders?

I go to take a hurried seat at the edge of my bed

but stub my toe on the frame, only making me angrier and more frustrated.

Shit!

My hand clutches around my throbbing toe as I bounce around in circles, screaming silently beneath my breath, still trying not to wake my mom and Brendan. I am no more ready to face them now than I was before my detective work.

Then the moment I sit down I can't help but jump up again. For how drained and despondent I felt only an hour ago, now I'm unable to sit still. My muscles feel like they're jumping underneath my skin.

I rub my hands against my arms, my hairs standing on end from the coursing adrenaline. My vision blurs in a sudden heatwave across my skin as I try to push away my biggest fears. My father was an elite, meaning I was more than just some rat caught up in their game. I was tied to it by blood. But just how deep that tie is… that's what I can't figure out.

All I have is the tree of hierarchy spelled out to me by Lily and these photos and records that indicate my parents attended WJ Prep, with at least one of them being an Elite. But a few of those things are more than what I had at the start of the day, and that's something. Right?

Up until now it felt as if I had no options. No choices for recourse or any way to fight back. And anything that could be pursued, who was I to even try it? I'm nothing around here. Worse than nothing, I'm hated by the people who run this town.

It baffles me even more to think my father was once one of them. Shouldn't that mean I'm on their side? That I inherited a sort of white flag or magic key?

But he isn't on their side anymore… He isn't even in the same town. Bringing a burning flood of more questions barreling up into my throat.

What went wrong? Why isn't my father still here living it up with his high school Elite buddies? Raking in the profits of the Jameson Automobile Company?

Worse than that…is he the reason I'm here? Why I was offered the scholarship in the first place?

Another thought sticks to my brain…the most irrational one, but the one my hormonal lusty side is distracted by the most. Did all of this somehow make my attraction to Emmett more justified? Was there something buried beneath these new revelations that excused his behavior?

If my mom could get past whatever my father's horrible faults were as a member of the Elites enough to marry him and have me, then surely, I could ignore Emmett's confusing hatred for me enough to give into our urges.

But that doesn't take away the fear. All he has

promised is punishment…punishment I would supposedly enjoy and want more of but abuse all the same. So why do I still want it? Why am I grasping at straws in the middle of this new evidence that would give me an excuse to act on my inescapable attraction to him?

After all, Vivian is more of an Elite than I am. Her parents are still all tied up in it and had never left. If bloodlines were to determine who went to bed with Emmett, she's obviously the front runner. Which is why he was kissing her in the garage…but then he was looking at me the entire time.

I try to shake my sexual fantasies away as my body shivers again. Really, I have no idea what any of this means, but it feels like the start of something. A foot in the right direction, and I am desperately willing to cling to anything that hints at an end in sight. I try to keep my grip on the momentum rather than tumble back down under the weight of what felt like a mountain in front of me. One where I can't even see the path up or down.

My eyes glint across shelves of trophies and medals, all of my running accolades that used to make me feel so big and proud. Now they just taunt me. They tell the story of all my potential that is now completely overshadowed by this Elites nightmare.

I look to the posters of Shalane Flanagan and my other favorite runners tacked against my wall and wonder if they ever had to deal with this kind of stuff. I have prepared myself for every kind of typical challenge or obstacle a runner could face. Shin splints, runner's knee, stress fractures, meniscus tears. A bad run at the worst time, like the one I had the day I met Emmett just before coming here.

But I had put so much energy into my sport, I had forgotten to prepare myself for the possibility of whoever my real father was coming back to haunt me. The missing chapter to my story I thought I might make time for some day…when I'm older and in the middle of an illustrious running career. Not now. But it seems I have no choice.

Suddenly, the ding of a new text causes me to jump. I look to the message from an unknown number.

Figure it out yet, bitch?

10

CHAPTER TEN

The next day, I am instantly hit with an uneasy sense of foreboding as I apprehensively walk into school, pushing strands of my ragged hair from my face. With a deep breath, I clutch my backpack and sweater and push myself forward.

My stomach turns in anticipation of what will be waiting for me today. I am expecting something awful in the wake of the crash with Emmett.

I am immediately caught off-guard at how unnoticed my entrance is. Everyone carries on like normal, not even glancing in my direction. I pull my jacket tighter, looking down as I navigate around other passing students in the halls.

But I don't have to do much to work my way through the crowd. Quite the opposite of being the center of attention as I expected. I keep my eyes glued to the floor, the tips of sneakers coming into view promptly step away as I move forward.

I glance up, expecting a sea of snarls and angry glares in my direction. But cheeks are turned with noses high, looking everywhere they can except for at me. It's like I have the plague.

I faintly hear one girl whispering to another, "Here she comes. Look away."

The elaborate game continues. What new way can we fuck with Ophelia today? Having run out of all their other tricks in their books, they seem to be waiting patiently for an idea of what to do next. Maybe that means I finally found some sort of advantage. I have, at least temporarily, outran their schemes.

Shoes squeak across the floors through the echo of everyone laughing and talking, clicking through their combinations and slamming lockers open and shut with thuds of their belongings being thrown inside. The moment the bell rings, the crowd disperses. But I'm in no hurry to rush off to class today.

The hair on my arm raises as my fingers graze my cold metal locker, taking the weight of the combination lock in my hand. The metal shows traces of my sweaty hands. Once I've thrown a few things in and taken a few things out, I look around again. Expecting the Elite mob to be stalking from a nearby corner, waiting to find me alone.

But I see no one. Everything is completely silent except for the muffled sounds of teachers starting their lectures.

My palm presses against the soreness of my neck as my eyes cut around the silent, empty halls. I roll my shoulders back against my neck, my fingers trailing up to fiddle with my necklace as I slowly step toward my first classroom.

I feel no better once I settle into class, the teacher and students around me carrying on as usual. I raise my hands a few times, even though I don't know the answers, just hoping to be called on so someone will have said my name or looked in my direction enough for me to know I'm still alive.

Did I die in the car crash? Was everything after that just my brain's weird way of fantasizing my life into continuance? And now reality's set in, my existence is fading into nothingness?

My mouth fills with the taste of wood from the pencil I have been gnawing at relentlessly, sparking an idea. I let the pencil fall to the floor, thinking someone will look up or pick it up to hand it back. But nothing. It quietly clicks against the floor as it rolls right out into the middle of the room, completely untouched and seemingly unnoticed.

My foot bounces wildly underneath my desk, my eyes darting to the clock on the wall every few seconds. I can't stop reaching down to dig through my purse, forgetting what I was looking for each time.

I blow out several short breaths, trying to steady my heart rate, but my fidgeting and noisy exhales don't bring a single darting glance my way. Even the teacher seems to be actively ignoring me.

I jump at the ring of another bell, following closely behind as everyone floods back out into the halls. Stopping at the edge of the door, my finger presses the button to light up my phone screen, wondering if another mysterious message will come through with a clue. Or even a menacing text from Emmett. But nothing.

My stomach churns and time moves too slow as the halls of the school seem to wind down to nothing in front of me, closing in on me. Normally I would welcome getting lost in the tide of students between classes. This is the kind of isolation I had expected when I first came here. But in this context, it feels wrong.

My hair is matted in the same ponytail as yesterday, tangled from restless tossing and turning in my bed all night. I keep my facial features blank, hoping that if I don't show any emotion they'll give up on the whole charade.

For a few periods, I tried looking as happy as can be. Smiling wide and whistling as I walked. But with no one to even notice, it started to feel ridiculous. So, I resorted back to calm nothingness. Apathy. Indifference.

For as calm as I look outside, inside I am falling apart. Frequently retreating to the bathroom to lock myself away in a stall. It feels better to be truly alone than to be surrounded by people who don't see me.

After an endless daze of morning classes, it's finally time for lunch. I'm certain something will happen in the cafeteria. The Elites had pounced on me for merely existing up until now. There's no way they'll leave what happened with Emmett unpunished.

At the very least, Emmett's car is mangled and in his warped mind, it's my fault. I expect to be punished. The silent build-up has to be part of their plan. Making me wither away in dreaded anticipation before they strike.

In the cafeteria, the bright florescent lights overhead flicker with a horror movie style buzz. I scan the rows of long tables and plastic chairs, ducking between lines of teens carrying their plastic trays. The double doors sway open and shut as more people flood in, each one's eyes looking everywhere but at me.

I know I can't eat, but I get lunch anyway, only to sit despondently and shove the food around on my tray with a fork. I guzzle down several bottles of water. Taking in liquids is the one thing I can do right now. I am parched no matter how much I drink.

I feel like an animal on high alert. Everything seems to be moving in slow motion under the gaze of the entire cafeteria. I hear every tiny little noise amplified…someone dropping silverware, the slop of food on someone's tray, students shuffling in their seats and clearing their throats. People chewing their food and the hiss of opening cans.

It gets to be too much, sending me bolting for the privacy of a bathroom stall yet again to eat alone. I duck into the first stall I can and flick the lock shut.

I quickly forget about my lunch as I hear a few girls flinging open stall doors that slam shut behind them with the flush of toilets followed by water streaming from faucets. They laugh as they fix their hair and makeup. The smell of perfume and hairspray fills the air as they gossip in hushed tones.

Finally, I hear my name. I half expect them to be discussing my tragic death. I study the sounds of their voices and their shoes from under the stall to try and discern who the girls might be, but I can't place them.

My eyelids blink rapidly as they talk, my body closing in and growing still to better hear them as the whirring hand dryers finally quiet down enough for me to make out their words.

"Can you believe it?" One girl chirps with a pop of her gum. "She's nuts. She was so determined to blow him right then and there that she made him run his car straight into the damn telephone pole."

Resentment and anger bubble up in my chest. I want to come barreling out and tell them everything that really happened. But once again I find myself stilling to see what else I can hear. Hoping for some hint at what to expect next.

"Tragic," another girl answers dryly. "So what now? We just ignore her?"

"That's what Vivian says. We're supposed to act like she doesn't exist. Which I'm happy to do. That'll teach her a lesson. Maybe the bitch will think twice before trying to blow someone else's boyfriend."

Jesus. What sort of punishment is that? I would take the relief of being shunned over the torture they had been doling out any day.

I bite my lip to hold back the questions bubbling up inside, nodding and blinking as they continue. That's why there's a lull in my torment. The Elites have told everyone to ignore me at all costs. For the rest of the semester. No talking. No looking. I am essentially a ghost.

My lips purse with raised brows, my fingers pinching against my chin. I obsessively check my phone once more, feeling half tempted to text last night's unknown number back. At least it'd be someone to talk to if nothing else. Still nothing.

The girls shuffle their plastic cosmetic cases back into their bags in a flurry of maniacal cackles as they exit the bathroom, the door swinging shut behind them to leave me in silence.

It couldn't be so bad, right? So, no one talks to me. Who cares? It'll be a relief in comparison to what I've been experiencing.

The isolation carries on throughout the day. I catch a few glimpses of Emmett, each time renewing my urge to feel his lips again. To hear the breathless groans he makes beneath my kiss. But the surge of hormones always dissipates into knots of anxiety as he effortlessly continues to not see me.

I choke down my desire for him, running through the list of everything he's done to me so that maybe I will finally come to my senses and be glad that I am exiled.

Walking through the halls, I feel the emptiness in the lack of strange and pitying looks I had grown used to. In their effort to shun me, even the whispers of my name have vanished. I'm not even a topic of gossip anymore.

Under doctor's orders, I still can't run for a few days. So, I'm relieved when it's time for gym. I need something to do to work off this anxiety. Some physical activity might calm my nerves.

I walk past the cinder block walls of the gym, scoffing at the school's name painted along the shiny wood floor. I hate that my name is somehow wrapped up in the legacy of this hellhole with the new knowledge of my father's attendance and former Elite title.

But his involvement disturbs me much less than my mom's. She is supposed to be a cornerstone in my life. One person I can fall back on when I have no one else. But now even she is tainted by the WJ Prep sickness. Not knowing to what extent only makes it worse, somehow.

My back aches from the lack of support on the bleachers retracting into the walls as I anxiously wait for the teacher to announce what we're doing today. I slump my shoulders at the revelation of dodgeball, the basket of balls quickly rolling in behind the words.

Great, that will be heavenly for my already sore and aching muscles. But honestly, I'll take it. The thrash of balls into my painful joints might be soothing somehow. Something to jolt me out of this haze of nonexistence. A reminder that I am alive.

With the blow of the teacher's whistle, the gym quickly fills with the sounds of sneakers squeaking across the floor and students calling out to one another. But my state of exile worsens. Every ball I try to snatch up is quickly taken right out from under me. Not a single one is thrown in my direction.

I stand with my hands on my hips, watching as the entire game races by without me. A comedic image of the bullied kid being a target and getting pounded with everyone's balls at once flashes through my mind. A scenario that I would almost welcome at this point. Somehow being ignored is worse.

Realizing my participation is null and void, I retreat to the water fountains to lap up as much as I can take in, partly to soothe my sudden unquenchable thirst, but mostly to avoid the awkwardness of being invisible.

The locker room is another place most girls would gladly accept a shroud of invisibility, but once again I am surprised at how much it bothers me. I sit on the long wooden bench in the middle of the lockers and stare down to the faint mildew spots staining the grout between the plain beige tiled floor, wishing I could find relief in all of this.

Surely being ignored is better than being tortured. I wanted an end to it, and now here it is. Served up to me on a silver platter. But it doesn't feel like a break at all. It's like the silent ghost town in a movie with crows cawing ominously in the distance, tumbleweeds blowing past. Quiet should be good, but you know it's just making space for whatever bad thing happens next.

Suddenly, I see a familiar pair of shoes in the corner of my eye. My heart leaps as I look up to see Lily huddled in the corner, drying sweat from her hair.

"Lily!" I rush over like an excited puppy, my voice cracking under the hours of not speaking out loud. "There you are!"

She doesn't respond at first, looking to her phone instead before finishing her preparations to head back out into the hall.

"Oh, come on," I huff with a laugh, assuming she's just messing with me ."Not you too."

My smile wavers as she looks straight through me, refusing to let her eyes meet mine. My hands wrap around my arms as I feel my face blanch. Before I know it, she's whirling right past me, stepping to the side to avoid our shoulders bumping. She is pointedly ignoring me right along with everyone else.

Left alone again, I tensely pace the locker room tiles, wringing my hands across the back of my neck. For the first time today, I want to cry. The one person I consider a friend is now against me. Everyone is avoiding me. I am completely alone.

My world quickly feels like it's closing in. With even Lily refusing to speak to me, I officially have no one outside of my parents. Between this new discovery about my mom and biological father and their ties to WJ Prep, mixed in with feeling like I couldn't tell them anything that was really happening at school, they feel like they're a million miles away even if they're right next to me.

I stand with my hand spread across the wall, my head bowing to take in a series of deep inhales and exhales, before reentering the halls to exit the building. My heart rate finally slows when I'm outside again, feeling the warmth of the sun on my cheeks. But even the cloudy blue skies seem ominous in my exile.

I hesitate in my pace with each person I pass in the parking lot, thinking someone will cave in and acknowledge me. But they've obviously done this before. It's like the Elites control a switchboard in everyone's brains and can simply flip it on anyone at any time, making them completely unperceivable.

I debate going to practice. I can't run away. But I had planned on at least stopping by to talk to Coach Granger. My mom had already called to let him know I'd be absent for a couple of days as I recovered, but surely he's above this vow of silence? He might be the only person left who would still speak to me.

A glimmer of hope shines through the clouds at the thought of him. He had said I could come to him for anything, and while I wasn't prepared to even begin explaining everything that had happened, a simple smile or hello would suffice. After this day from hell where every other teacher played along as Vivian's pawns.

It was disgusting the way the entire school staff, and even the police, just sucked up to the Elites, going along with whatever new dumb thing they demanded. Even if it meant pretending I didn't exist. It was that extent of their power and influence that kept me silent. Especially after seeing my mom playing chummy with Trey and Vincent.

By not telling anyone, even my parents or coach, I still have some distant hope of confessing to them as a last resort. If I play that card too soon only to find it did nothing, I would feel too hopeless to go on.

I can't find Coach Granger at the track, and of course no one will answer me when I try to ask around for him. But finally I catch a note on the billboard informing everyone that he'd be absent today and to run the usual laps.

Fucking of course. Of all the days he could be absent, it had to be the one when he might have been the only person who would acknowledge me.

With each new instance of being shunned, I want to take off running to my car. But I'm too sore and tired. I walk slower than a turtle, kicking pebbles as I go. By the time I do reach my car, I decide to keep walking. I already feel claustrophobic with a lingering shock from the crash. I can't stand the thought of getting in. I'll walk home.

My mind races as I go, drenched in self-loathing of my own hypocrisy. From day one all I wanted was for everyone to forget me. Move their target to someone else's back. I just wanted to run and focus on my grades, hoping if I stayed out of their way they'd stay out of mine. And now that my wish is finally granted, I can't stand it.

When I get home, the house is dark and quiet, only worsening my feeling of seclusion. I remember Mom saying she would be working late. I collapse into bed, not even bothering to change out of my uniform. Sprawled out across the bed, my hand grips the phone, waiting for any kind of message. Even a bad one. Anything at all.

The long, gray day fades as I drift into a light nap. The kind that comes from boredom and restlessness, where every tiny sound or thought wakes you up again. Denying you the escape of sleep.

11

CHAPTER ELEVEN

I don't know how long I've been awake before I finally resign to having to open my eyes. I had half-hoped I would just fall asleep again and wouldn't have to worry about it, but it became apparent that wasn't going to happen this time. The room is still mostly dark, but the harsh rays of light darting through the openings in the curtains tell me it isn't early morning anymore.

I look over to the nightstand. 12:00pm. Shit. I slept in again. This is becoming a more frequent pattern, seemingly beyond my control. I lay here for hours, tossing and turning, not falling asleep until it's almost dawn. Then I'm unable to stay awake when I should be getting up.

One week has gone by. Still nothing. No one will

look at me. No one will talk to me. Aside from the moments I desperately cling to with my mom and Brendan, which are scarce around their busy work schedules, I am completely alone.

I slide out of bed, my still-tired body aching with each movement. My legs seem to buckle underneath me, not wanting to cooperate. I go downstairs, finding the house to be empty. My parents have already left for work.

I make it into the kitchen and see that it is mostly empty. Well, not exactly empty. There are eggs and bacon and bread for toast. A normal person would jump right in to making a nice breakfast, but the thought of cooking right now repulses me. I have zero appetite or energy to prepare food.

I throw on a t-shirt, secure my hair up into a sloppy bun and put on a pair of leggings and tennis shoes. Most importantly, I put on sunglasses to hide my tired eyes from the world. Walking out into the sun is painful. It burns into my eyes, my head and every bone in my body.

Once I'm at school, I wander through the halls, accepting my fate in exile. At least no one cares that I'm late. I look around and see a gangly kid approaching me with an apologetic look on his face. Finally, this is it. Someone is going to talk to me. But instead he just rushes past to his friends on the other side of the hall.

Coach Granger has been absent for a family emergency. And none of the other teachers will acknowledge my existence. Even when I try to corner them with direct questions, the other students always find a way to distract them or steal the attention back.

I am completely and utterly alone.

A state that at times, especially recently, I thought I wanted. But now that it is happening, I am more miserable than I have ever been.

I understand the concept now of children misbehaving for attention. Because negative attention is better than no attention at all. They would rather be punished than be ignored, and that is exactly how I feel right now.

I miss the punishment of the Elites. That's how insane isolation has driven me.

It's lunchtime, and I am over hiding away alone in the bathroom. I thought if I faced down being ignored, something would change. But then I realized it didn't matter if I tried to hide or put myself out in the middle of everything. The result is the same. So there's no use in hiding.

Instead I sit here in a room full of people completely alone. I can hear cackles from the Elite table. And it makes me want to smack each one of them in the face until there's nothing left to laugh about.

That's it. I have reached my breaking point. Finally, I'm so desperate for human contact that I decide to do something drastic. Something that can't be ignored.

I scan across the room, inevitably landing my sights on the Elites' lunch table. I hate how happy and arrogant they look. They don't deserve to be so carefree with the misery they inflict on other people's lives, and I've finally had enough.

I can feel my muscles quake as I stand from my seat and charge straight for them. My nostrils flare as sweat beads across my skin. My shoulders bump against people as I go, which they still do their best to ignore, and I don't stop until I'm at the edge of their table.

They keep looking everywhere but at me, but I see their eyes give the faintest glint in my direction. Everything closes in around Vivian in pure tunnel vision. She is the only thing I can see now.

I bare my teeth and with one sweeping, swift motion, I slap Vivian right across the face. A violent clap echoes through the silent lunchroom as my flat and stiffened palm strikes her cheek.

Vivian looks up to me with a vicious growl, her hand still pressed against her red cheekbone in shock. Her eyes bulge out of her head so far, I think they might burst.

Before I can think or do anything else, she is pummeling toward me. My body slams to the ground beneath her attack, her hands pinning my arms down long enough for her to break free and go for a punch.

I am too high on jealousy and anger. My adrenaline is pumping, giving me what feels like special powers. I am alert and sharp enough to catch her blow midair with my hand gripped around her wrist. I roll over, reversing our positions so that she is now the one pinned below me.

I go into a flurry of punches. One right after the other. Anywhere I can manage. Her face, her ear, her side. She knees me a few good times, but other than that is completely helpless beneath my rage. I can't even feel the scratches she manages to get in across my hands and arms in defense.

I stare ahead blankly, cold and hard as jeers and taunts swell up around us. Finally, I think. At least they're acknowledging that they can see me. I don't even care that they are cheering for Vivian, encouraging her to get the upper hand again.

I'm surprised that no one jumps in to stop me, but I imagine I look like an absolute mad woman running on nothing but pure anger. They're afraid of me. I also like to think everyone secretly wants to see Vivian get the shit beat out of her.

Finally, an arm across my chest snaps me from my

red blur of fury, but barely. I feel a man's firm chest push to my back as I'm raised into the air, my arms still flailing viciously. Just before I'm hauled through the swinging cafeteria doors, I see Vivian glaring as she's left to pick herself up off the floor.

I don't know who is carting me off until he's pushing me up against the wall of an empty classroom. Emmett.

His hand grips around my neck, his own neck muscles bulging and his breath heavy through his nose. I don't recoil as I normally would. I'm so desperate for his eyes to be burning into mine. His hands across my skin, even if they are holding on too tight. Instead I melt into him, drawing my chin up to meet his gaze.

The desperation in my eyes softens his touch, drawing the curve of his finger across my jaw.

"What the hell were you thinking?" he hisses, his skin roiling with desire. I can feel it coursing through his fingertips, and I know how it is burning into him because I feel it too.

"You can't do this to me," I respond breathlessly, his fingers clutching harder into my neck as I speak. "You can't just pretend I don't exist."

"You did this to yourself," he groans, his head swaying with the rhythm of my squirms. "If you had just been a good little pet and done what you were told…"

"Enough of that shit!" I try my best to shout, but it cracks into a whisper. "I'm no one's pet. Not even yours. All I've done is defend myself."

"Oh no?" he grins devilishly. His hand drops below my neck, forcefully pressing down every inch of my chest before resting across my abs. "You're not my pet?" His eyes move hungrily over me from top to bottom, taking in every inch of me.

I want to scream no, but I can't say anything. I'm too high on the ecstasy of human contact.

"I like you like this," he croons softly, leaning closer to my ear. The soft graze of his lips sets my skin on fire. "Broken down…desperate. I bet I could do anything I wanted to you right now, couldn't I?"

"Key word being *want*," I shoot back in a moan. "You do want me. You have wanted me this whole time."

I don't even care anymore how sick and twisted this whole thing is. His desire is all I care about right now. I need the validation. I need to know I am real after this week of feeling non-existent. And I know that's what he gets out of all of this. I don't know if his motivation for making my life a living hell is the same as Vivian's or any of the other Elites, but I know the benefit is that it leaves me like this…putty in his hands.

When he doesn't answer, I push forward to run away,

but his palm quickly juts across my chest and slams me back again. His breath quickens even more, and I can see him trying to resist as his finger trails across my face.

All at once we both surrender, our lips colliding and opening wide as our tongues crash across each other in firm waves. I can't help but whimper into his mouth, sparking an earnest groan from his in return.

"When I saw you storm up to our table, I was hoping we would end up like this," he mumbles into my lips, barely breaking us apart to speak. "I was expecting you to put up more of a fight. We really did get to you this time, huh?"

I almost think I can sense a tinge of pity in his voice. Not the degrading kind, but a sincere sympathy for what they have put me through. It makes me lose myself in him even more, my hands sliding across his back, up his neck and clenching into his hair. His hips push against mine, keeping me pinned firmly to the wall, and I can feel his hardness straining against his paints.

"Touch me," I plead, biting his lip.

He pulls back, his eyes lighting up with a yearning fire as he studies me. He's surprised I'm so willing right now. I saw it in the moment his eyebrows raised ever so slightly.

But rather than give in to what we both want, his

grip tightens around my neck again, pulling my lips from his.

"You know I can't just let you get away with what you did to Vivian," he says almost apologetically. "They'll never let me."

"So…what? You're just their puppet?" I tease defiantly, expecting a swift reprimand for challenging him.

The way he stills suddenly frightens me. I can see a new touch of humanity in him. One that really does feel sorry for me and all he's done to me. Could it be that none of this is Emmett's choosing? Is he just caught up in the game like I am and doing what he's told?

His hand loosens from my neck, falling limp to his side as he steps back in surrender, still saying nothing.

My mind flashes with all that he's done. The physical and emotional abuse. And all at once I remember there's no way he's just an Elite pawn. He is one of them through and through. And even if part of him feels regret now, he was completely in charge all the times before when he caused me harm.

And it all served the exact purpose it was intended to…to leave me so fucked up and desperate for anything that I would willingly give myself over to him. Admit to the things he makes my body feel, no matter how much it repulses me.

I'm overwhelmed with it all. I can't believe this sad

puppy act he's putting on all of a sudden, and I don't want to fall for it. Unable to fight the single tear spilling down the side of my face, I push past him and run away down the hall as fast as I can.

I don't stop until I'm halfway to my car. Fuck this day. Fuck school. The way the teachers have been acting I'm not even entirely sure they're counting my attendance or grades anyway. I might as well give up and go home.

But once I reach my car door, I still don't stop. Running feels too good right now. It's what I need. I keep barreling forward, right past my car, all the way to my house. I'll figure out the rest later. Right now I just need to run.

The cold sting of air bursts in my lungs as I go, burning with tears that I try to fight back as hard as I can. Every time I feel the pulse of his lingering touch, I run faster and harder. Hoping the swift wind against my body will blow it all away.

By the time I collapse on my bed in my room, all I can feel is the need for his warmth against me again. The fantasy of him falling on top of me in my bed is so palpable that I almost reach for my phone to message him. Beg him to come finish what he started.

I swear I hear a drum beating in my ears, but I quickly realize it's just the steady severity of my own heart. Pounding through me as the most tangible images of Emmett flash through my mind. I can see exactly what he would look like right here right now… towering above me in this light as he takes off his shirt.

I roll into my hands, covering my eyes and wishing it would all go away. Somehow my desperate need to punish Vivian and to get some kind of attention rapidly crumbled into a completely unhindered lustful need for Emmett. More strong than I have ever felt before.

The way he sounded so sorry… It reminds me of how he sounded before I got into his car. I remember now that's why I followed him in the first place. He sounded so sincere. So normal. Maybe even kind.

It was the same boy I met at that track meet before coming here. Maybe I don't have to beat myself up so much, or maybe I'm just grasping at straws. But I have seen small glimpses of a decent human being in him. Ever so brief moments when he doesn't seem demented or sadistic. And each new taste of it seems to cause my longing for him to erupt. It clouds my judgment. Makes me do everything I swore I couldn't.

It makes me surrender completely to him.

Completely exhausted, I close my eyes and hope to dream of something…anything else.

My brush with Emmett was exactly what I needed to set my head straight in a weird way, because now I am more than happy to embrace my isolation. I'm resting in it like a shroud.

I gladly walk alone and eat alone yet again when I return to the lunchroom. But it seems now that I want the isolation, they're ready to take it away again. Because I can see the Elite pack marching right toward me in the corner of my eye. I don't look at them, staring down at the sandwich in my hands instead, hoping they will just walk right past.

And at first, they do. But then Emmett's hands reach around and spread out on the table before me, his chest leaning into mine with his lips next to my ear. Reawakening every spark I felt the day before and had worked so hard to erase. Only now, Vivian is just a few feet away, watching our every move.

"Get up and come with us," he demands with the best growl he can muster, but I can still hear the lingering pity and reluctance. I tell myself he doesn't want to be doing this. He said he couldn't let me get away with it…that they'd never let him.

Before I can protest, his hand grips my arm and lifts me to my feet with a subtle jerk. Just enough to let me know I don't have a choice without outright manhandling me in front of the entire cafeteria. My sandwich drops to my tray and before I can say or do anything else, I'm being led back to the same classroom he and I took refuge in just the day before.

He pushes me inside as the rest of them file in behind him. I catch one last subtle "I'm sorry" look from him in my direction before he turns to lock the door and close the blinds. Instinctively, I start stepping back away from them, quickly meeting the edge of a table that stops me from moving any further.

I lean back to brace myself and consider attempting to dart away between the table and chairs, but they're surrounding me like a pack of hungry dogs. I know it's no use. Trey and Vincent surround me on either side, each grabbing an arm and carrying me to the wall.

The memories of Emmett pinning me to this wall almost make me immune to my fear of whatever is about to happen. I glance over to him, but before our eyes can meet, he quickly looks away. By the time I look back up, Vivian is storming toward me.

I brace myself for a revenge slap and am instead met with the blow of her fist, shooting straight into my nose and up between my eyes with streams of tears. Followed by a warm trickle of blood from my nostrils.

I feel the physical sensation of the pain, but barely. I am numb to them now. My apathy scares me more than they do as I look back to her blankly, unmoved by the punch. It only eggs her on. She delivers another swift blow to my gut.

"You had enough yet?" she growls into my ear. "You ready to talk?"

"Talk about what?" I shoot back, defiantly spitting the blood from my lips in her direction.

Her palm strikes my cheek, the sting echoing into my eardrums.

She steps back with a half-hearted smirk and looks me up and down, nodding to Trey and Vincent to let me down. I collapse to the floor, but quickly pull myself back up. Ready to stand and take more of a beating if that's what she insists on. I'm over backing down to them.

"Well?" Vivian snaps expectantly.

I don't know what she wants from me, but I'm positive I wouldn't give it to her even if I could.

"What!?" I cry back in frustration. "What is it you want from me?"

"You know damn well what we want," she sneers, pacing in front of me. "Don't play dumb."

I consider telling her what Emmett and I did in here the day before, and again before that in the hospital room. My eyes glint toward him at the prospect, but he still refuses to look in my direction. His hands are in his pockets shamefully, looking down to the floor as if he has nothing to do with any of this.

But I know, no matter how sorry he may be, that's not entirely true.

And anyway, telling her about those moments will only ensure they never happen again. However fucked up it may be, it's not a bridge I'm willing to burn just yet.

"I don't know what you want!" I bark back at her, clutching the ache in my gut. "I haven't known what you've wanted this whole time! You're all fucking crazy! Ganging up on me for no reason!"

"Is that what you think?" she smiles arrogantly. "That we don't have better things to do with our time than chase you around? Get over yourself. We'd be happy to just forget you ever existed like the meaningless nothing you are. But we have to protect ourselves. So here we are."

"Protect *yourselves*!?" I scoff in disbelief, my voice betraying me with too high of a pitch. "What the hell do you need to be protected from? I'm the one that's being treated like some kind of prey. You've gone after me relentlessly from day one!"

"I'm not an idiot," she growls back. "You know more than you're letting on." She nods back to Vincent and Trey who promptly scoop me back up against the wall, my stomach muscles still clenching in pain from the time before.

I grit my teeth to bear another round of blows to

my face and stomach, punctuated with a crippling kick to my shin. The sting sends me into a panic.

"Stop!" I scream in anguish. I can take a beating anywhere at this point, but not my legs. I have lost enough time on the track because of these assholes. I won't lose any more. "Not my legs! Please! I don't know what you want from me…but whatever it is, I'll try. Just please not my legs."

Vivian's lips curl. She's pleased that she struck a nerve. Found a weak spot. She steps forward, her foot rearing back again, but Emmett grabs her.

"Vivian, no," he commands, shaking her by the shoulder between his hands. "She said she'd talk."

Her eyes burn into him, giving me the feeling that he'd pay for that later. But for now, she complies and turns her attention back to me.

"You're gonna have to do more than try," she grunts. "When's the last time you talked to him? I want to know everything he has said recently. About us."

"What the fuck are you talking about?" I sob in exasperation, feeling completely clueless. Like they have the wrong girl. I'm being framed. I have to be. I don't know whatever it is they think I know.

"Give it up already, Ophelia! Your fucking dad!!" She barks back, my heart stopping as the words roll from her tongue.

My fucking dad, indeed. I should have known this

entire vendetta against me had something to do with him from the moment I found out he was once an Elite. I suddenly wish I had kept digging. That I knew more by now. But I was too distracted with the exile they placed me under.

I can feel my blood boiling beneath my skin. Of course this man who my mom considers to be the scum of the earth…who has been completely absent from my entire life…is now somehow responsible for all the torture I've been enduring.

12

CHAPTER TWELVE

My brain sparks, rapidly trying to connect everything enough to make some sense of her ranting. Wrapping my head around my dad being an Elite in the first place was hard enough. But that was in the past…and he seems to be long gone now. But Vivian is acting like he's still around…playing all of their games. I'm screaming inside, wishing I could escape being involved at all.

My eyebrows gather with a heavy sigh as my mind drifts to all the places I'd rather be. Anywhere but here. Running. Laying in my bed. Eating in the cafeteria.

I hate myself for slapping Vivian yesterday, even if it was rewarding. And even if it did get Emmett's lips pressed back to mine, if only for a few moments.

I knew there would be a price to pay. But I'm not

so sure the benefits were worth the cost as I stand here now with the Elites circling me like vultures, working my stomach into knots.

My feet point toward the door as my dull eyes drift to its window, wishing I could catch sight of a teacher passing by. Or another student. But I know better. Even if someone did walk by, they wouldn't help.

I'm completely stuck. Cornered. The only way out is to bend to their will, and even that isn't a way out. It's just more of the same. No matter what I do…I am their pawn. Or, their "pet" as Emmett likes to say.

I want nothing to do with the Elites, especially if it helps them. The only thing I can think I want less than working with the Elites in any way…is to have anything to do with my biological father. In fact, it seems more and more that those two things are one and the same.

The sun is shining in through the classroom windows, and I can see the track field off in the distance. I would do anything to be out there running right now instead of in here being threatened and tortured.

I think back on Coach Granger's offer…when he told me I could tell him anything. I am kicking myself for not having the balls to talk to him then.

But now here I am piecing this all together on my own. All of this has something to do with my dad.

I guess it's better than having to think the Elites are so incredibly bored and desperate for something to do that they make people's lives miserable just for fun. These people have power and money, and they're willing to do whatever it takes to protect their positions in life.

I want this new motive to redeem Emmett. All of them, but mostly him. I know I wouldn't have liked Vivian and Bernadette even if they hadn't attacked me before I even set foot on campus.

But my crush on Emmett was strong. I thought we had potential…until I realized who he really was. Does having some insight to the motive somehow excuse everything he has done?

I can't believe my father used to be one of them and that he is apparently still chasing after them in some way. Enough to have them all riled up.

My mother is completely the opposite of anything the Elites stand for. She's worked hard to give me a good life. Brendan does too. But at the end of the day, all they care about is family. Money and things have never been top priorities for them. And they would never betray their friends or family, or bring physical harm to someone, just to protect some perceived entitlement to social and financial standing.

I look to the clock on the wall, gulping as I realize lunch period lasts for another twenty minutes. Then the students will crowd back into the halls and this classroom will need to be used.

It's a relief to know there is an end in sight. They could have thrown me into one of their cars and drove me off somewhere. At least this way I know we have to be done in twenty minutes or less. But a lot can happen in that amount of time.

"Just tell me what you want," I hiss with tired eyes that are dead and flat. I'm over the secrecy and vagueness. Maybe if I hear them out it will give me more information on what my dad has to do with all of this.

"You're just collateral, sweetie," Vivian answers smugly, her voice chiming sweetly in a mocking tone with her pinched face and sour expression. "Just be a good little bitch and do what we tell you, and we'll take it easy on you."

"Ha!" I scoff, finding it hard to believe they'd ever take it easy on me. "Now I really don't know what you're talking about."

They've hurt me. Humiliated me. I've suffered greatly at their hands and now…they want my help? I look away, feeling at a loss for words.

"Let me put it this way," she continues menacingly, jutting out her chest and crossing her arms. "If he doesn't stop playing games, you're dead. So, you might as well save your own ass and help us."

"You're out of luck, Vivian. I've never talked to my

dad. I don't know the guy. He doesn't even know I'm here, so this is just a waste of your time," I fume, rolling my eyes, my head hanging heavy, in hopes that this will be the end of it. But I know better. They'd never give up so easy.

"I find that hard to believe," she fires back with a look of superiority, projecting her voice just to show she has the upper hand in a determined strut around the room in perfect posture. "We know he saw the press release about your scholarship and you attending WJ Prep."

"And how would you know something like that?" I groan with an upward glance, a dramatic breath rattling my lips.

"Because we sent it to him, you dumb bitch!" she shrieks impatiently, her fingers retracting into claw-like fists.

"Well then that's on you, isn't it? Still has nothing to do with me. And if anything, it just proves my point more. So, you made sure he knew I was here, but he still hasn't contacted me," I explain condescendingly, settling my back to the wall and crossing my arms.

"Trust me, he knew exactly where you were long before we sent that release," she continues with a loud blusterous voice. "We just wanted to make sure he knew we were on to him. I think he's been more present in your life than you originally thought. And if it comes down to it…we'll kidnap you and use you as a bargaining chip. He's not going to get away with his bullshit."

"This has nothing to do with me, Vivian," I plead cluelessly. "I don't know what's going on with you and my dad, but whatever it is…it's just between you two. He's not in my life and I'm not in his. And I'd like to keep it that way."

"You don't have a choice, Ophelia. Just by existing, you're wrapped up in this. You're the only key we have to him, and we'll use you however we have to." Vivian turns away snidely as Trey and Vincent circle me.

"Use me for what!? What is it that he's doing!?" I keep looking to Emmett, but he is still and blank. No one answers me. "I'll just go to the police," I try to reason uselessly. Knowing as soon as the words fall from my mouth that it's a futile remark.

"The police work for us just like everyone else in this town," Vincent sneers with a crack of his neck.

"Of course, how could I forget," I say sarcastically with a sharp, hopeless exhale. "This is fucking useless."

"You're still dumb enough to think everything is just happening by coincidence," Vivian sneers. "There's a reason you're here, Ophelia. At this school. Your father waged war with our families before you were born, and it's still going."

"How!? What did he do? I don't know anything!"

"I'm sure you'll figure it out in time," she smiles. "But for now…you have one job. Get him to stop coming after our parents."

"Great…except I have no clue how to do that," I fire back dryly. "You don't seem to be getting it. We have nothing to do with each other and I don't know anything about this supposed war he's in with you and your stupid fucking families."

"You don't have to know anything. You just have to get him to respond to our messages. Or else you're dead," she turns her back to me impatiently.

"Ophelia," Emmett finally chimes in, practically begging me to comply. "You'll help us. Or we'll kill you. And that's the end of it." It almost sounds like he wants me to give in so I'll be spared any more torture.

"I'm not helping you with anything," I growl, sparking a pleased grin across Emmett's face. It's as if he wants to kill me. Maybe that'd be easier for him than dealing with whatever's going on between us.

Trey and Vincent lunge forward again, their rough hands twisting into my shoulders and wrists. I'm still sore from Vivian's beating, but try to buckle down and brace myself against the wall the best I can, but they're too strong. My teeth grind as their hands circle my arms tightly, burning and pinching the skin as they go. I wince and take tentative steps beneath their grip, my eyes watering up from the sensation. They don't stop.

My head flails back against the wall with my face twisted into a grimace.

"Let me go!" I scream in a panic in between grunts and pained hisses, wondering if they really do have the balls to kill me right here and now. That might be better than having to help them or have anything to do with my father. Their fingers twist into my skin with a burning sensation. "Stop! Just leave me alone!"

My breath saws in and out rapidly as Vivian marches toward me again, sending her foot back into my shin despite Emmett's disapproval. I yowl out in pain as I crash back down to the floor.

"Fuck!" I cry, rubbing my hand across my stinging leg bone that is already turning purple. Within seconds, I am lifted back into the air, propping me up for more of Vivian's blows. But to my surprise, Emmett appears just a foot away from me. I wonder how he felt about Vivian denying his orders to leave my legs alone. After all, he enjoys looking at these muscular legs of mine. If I can't run, they go to flabby shit…which just isn't in his best interests.

He scowls toward the others, prompting them to back up. It's as if he watched for as long as he could, but now he has to have me to himself again. Whether Vivian is watching or not.

"Quit fighting us," he barks. "Just make sure your dad responds to our parents. And do what we tell you."

"I don't even know how to reach him," I growl, fighting back sobs.

His feet inch closer to me, propelling me back to the day before. We were exactly like this. Him seething before me as I was pinned up against the wall. My eyes dart over to Vivian as I wonder if I should kiss him again right in front of her.

"We can take care of that," he murmurs into my ear. "You just need to be a good little pet and do as you're told."

My eyes dart back to the ticking clock hands every few seconds, noting how painfully slow they are moving. Almost backward.

I hate that we're back to this and I feel stupid for believing even for a moment that he could be innocent in all of this. Just as stuck as I was. No, he was a willing participant. Getting off on it all just as much as the rest of them.

But as I consider how trapped I am, the bigger questions at hand flood my mind. What could my dad possibly be doing to have them this riled up? And what kind of ultimatum was he being given?

"And if I can get him to respond?" I test lightly with my brows raised, purposefully keeping my face too close to his in hopes that it will drive Vivian insane. "If I do whatever you say and get my dad to do what you want…when all of this is over…do I ever get to be free from this bullshit? Are you ever going to leave me alone?"

"Do you want me to leave you alone?" he whispers boldly into my ear, his hot breath rolling down my neck. "Don't waste your time asking what happens if everything goes right. You're better off focusing on what's going to happen to you if it doesn't."

"But I don't know how to help you," I try again through gritted teeth, spurring him to push into me harder.

"I think you do, baby," he jeers in a low tone that burns straight into my gut.

Baby. The sound of it on his lips used to make me sick. And it still does, but now my stomach twists with nauseating desperation.

I sigh dejectedly, slumping my shoulders. My eyes meet his with blank features, stooping below him as my feet shuffle to steady myself against the wall. "Okay, so what happens next?" I resign with a monotone voice, my chin trembling.

Emmett's lips curl into a pleased grin, his gray eyes piercing across my skin as he looks me up and down, violating me with his gaze in a way only he can.

"Emmett!" Vivian barks disapprovingly from over his shoulder. "Let's get on with it already!"

I can't help but smile at her impatience. She can't stand to see Emmett lusting for me so fearlessly, right in front of her and everyone else. We struck a nerve, and for once she wasn't able to hide it.

"What's wrong, Vivian?" I fire back with a cocky grin, placing a hand on Emmett's arm. "Jealous?"

"Jealous?" Vivian laughs. "I could never be jealous of a little worm like you. I have nothing to worry about. I'm just bored and ready to see you bleed some more."

The faintest crack in her voice tells me that she is trying to convince herself just as much as she's trying to convince me.

"You don't sound so sure, Viv," I tease back, buckling my hips forward subtly. Just enough to be closer to Emmett's body with my hand still draped over his arm. "Maybe we should ask Emmett if you have anything to worry about."

My eyes turn to his with a devilish spark. My hair may be a dirty, disheveled mess, and I can feel the drying blood caked above my upper lip. But a flick of his tongue across his lip tells me all I need to know. He still wants me. And restraining himself with his girlfriend in the room is torture.

"Stop causing trouble," he remarks apathetically, his smile betraying him.

"But you like me when I'm causing trouble." I flash him a smile, and I wonder if he'll smack me or kiss me. "Or at least you sure seemed to yesterday."

If I have no choice but to play along with their games, I at least want to have some fun at my own funeral.

I watch Vivian's confidence crumble. "What is she talking about!?" she snaps.

"Nothing, baby," Emmett dryly responds, not even bothering to look at her. His eyes are glued to me, and I know he's getting off on my defiance.

"Yeah, Vivian," I smirk. "Nothing at all."

"Emmett, I don't know what she's talking about, but if you don't make her shut up right now, I'm going to kick her fucking ass," Vivian threatens, desperately wanting to cling to her ignorance.

The Elites think they need me for something, which means momentarily they are going to avoid killing me at all costs. I know it must be driving Vivian insane. But I am loving getting to torture her some in return.

"How will you make me shut up, Emmett?" I provoke him coyly.

His fist slams next to my face so hard that the vibration in the wall hurts my skull. He is growling through his throat, holding back desire.

"Come on, Emmett. You've had no problem roughing me up in the past. I don't know why you're having trouble with it now," I continue, causing his face to wince. He's torn between Vivian's demands, his need to hurt me and his want to fuck me. I dart my eyes over to Vivian and then back to his. "You wanna tell her what happened in here yesterday, or should I?"

"Shut your fucking mouth, Ophelia…or I swear to god," he fumes, leaning in closer to intimidate me, but it only intensifies the heat between us.

"Make me. Or is that something you can only do when your girlfriend isn't watching?" There's a hard lump in my throat reminding me that I shouldn't be so bold.

They are going to make me pay for every cocky word coming out of my mouth. But I can't help it. Now that I know they need me…I can't resist taking advantage and turning the tables for once.

"Emmett, I swear to god…," Vivian grumbles viciously. "If you've been messing around with this filthy whore you're never touching me again."

"I don't think he'll be missing out on much," I quip softly, smirking to myself.

"Enough! We're not here for some stupid catfight," Emmett snaps, slamming his hand to the wall next to my head again. "Though I'd love to watch you two fight over me all day. We're here to get you to get your father under fucking control."

"You're going soft on us, bro," Trey mocks from the other side of the room. "She's not even scared of you anymore. That's why she's giving us so much trouble."

"Yeah, let's just get on with this already," Vincent adds in agreement, looking bored. "Just hurt her some more and she'll do what we ask."

"You're all good for nothing," Bernadette chimes in suddenly from the other side of the room, slamming her cell phone to the table in exasperation. "Let me take a crack at her."

She sways her hips in a dramatic fashion as she strolls up to me, popping her chewing gum in a big bubble. "You think you're tough as shit now, huh?" she taunts in my face, trying to squeeze in between me and Emmett but he's not budging. "Well regardless of whatever gross pussy magic you think you've worked over on Emmett here…the rest of us still see you for exactly what you are. Disgusting white trash. You don't belong here. Your father didn't belong here. And when we're through with you…you'll go right back to whatever dump you came from, penniless and worse off than before you came here."

All I can do is smile, reigniting the flames in all of their eyes. Funny that they think running me out of town is some form of punishment. At this point, it's what I'm praying for.

Fuck my scholarship. I just want to be done with these assholes.

13

CHAPTER THIRTEEN

"I'm done with your bullshit," Vivian huffs, marching up to us and flinging Emmett and Bernadette out of the way, wagging her fingers viciously in my face. "As long as daddy dearest responds to the ultimatum our parents sent, you won't get hurt."

"What ultimatum?" I ask, wishing I had more of a clue as to what was going on. "If my life depends on my ability to help you, wouldn't it be better for all of us if you told me what was actually going on here?"

"I don't buy this little innocent naïve act of yours for one second," she barks back, practically spitting in my face between her gritted teeth. "I'm not going to stand here and waste more of my time and energy explaining things that you probably already know. You're just trying to get more out of us so you can tell your shitty dad how much we know. And *that* is a biiiig mistake, you little rat."

"I wouldn't know how to reach him to tell him anything anyway!" I remind her, my voice shrill in frustration. "Much less how to reach him and tell him to do whatever it is you're wanting. I don't even know where to begin."

"Well, you better start figuring it out, princess," she walks away carelessly. "I'd hate for your first meeting with Daddy dearest to be at your funeral. That's if he even makes it out of this alive. Which is doubtful at this point."

My blood chills. She's not fucking around. And she's also not budging. Her death threats make me want to threaten to go to the police again, but I know that means nothing to them. They're completely fearless.

Well, almost. My dad has managed to do something that has them afraid. Something I know nothing about but am somehow expected to stop.

She tosses a phone in my direction, sending my arms flying to catch it so it doesn't hit me in the face. Once my hands wrap around it, I lower my arms to study the device.

It's not just any phone. It's *my* phone. Again.

"How did you get this?" I murmur in confusion.

"Oh, I hope you don't mind..." Emmett answers tauntingly. "I borrowed that from you yesterday."

"No...you couldn't have...," I reason out loud, but then I start connecting the dots.

I was so upset after our encounter I had raced straight home and never even bothered checking to see if I had my phone last night or this morning. I slept straight through and then came to school in a daze. He had it the entire time.

Had that been the only reason he got so close to me? Why he kissed me again? Was it all just a ploy of distraction so he could swipe my phone right out from under me?

I shake away my doubts, filing them for later, as I bring myself back to Vivian's demands.

"Well, can you at least tell me when my dad needs to respond to the ultimatum by?" I try again, hoping for any small hint of where to even begin.

There's no response. Vincent and Trey are approaching once again with frightening smug grins. This isn't just another round of roughing me up. They're closing in on me with a purpose, one that they're too pleased with.

My eyes dart to the door as I contemplate making a run for it. They may be stronger than me, but I doubt they're fast enough to outrun me. But I know I won't be able to build enough speed between where I stand

and the door. They'd have me back in their arms before I could make it out.

And even if I did get away…they don't sound like they're going to let all of this go easily. I'd escape only to be haunted by the constant looming threat of when they'd try again. And since this business with my dad seems to be of a time-sensitive nature, I might as well try to get this over with.

"I'll just ditch my phone!" I jeer, swallowing down my fears about how pricey a new one would be. "I can get a new one. You're not going to keep tabs on me."

"Oh, don't worry," Vivian grins. "We've got a back-up plan."

Trey and Vincent snarl and cackle as they grab onto me again, Bernadette joining in. They sound like wild hyenas who've just landed their prey.

"Get away from me!" I protest hopelessly as they each take an arm and lift my feet from the ground. I kick aimlessly into the air, but it's no use. My struggling doesn't doesn't faze them and I'm at the mercy of their hard grip around my shoulders.

With a painful thud, they slam my chest and face down onto a table. One hand spreads across the side of my face while another set of hands holds my arms behind my back.

"Move over," Emmett grunts. "Let me do it."

"I'll do it," Vivian protests. "I don't want you putting your hands on this filthy little cunt anymore."

Her jealousy gives me a momentary thrill, but I'm quickly brought back to the danger I'm in.

I hear a scuffle from the two of them fighting over something, but barely. One of my ears is sharply pressed down beneath the weight of my head, and my other ear is being crushed underneath Vincent's hand. All I can hear is the fierce and rapid pounding of my own heart in fear of whatever it is they're getting ready to do.

With a quick and sudden pull to my top, I hear the fabric rip around my right arm. I assume their motives are perverted and sexual, but then…

"What the fuck!" I cry out in a shrill sob as a sharp, searing pain cuts into my shoulder.

I can tell by the size of the hands that Emmett won out over Vivian, which I want to take some small comfort in. He seems to be leaning toward taking it easier on me. After all, if I'm dead, he can't fuck me. So, in a weird, twisted way, he's on my side, right?

But it doesn't feel like he's on my side as a cold blade digs deeper into my skin. I try not to notice the way his hips press against my ass as I squirm beneath him, but I feel a hint of that familiar bulge from yesterday. He's holding back, but he can only do so much.

He's getting off on pinning me down from behind like this.

I can't believe my mind is even going there with the cold pain slicing into me deeper and deeper. A warm trickle of blood causes my skin to shiver and flinch as it trails down my side.

"What are you doing!?" I cry out again, jerking harder in their hold.

"This is a tracking device," he responds coyly, tinged with satisfaction. "Tucked away under your skin. So, you could ditch your phone…but it'd be no use. We'll still be able to keep an eye on you."

I scream and cry, kicking more violently, as I feel the distinct tug of a needle and thread working its way around the incision.

"Now, do yourself a favor and don't bother trying to get it out," he rants like a mad scientist at work. "It's too deep. You'll never get it on your own. And I don't have to tell you what would happen if you were stupid enough to try and get someone to help you."

"A doctor!" I protest. "I'll go to a doctor! Whether they work for you or not, they'll have to help me!"

Vivian laughs wildly from behind Emmett. "You go to a doctor whining about tracking devices being implanted in your skin and they'll have you committed!"

With a painful pull of a knot followed by the snip

of scissors, they loosen their hold on me. My hand reaches to feel the wound, but it's just out of my reach. And the more I try to stretch around to it, the more everything hurts.

"That's all for now," Vivian chimes with a deceptively innocent smile, looping her arm into Emmett's before turning on her heels to exit the classroom. Trey, Vincent and Bernadette follow closely behind.

Emmett flashes one quick subtle look over his shoulder in my direction, but it's unreadable. And I can barely stand the sight of him right now with Vivian draped back over his arm like nothing happened.

My chest heaves in hyperventilation as they leave me struggling to regain some semblance of composure. I have given up on trying to feel my way around the implant in my shoulder. My uniform is still ripped and I'm covered in bruises. My shin has turned black from where Vivian's foot struck against it.

What was Emmett thinking, standing up for me like that? It may have been subtle, but it was a bold move on his part. One that leaves me even more confused than before.

I wonder if Vivian will continue their conversation about me later. If she'll ask him about what I implied over our private encounters. I'm just happy I managed to do something that got under her skin for once…no matter how briefly.

But none of that changes the spot I'm in now. Once again, I feel stupid for getting caught up in this high school romance drama over the same guy who is threatening my life, with his girlfriend by his side.

I look around the room in disbelief, blowing sharp breaths through my cheeks as my fingers press to my temples. I try to collect my thoughts.

All I gathered from our little encounter is that my deadbeat dad is somehow responsible for the entire nightmare. The hell I've endured since coming here is all because of him. And now I'm expected to do something to get him to respond to the Elites. What that is…I have no idea. Not only do I not know how to pull that off, but I don't even know how much time I have or what it is he's responding to.

Regardless of all that, now my every move will be tracked. No escape.

Fuck. I can't imagine things getting much worse than this, but I'm learning not to even dare to think such a thing. Before I could so much as blink, the Elites would be rushing back in here to find some way to prove me wrong.

I try to shake it all away as I snake over to the doorway, peeking out to see if anyone is in the hall. If I thought anyone would help me, I'd march right out in front of them with my wounds and distress on full display. But knowing it'd be no use; I decide to try and sneak to the bathroom with at least a tiny shred of my dignity intact.

Once the halls are empty and silent with the last few stragglers disappearing around the corner, I limp across the scuffed floors in between the walls of lockers. I stare ahead resentfully, blazing right past the trophy case commemorating the Elite scum who built this school.

But something about the case of school accolades stops me. I turn to the sea of carefully pinned metals and plaques and study the framed photos for a moment, skipping across the black and white faces in vintage sports uniforms.

I locate Theodore Nickelson in a few different places. Just another face in the rows of other clean-cut young gentleman. Thomas Jameson and the other Elites usually only a few spots away from him. My fingers graze the glass that rests in front of his face.

"It's easy to find you in pictures," I mumble under my breath. "Now if only I knew how to find you in real life."

A renewed surge of rage bolts through me as I consider how absurd it is that some man I've never even met is so influential on my life today. The contribution of his sperm aside, he's had nothing to do with me…that I've known of. But now it seems his entanglement with the Elites didn't end whenever he left town. It was still alive and well and fucking up everything in my life.

My hand falls back to my side as I turn to continue my listless walk to the bathroom. The classroom doors shoot past the corner of my eyes, one after another, but I keep my eyes glued to the floor, noting the random bits of food wrappers and crumpled papers. The janitor up ahead will work his way to these things by the time I've reemerged from the bathroom.

Nothing in this ridiculous school stays dirty for long…at least not on the surface. The smell of his mop solution wafts through the halls, mixing with the lingering food smells from the cafeteria, creating the most nauseating aroma.

As the adrenaline rushes from my body, leaving me cold and shaky, I half wonder if I'll need to puke by the time I make it to the bathroom. I never was able to finish my lunch.

Aside from the nearby custodian, a few teachers make the trek between offices, classrooms and their lounge. Not a single one even bothering to notice how roughed up I am, much less stopping to ask if I'm okay. The occasional stray student I pass here and there ignores me just as adamantly.

I want to scream out, "Haven't you heard!? The

Elites won! They made their point! And now I'm working with them! You can admit that I exist again!"

It's just as well. I'd rather not be seen in my current state. But then…

I feel a sudden hard tug to my side as another body pushes past.

"Watch where you're going, cunt!" A guy spits at me as his shoulder bumps into mine.

Wow, I guess word does travel fast. Guess I'm out of exile after all. Which is a relief, but I don't know if being held hostage as a bargaining chip in my father's charades with the Elites is any better.

His choice of words are ironic, I think with a half-hearted chuckle to myself. I actually don't have to watch where I'm going anymore. The Elites are doing that for me now.

The reality of it is daunting. Wherever I go, they can find me. There's no escape now. No retreat. No hope of losing them. They can show up anywhere at any time and continue my torment.

For the first time, I notice all of the safety signs around the halls. Yellow a-frames cautioning for wet floors. Print outs alerting us what to do in case of fire, flood or tornado. Even a few posters warning of the dangers of unprotected sex and STDs.

But nothing that could have prepared me for any

of this. Nothing that tells me what to do to stay safe from the Elites. And from my father.

Once inside the bathroom, I don't even bother looking at my reflection before bending over the sink to take in handfuls of cold tap water. It's stale, but anything is better than this dry, hot, iron taste. Toilets gurgle with refilling water behind me as I look across the pink soap specks dripping down the sink.

The simple task of washing my hands becomes meticulous and important. Any small little chore to make me feel in control. I move through the motions slowly and carefully.

Fucking absurd. I glance up just enough to notice my hair sticking out in every direction, matted into nests. My skin is blotchy and bruised around my bloody, ripped uniform. And here I am, washing my hands of all things, like it's the most important thing in the world.

Get it together, Ophelia. You're cracking. Don't let them get to you.

When everything falls still and silent again and I've turned off the faucet, I hear the faintest whimper from the corner stall.

"Hello?" I call out timidly, convinced whoever it is won't answer me anyway. I'm too newly released from exile.

Two feet appear with a plop under the stall door as

the lock slides slowly, faintly covering the sound of sniffles. Finally, the door opens, and I see Lilly standing there with black mascara circles under her bloodshot eyes. Her cheeks shine with wetness under the fluorescent lights.

As upset as she looks, I know I have to look worse. And I'm kind of glad. I can't help but feel angry as I remember the way she ignored me right along with everyone else. I had my ass beat when I stood up for her, and she couldn't be bothered to do the same for me in return. I hope my bloody and bruised image makes her feel remorse.

But she stands there frozen and blank, not saying a word, and I can't tell if she's angry with me or just afraid.

14

CHAPTER FOURTEEN

The moment the Elites left me, I slowly sank into a pit of numb hopelessness. Too overwhelmed to fully feel anything. But now that Lily is standing in front of me, my heart surges with emotion. Hope. Maybe she can help. Whether she can or not, I need to talk to her. She's the only one who can even begin to understand any of this.

I contemplate telling her everything. All that I've learned about my father and his ties to the Elites. How they think I am somehow their key to getting him to leave them alone.

I can feel the desperation rising too quickly in my hot chest. If I pounce on her like this when she's already upset and hasn't been speaking to me for over a week, she'll shut me out. I have to tread lightly. Handle this carefully.

I calm myself down and focus. My hand reaches for the faucet again, turning it on to muffle my voice as Lily walks over to the row of sinks. Her movements are rigid, her head and shoulders pointed straight ahead as she tries to avoid eye contact with me.

"You ready to talk to me yet?" I offer, extending my hand to give her some paper towels.

She snatches the crumpled tissues from my hand, huffing toward the mirror without a word. "That's the last thing I need to do," she barks.

"Why? What are you talking about?" I ask, blotting my own bloody lips. "What did I ever do to you?"

"Oh, absolutely nothing, Ophelia," she sings in a resentful, sarcastic hum. "You've only ruined my entire fucking life!"

"Whoa!" I smirk, too traumatized and desperate to feed into her misguided anger right now. "Do I look like someone who is ruining lives? Or isn't it more accurate that my life is being ruined right alongside yours?"

My eyes cut over, watching her shake her head and scrub her hands furiously, muttering under her breath. I decide to try again, more gently this time as I reach out to place my hand to her shoulder.

"Come on, Lily. You know I'm on your side

here…" the words purse my lips as I remember how she had very recently not been on my side, but I try to push down my bitterness. "We're all just doing the best we can in this Elites hellhole."

"They've ruined my life," she sobs, blackening the same spots under her eyes she had just cleaned up. "Every college I had lined up for piano scholarships has rescinded their interest. I know those Elite assholes did this as punishment because I was nice to you."

"I'm so sorry, Lily," I blurt out, not even fully grasping the magnitude of the situation before the words spill out. I just want to say something…anything as fast as I can to comfort her.

I guess it shouldn't be so surprising that people of their financial and social standing would have the power to sway such prestigious institutions. But it angers me the same way the cops and teachers around here do. Certain things should be above social sway. A girl's entire education shouldn't hinge on whether or not she's in some rich teens' good graces.

"I can't believe they'd stoop so low," I add, brushing my hand on her arm as she cries over the bathroom sink. "I mean…I guess I can. They're monsters. But still….fuck."

She doesn't answer. I can see the lump in her throat and the tightness of her chest, and I know exactly how she feels. The Elites are especially skilled at reducing people to their lowest low. Taking away the things that matter most to them.

Or hitting your most sensitive nerves…as they are currently doing with my dad.

"My parents insist they can just send me to a West Coast school…somewhere far away. A place they maybe won't be able to have an impact on," she continues through her tears, her voice rasps in a way that only comes after several straight days of crying. "But I had my heart set on Julliard. Now that's completely ruined."

She slams a paper towel into the sink, but it catches in the air and lands with a disappointing lightness.

We're silent for a few moments as I think over all of the new developments. I want to tell Lily what they've done to me. How they're forcing me to help them negotiate some mysterious thing with my dad. But somehow, it doesn't seem like it will help either of us right now. I worry it will only upset her even more. Though I do wonder if she may know something that could help me understand exactly what it is I've signed up for…even if I didn't have much of a choice.

"Listen to your parents," I encourage her softly. "The West Coast will be wonderful. You'll be far away from all of this bullshit. I mean, just look at everything they've put you and your family through. Aren't you ready to get away from it all?"

"Yeah and go running off to the other side of the country like a cowering dog," she scoffs. "It's exactly what they want."

"Don't think of it like that…"

"I wish you had never stepped in that day!" she snaps suddenly, turning her anger to me.

I recoil, thinking back on that day in the hall when they were covering her in trash. Her only offense was that she tried to help me. An unforgivable sin in their minds…which makes more sense now that I know they have some sort of vendetta against my father.

"I had to, Lily," I defend, knowing it's probably no use. "I couldn't just stand back and watch them treat you that way any more than you could stand by and let them harass me without at least explaining who they were."

I shiver at the memory of realizing Emmett was at WJ Prep…and that he was with the gang of offenders. That brief moment when I didn't fully know what was going on. When I thought I was just lucky enough to end up at the same school as my biggest crush. The guy I thought I had met purely by accident, but now I know it was all set up.

"Well, we both should have kept to ourselves!" she shouts, crying harder and snapping me abruptly from those memories of Emmett.

"But I can't imagine how I would have got through

any of this without you," I argue back, the idea of it causing my bottom lip to quiver.

Lily was the only thing keeping me sane at times. In fact, her shutting me out during my exile was what pushed me over the edge. That was what made it so unbearable.

"It wasn't worth losing my dreams over," she answers with a low groan, her face stilled with seething anger.

"Lily…there's so much I want to tell you," I hesitate, my hand frozen in midair. "You have no idea what's going on. It's so much worse than I thought."

"I don't care what's going on with you, Ophelia! That's what got me into this position in the first place!" she turns her shoulder to me, trying to be strong and cold. The way she wishes she would have been from the beginning.

"But don't you see this is what they want!?" I persist. "If we let them isolate us and pull us apart then we don't stand a chance. We have to stick together. I know what they did to you was terrible…but it's not my fault."

She whips back around, her eyes big and wild with anger. "The Elites were bored and done with me before you showed up. Now I'm one of their main targets again and have been ever since your first day. How is it not your fault!?"

"Because you know I would have stopped them if I could have. Just like I'm sure you would stop them from everything they're doing to me if you could. But even if we can't stop them…maybe we can at least help each other cope with their wrath…" my voice trails off, breaking. More than anything, I just need someone to talk to, and I wish she would listen.

"There's nothing to cope with anymore," she says softly, her head shaking. "I'm being ran off to the other side of the country, and everything I've been dreaming of since I was a little girl has been taken away from me. I don't care anymore. I just hope they're done with me and talking to you will ruin any chance of that."

"Lily, please…don't shut me out. I need you more than ever now. Maybe if you can help me get to the bottom of this, we can undo some of the damage. Find some way to get them to take it back so you can go to Jilliard and…"

"Enough, Ophelia!" she cuts me off. "Just let it go, okay? Game over."

"Please, Lily. You're the only one I can trust," I beg with tears streaming down my face.

I want to argue back more. Tell her to stop giving them so much power by giving up that easily. To stop letting them come in between us. Say again that by isolating ourselves out of fear, we only made it easier for them to fuck with us. But I can see she's in no mood to fight back. They've completely broken her.

Just as I part my lips to speak, not even entirely sure of what else I can say, she snatches her purse and storms out. I know better than to try and follow her. The Elites can track my every move now, and it will only make things worse.

I watch despondently as she storms out, leaving me feeling more alone than I ever have before. Even during exile. Lily is even more against me now than she was before. Now there is no one I can trust. She is the only one who can understand and relate to what I'm going through and she hates me.

I try to fix myself up the best I can. Just enough to make it home without being questioned by my parents. On the way home, I drive recklessly, my music blasting. I need to feel the vibrations of the music. The rise and fall of my heart as I speed too quickly around each and every turn, accelerating more every chance I get.

I need to feel anything intense I can get my hands on to fill this gaping hole and fear and powerlessness. I have never been so irritable in all of my life.

My mind goes through the possibilities. I could run away. I could catch a bus out of town and just ride it until it stops somewhere interesting. I could drive my car until it runs out of gas and just stay wherever I break down at.

But no, that would never be far enough away to keep me safe from the Elites. I have a feeling no matter where I try to run to, they'll hunt me down and find me. Especially now that I know they're motivated by some vendetta against my father.

I think again about telling mom and Brendan. But that thought is quickly squashed by the memories of her playing nice with Trey and Vincent. She was friends with their mom. I doubt she has any clue what these kids are really like.

Unless of course the Elites were like this back in her day too. I hope she never treated people like this. I can't imagine it. But then again, I can't imagine her being with an Elite either. Then of course I have to kick myself, knowing full well that if Emmett could be kind to me I would be his in a heartbeat.

I feel like if I even try to tell anyone outside of the Elites' range of influence, they'll think I'm lying. Or that I encouraged Emmett's assault in some way. I am convinced my attraction to him is written all over my face.

The thought of explaining what is really going on with Emmett to anyone makes me sick. Even Lily would judge me for that, especially now. My mom would probably think I'm a freak and disown me. Brendan would be ashamed. I'm sure they think I'm smart and strong enough not to fall for someone so fucked up who treats me so terribly. Hell, I used to think I was too smart and strong for that, too.

When I get home, I hear my mom and Brendan rustling around in the living room. They're home early. It sounds like they're putting on a movie and settling in with some popcorn. I want more than anything to join them, but I'm too upset. I can't hide it, and I can't tell them anything.

I feel completely helpless. And as tired as I am of going through this alone, the only time I feel safe is when I'm alone. And even then, I'm plagued with paranoia over what will happen next. Especially now with this tracking device in my arm. I feel broken. Like something is wrong with me. I don't know how I can ever go back to living a normal life after this.

Thankfully, I'm able to avoid my parents as I race to my bathroom. The spot on my shoulder where they sewed in the implant is still bleeding, and I have to bandage it up just to keep the blood off of my clothes.

I decide to take a bath to soothe my aching muscles, filling the hot steaming water with every bath product I can find that might bring me some peace and comfort.

I lay back into the bath water, my body still tingling and my legs feeling almost numb. The lavender scented steam rising up should comfort me. But nothing seems to be able to do that anymore.

I think back on the life I had before coming to WJ Prep and this Elites nightmare. I had friends to hang out with. People to talk to and go to the movies with. We goofed off at the park. Took bike rides. I had friends to jog with. I had fun. But now it all seems so far away.

I would give anything to have my regular running schedule back. I thought I knew what torture was. With what I used to put my body through. The hard, painful monotony. But those kinds of words have taken on a new meaning for me now.

I miss the thrill and sense of accomplishment. Since the Elites got their hands on me, I haven't felt like I could do anything right. I remember the way I would sweat and the way my muscles would ache. Those sensations come for very different reasons these days.

God, I miss running.

I miss the satisfaction of it.

The pain that was gratifying…not relentless and out of my control like what I've come to know.

When I ran, I was in control. How fast and far I went was all up to me. A kind of freedom and responsibility that has become almost foreign to me.

I wonder when all of this is over…if it's ever over…how hard I'll need to run to wash all of this away.

I miss my old routes in Oklahoma. The newness of Jameson wore off quick. Any thrill of it was chased away by the Elites. And I can't let myself forget the role that Emmett has played in that.

I should have known better when I first received that phone call from the Headmaster of Weis-Jameson Preparatory Academy. That scholarship was too good to be true. I wanted to think I had earned it. But now I know better. It was all just a part of the set up. The game.

I miss how hopeful and surprised I felt before school started. The exciting challenge of Coach Granger's workouts.

Those memories all vanish before my eyes into some far-off distant haze, like the Epsom salts in my bath water.

Once I'm clean, I stare despondently around my room. Unsure if I should try to sleep or face my parents long enough to get some dinner. Nothing sounds appealing right now.

Instead, I find myself staring blankly out the window at some kids playing in the yard across the street. I watch as one kid takes the other's two before they break out into a playful, but angry, wrestling match. I wonder if it's just human nature for us to be greedy and hurt others to get what we want. It sure seems to be around here. In the land of the Elites.

Where no part of the town seems to be untainted by their evil ways.

I finally collapse back onto my bed, my eyes glued open wide but blank. I know I won't be able to sleep even though it's what I want the most. Instead I am stuck in a state of waiting. And I don't even know what exactly I'm waiting for. I'm at the mercy of whatever gets thrown my way next.

15

CHAPTER FIFTEEN

I am so close to finding escape through sleep. At least I think I'm falling asleep and starting to dream. I'm back in the classroom, pinned to the wall by Emmett. It's just the two of us. He's kissing me, but this time he doesn't stop. I push his hand away as his fingers trail between my legs, but he slams my wrist to the wall and carries on with his other hand. I should be angry. I should feel violated. But instead I'm just incredibly turned on.

When suddenly my phone starts ringing, jerking me awake.

"Great," I think, rubbing my eyes as my hand blindly fumbles for my phone in the dark. "My only vacation from this nightmare is sleep, and I don't even get that."

I try to ignore the pool of wetness in my underwear as I answer.

"Hello?" I grumble, pressing the phone between my cheek and shoulder as I stretch.

Nothing. The line is silent aside from the faint shuffling that tells me someone is on the line. They're just not saying anything.

It beeps and disconnects just as I am about to speak again.

Emmett wouldn't call from an unknown number. He'd want me to know it was him. Any of the Elites would. And yet some mysterious person keeps contacting me. I'm fed up with not knowing who.

My heart stills with a chill that rolls over my skin. Vivian's words echo through my ears. She had said my father was more involved in my life than I thought. What the hell was that supposed to mean? She obviously knows something I don't.

He has to be the one calling and who sent the cryptic messages before. I used to think it was the Elites, but they have no reason to hide. They'd be much bolder in any attempt to make contact. They don't fuck around.

No, this has to be my father. And I am not going to brush it off this time. After everything that's happened, this fucker owes me an explanation. More than that, he owes it to me to do whatever it is the Elites are asking of him. Whatever it takes to get me off the hook. He has never done a thing for me, and I sure as hell don't deserve to go down for whatever mess he's gotten himself into.

My phone dings again. This time with a text. I race to light up the screen and read it, certain the message will be from my father.

You're being watched. Close the blinds. Put on running clothes. Go to the living room and await further instructions.

What the fuck. I hesitate to do anything some random mystery texter tells me. Especially without any kind of explanation.

My hands shake as I quickly type my response. **Who is this?**

No response. I look around nervously. Sure, I know the Elites are tracking me. But now I'm being watched by someone else too? I'm not even safe in my own home anymore.

I try again. **Who the fuck is this?**

Still nothing. My nerves get the better of me, and I decide there's no benefit to the risk of ignoring their guidance. The Elites said we're on a time limit. I don't know how long they'll give me to produce some kind of result, but right now I have nothing to work with. I'll take what I can get. Any kind of stab in the dark to get some momentum.

I walk in the darkness and rush to close all of the blinds, looking up and down the dark streets as I go to see if any cars or people look suspicious. I see nothing out of the ordinary. The neighbor walking his dog. A woman taking her trash bin to the curb. Only the usual cars parked in their driveways. People carrying on with their ordinary lives. People who don't have to worry about being stalked, tortured and tracked. I'm filled with envy.

I flip on my lamp and scramble to snatch up my nearest pile of running gear. I feel sick as I slide the clothes over my trembling body.

"Get it together, Ophelia," I huff to myself as I shake my hands, wishing they'd steady themselves.

I check my phone again anxiously, but there's still no further reply. With a few more paranoid, narrow-eyed glances out of my blinds, seeing nothing that gives away who could be watching me, I reluctantly make my way downstairs to the living room.

Mom and Brendan are still quiet and distracted with the couch and TV in the den. I try to be as quiet as possible, so they don't rush in and start asking a bunch of questions.

My phone dings again almost the moment I enter the room, causing me to jump. Fucking ridiculous. They're warning me I'm being watched while they're watching me.

Drive to a McDonald's and start running.

Perfect. That's just what I want to do. I wish I could take comfort in knowing the Elites are tracking me. At least someone would know where to find me if I came up missing. And I have to assume they would come find me since they need something from me.

I blow a long, sharp breath from my cheeks, closing my eyes as I picture getting into my car at night and running from a dark and empty parking lot. With my luck lately, it's the last thing I want to do. I'm convinced someone will be waiting to attack, but it feels like I have no other choice. I may be scared shitless, but I'm tired of being a pawn. This could be a way out, or at the very least, a way to get more information.

With a deep breath, I clutch my keys to my chest and swing my bag over my shoulder before heading out to my car. I don't even turn on the radio as I drive. My thoughts and nerves are loud enough as it is. Any more noise would only make my never-ending headache worse.

Just as I was instructed, I drive to the nearest McDonald's, park, and get out to look around. With no obvious threats around, I take off running. In a way, it's exactly what I need. All of this drama has been leaving me too exhausted at the end of the day to take any evening runs. I have been longing for this kind of release ever since I laid soaking in the tub earlier this afternoon. And now here it is. If only it wasn't under such crazy circumstances.

I relish in the feel of the night air swishing past me. The wind is numbing, biting at my ears and cheeks, but I love it. Right now I'll settle for any kind of physical sensation that doesn't come from the hands of the Elites…the hands of Emmett, specifically.

With each step, I want to feel like I'm closing in on something with this strange new development. This mystery caller. Maybe this will lead to a light at the end of the tunnel. Either that or finally put me out of my misery.

As soon as I get into a good stride and feel a moment of release, an expensive-looking black sports car rolls up beside me, speeding my heart to an alarming rate. As it squeals to a stop, I half expect the window to roll down and a gun to just start shooting. That's how paranoid I've become.

I slow down and look over to see the driver's side window rolling down, revealing a familiar face.

Malcolm Henderson. A satellite Elite from school. And he doesn't appear to have a gun. So at least there's that.

"You!?" I yell out in exasperation, feeling even more confused than before.

"I've been sent by your father," he explains curtly.

Of course. I knew it. I knew this whole thing had to be his doing.

"How the hell do you know my father!?" I quip back, feeling too strung out for niceties.

"Everyone here knows your father, Ophelia," he glares ominously. "I thought you would have figured that much out by now."

"I guess I'm starting to. But you'd think that'd make things a little easier on me. If he's such a big and important guy around here," I lament bitterly.

"Well…I said everyone knows him," he raises his brows, tilts his head and lifts his fingers briefly from the car door. "I didn't say people like him."

"And what about you?" I ask, leaning over with my hands on my knees as I catch my breath. "Do you like him?"

"My father and your father are very close. So, I suppose you could say I like him. Or rather, we're helping each other out at the moment." He reaches to his passenger seat and grabs a bottle of water, quickly tossing it in my direction.

"I didn't think my father had anything to do with this town anymore," I explain, twisting the cap of the bottle with an appreciative nod. I know I should be more hesitant and distrusting with Malcolm, but I'm too tired to put up any airs. "I thought he was long gone."

"Get in," he commands with a flip of the car door locks. "It'll all start to make more sense if you come with me."

I roll my shoulders and step toward the road to walk around the car, but something stops me. I remember the last time I followed a boy into his car. I duck down and peek into the backseat for an arsenal of weapons or any sign that he plans to torture me the way Emmett would after inviting me to take a ride with him.

It's spotless. I take a deep breath and get in, against my better judgement.

The car speeds off, leaving me at Malcom's mercy. I watch the familiar increase of house size fly by my window. The landscaped yards and all their pretentious ornaments. Giant mansions. Filled with haunting secrets, most probably connected to the Elites. Everything in this town is, especially anything bad and hidden away.

I grow nervous as he takes a dark side road, avoiding a fallen powerline. I wring my clammy hands around my cell phone, noting its loss of bars as we drive further away from civilization. What have I done? I am completely screwed.

"Relax," Malcolm says, his eyes darting at my shifting arms and legs as I squirm in my seat. "I'm not going to hurt you. Nothing bad is going to happen, I promise. Quite the opposite actually. This will shed some light on a few things for you."

"Oh, forgive me for not being so trusting," I quip back sarcastically. "This town hasn't exactly treated me well since I arrived." My fingers graze across my bruised arms before I turn to look out the window again. "So, the calls and texts from before? Were they all you?"

"Well there's no telling what all has been sent to you, but yes. Most of them probably were. I was hoping you'd catch up to things in time," he explains, shifting the gear to accelerate faster down a dark and winding road.

"Catch up to what!?" I groan, stroking my forehead in exasperation. "Everyone is acting like my role is so important in whatever is going on. But I don't know anything. And no one seems to want to tell me anything."

"Be patient," he insists with a frustrated huff. "I said this meeting will help with all of that."

"Can you at least tell me who you're taking me to meet with?" I ask earnestly, but he shakes his head in silence.

I press my head to the window in exhaustion, trying to push down the nervousness bubbling in my gut. I wrack my brain for what Malcolm Henderson and I could possibly have to talk about on this little road trip, since he seems intent on not discussing any of the things I need to know.

"I guess the Elites did all of that?" He nods toward the bruises I had been fidgeting with just moments ago.

Well, I guess that solves the issue of what we should talk about. But it's also not a very fun topic of conversation.

"You say 'the Elites' like you're not one of them," I grumble resentfully, remembering Lily's little chart of hierarchy that featured Malcolm and his family prominently.

"I'm not," he states bluntly. "We're tolerated by the Elites. More so than someone like you that's blacklisted, but definitely not regarded warmly. My family's fortune was built from the ground up in more recent generations. We can't touch the old money of the Elites. But they work with us so long as we provide them with something profitable."

"And what is it that your family provides for them?" I ask curiously, secretly delighting in a conversation with someone that doesn't involve beating or shouting. But of course, it still has to revolve around the great and mighty Elites. That seems to be all my life is about anymore.

"We own a software company that services the Jameson Automobile Corporation," he explains. "Open the glovebox." I pull the compartment open, grabbing a brochure that he motions to. "That tells you about our company."

I nod in a sort of stunned silence as I flip through. The ties to Jameson Automobiles really are endless. It's like the whole town is just one giant web with that one company smack dab in the middle. You either work for them, are controlled by them or hated by them. There doesn't seem to be any other way to fit into this elaborate social circle.

Something resting beneath where the brochure just was catches my eye. It's a strip of photos from the booth at the mall, featuring Malcolm making a series of funny faces. He must be a few years younger in them. But then I notice the face next to his in the photos that causes my hand to shoot out and snatch the strip up to take a closer look.

"What the fuck," I whisper, thumbing over the second figure in the photos. "Is this Emmett!?"

"Yeah. That feels like ages ago," he answers dismissively, shaking his head.

"You and Emmett are friends? I never see you together at school," I study the pictures more closely, taken aback by how happy and carefree Emmett looks. A side to him I have yet to see.

"Used to be," he replies with a tinge of sadness. "When we were younger, our parents didn't care if we were friends or if we hung out. My family has money after all, and that's all they care about. But his dad and my dad had a falling out. And then as we got older, it became less socially acceptable for us to be seen together as much."

"A falling out about what?" I ask, knowing it's a reach, and am met with another quiet shake of his head.

"Their businesses," he grunts, brushing a finger to his nose. "That's all you need to know."

"Asshole," I grumble disdainfully, tossing the strip back into the glovebox and slamming it shut.

"It's not his fault," Malcolm shoots back sharply.

"What the fuck do you mean it's not his fault!?" I shriek with more emotion than I mean to. "Don't tell me you're brainwashed by them too. Everyone's so afraid of them they just go along with their bullshit and let them get away with whatever they want. Treating everyone like shit."

"I'm not saying the Elites aren't capable of horrible things," he defends. "You don't have to tell me. I grew up with them. Vivian, Bernadette, Trey, Vincent… they're no good. But Emmett's always been a little different. That's why we were buddies. He's not like the others."

"Maybe he wasn't," I answer lowly in disdain, tugging at my shoulder. "But he had no problem writing you off when he got older. And some time after that, he became a monster just like the rest of them."

"He hurts you?" Malcolm asks, his face slightly twisted.

"They all do."

He shakes his head, turning briefly to the driver's side window with his lips pursed before refocusing on the road. "That's not like him. I know it's going to be hard to convince you…but anything he's doing is just out of fear. He didn't ask to be born into that fucked up family of his. He's just as much of a pawn as the rest of us."

I stare at him as he drives, searching for some sign of an ulterior motive. Doubt. Anything that tells me he doesn't know what he's talking about. But he's filled with resolve. Completely confident that Emmett is somehow different than his flock of abusers.

My head flings back against my seat. I can't handle this right now. The last thing I need is another gnawing voice in my ear trying to convince me that Emmett's behavior is excusable.

I've watched him dump trash on Lily's head. He manhandled me in front of his asshole Elite friends. He's verbally abused me. Humiliated me. Threatened me. Not to mention whatever he planned to do with me with that rope and gloves before we crashed his car. The list goes on and on.

I clench my fists, needing the reminder of it all to dig into me as deep as my fingernails dig into my palm. I don't care what Malcolm says, or what flash of pity I saw in him recently. He's one of the bad guys. He's hurt me. And my fucked up attraction to him is just that. Fucked up. It has to stop. I have to make it stop.

"I promise you, Ophelia," Malcolm continues, jolting my attention back to him. "Things are about to change. The days of the Elites' reign are numbered. They're on thin ice. And when their little hierarchy starts to shift…you'll see the real Emmett."

Emmett's angry snarling face flashes before my eyes. I have plenty of memories of him like that. Staring me down with pure rage and hatred. Saying terrible things to me. I can't let myself believe that there's anything more to him than that.

"We're almost there," he announces, pointing a finger over the steering wheel to an ominous looking vacant lot in the distance.

I gulp down a hard knot, unsure if I should be relieved or terrified. Either way, he claims this will be informative and good. So I try to hold on to that with any ounce of capability I have left to trust someone in Jameson.

16

CHAPTER SIXTEEN

Malcolm drives us to what looks like an abandoned warehouse on the outskirts of town. The parking lot is dark, lit up by only one streetlamp that rests near the large garage door entry. He flips a switch, causing the metal door to clatter as it rolls up.

I am certain I should be afraid of dying. This could be how I go. But Malcolm doesn't seem threatening. His meager and slender build makes me think I could take him if it came down to it. But it doesn't make him unattractive. He has creamy pale skin and long legs leading up to a well-chiseled narrow chest. His light sandy blonde hair is cut and styled into spikes, complimenting his pale blue eyes that seem kind.

It's a shame I can't be attracted to him instead.

He's shown me more kindness than anyone else around here, aside from Lily.

Or maybe my concept of kind has just shifted after enduring the torture of the Elites. In my book, he is still one of them by proxy after all, no matter what he says. Now it seems anyone who doesn't instantly attack me seems nice in my book.

The inside of the warehouse is even darker, with only the moonlight shining through a large opening in the back to give me any clue as to where to step. Malcom places his arm through mine, startling me as my eyes dart to his in suspicion.

"I told you I'm not going to hurt you," he assures me, nodding to his gentle, friendly touch.

"Sorry. I know," I groan, letting him lead me. "I'm not used to someone being nice to me. Trying to help." My mind drifts to Lily. I wonder if he knows how risky it is to be doing anything but treating me like shit. "In fact, you may want to be careful. The Elites tend to make anyone that helps me regret it. They may turn on you."

"I'm not afraid of them. At least not in the way you think," he huffs, guiding me toward a figure standing in front of a window so that all I can make out is the silhouette of what looks like an older man in a suit.

His tall slender legs mimic Malcolm's build, but he

has a much bigger gut jutting out from his suit jacket. I can see a glare across his balding head as he wipes his forehead with a handkerchief.

I look up to him nervously, hoping and praying I haven't been duped yet again.

"Ophelia," the man calls out. "Thank you for coming. Sorry to have to drag you out of the house so inconspicuously, but as I'm sure you've gathered by now…there are some dangerous forces at play around here."

"Who are you?" I ask, squinting my eyes to try and make out his face.

"This is my father," Malcolm explains. "Meet Liam Henderson."

I have no idea what to think. What on earth could both Malcolm and his father want with me in this abandoned warehouse out in the middle of nowhere?

"Your father could not be present, but he says hello," Liam adds, firing the synapses in my brain.

My father. Of course he wouldn't bother actually showing his face, but at least he's making some form of contact. It's about damn time for how much trouble as he's caused.

"Well, that's a first," I jeer in bewilderment. "I've never even met him."

"I'm afraid this will have to be brief," Liam continues, ignoring my bitterness. "We can only block the signal of the tracking device in your arm for so long."

My eyes widen and glance toward my shoulder. I'm amazed that they can do something like that…and that they even know it's there in the first place.

"How did you…"

"I'll get straight to it," he carries on after clearing his throat, cutting me off. I still can't see his face as he stands in front of the backlit window. "Maybe you're aware that I write code and create software for a living. The programs I've designed have been used by many fortune 500 companies for many different purposes. I've been very successful."

"Yeah, Malcolm filled me in on some of that on the way over," I nod, still confused as to what this has to do with me. Or my father.

"Unfortunately, the Jameson Automobile Corporation has been using my software to run extortion rings of politicians," he continues with a disappointed sigh. "It's also been modified to create a black market for underage girls. I'm sure a smart girl like you can understand why that's big trouble for me."

"Sex trafficking?" I blink, staring ahead blankly. I want to be as smart as he thinks, but I'm too taken aback to piece anything together on my own right now.

"Since I'm the creator of the program and one of the top employees of the company, my reputation and career would be seriously harmed if this information came to light. Which is what brought us to the aid of your father, Theodore Nickelson."

His name hangs in the air like a plague. I hate the sound of it.

"I can't say I'm making that leap with you," I confess. "What does any of that have to do with my father? Or better yet…me?"

"How much do you know about him?" Liam asks, slightly stunned.

"Nothing," I shrug. "I told you. I've never even met him."

"Ah," I see the shadow of his brow wrinkling in the light as his head drops. "As I said, we don't have much time, but have a seat. I'll explain what I can for now." He motions to some nearby shipping crates and follows me over to take a seat. "Your father, Theodore Nickelson the Third is the only grandson of one of the Jameson Automobile Company's founders."

I shake my head vehemently, excited to finally be getting some kind of real information. I'm so wrapped up in every word he's saying, I can barely process the scope of it.

My father. One of the Jameson Automobile bigwigs.

"Therefore, he inherited a quarter of the company's shares," Liam continues. "But in the early 2000s, he mismanaged millions of the company's funds. He had used the money to fund his own private gambling problem. So, the Elites cut him off. He tried to go public with Marissa Jameson's affair with the gardener, which only got him blacklisted at every public establishment, sued for every penny he had, and his entire reputation was completely tarnished for good."

"Wow," I marvel out loud, still hanging from his every word. "All of that for a gambling habit."

"He fled town with your mother, Lala," Liam continues. "Theo trained as a private detective on the West Coast, but he could never let go of his hatred of the Elites. He built his fortune from the ground up through stocks, purely out of vengeance. And he vowed to come after the Elites in whatever way he could to make them pay for taking away all that he had."

"Seems ridiculous," I blurt out dryly. "It was his own gambling problem that put him in that spot. And he ended up making it all back anyway, so…why not just let it go?"

"Maybe you can ask him that yourself one day," Liam replies dismissively. "But for now, you can see why we would want to work with him."

"You both hate the Elites?" I offer.

"If this sex trafficking and pedophilia thing breaks, it could be a huge federal case," he barks, growing impatient with my seeming lack of interest. "All of the Jameson founders could be found guilty and sentenced to life in federal prison. But we need a verbal confession to really tie the case together. The evidence now is compelling, but it could be overwhelming with such a confession. And according to Massachusetts recording laws, it's illegal to record someone without their consent. This is the only reason there hasn't been any movement forward. Thomas Jameson isn't stupid enough to go to other states and say 'Yes, I'm the one who has done these horrible things'."

"So that's why the Elites are trying to get him to back off?" I think out loud. "They know he's not going to stop until he puts them all behind bars."

"Precisely," he nods, scratching his fingers across the five o'clock shadow on his chin.

"Well, now the Elites are up my ass," I commiserate, rubbing my bruised shin. "So you can tell my dad he has to respond to whatever ultimatum they gave him or else they're going to make me pay."

"I'm sorry they've been so cruel to you," he says softly, his face grimacing at the bruises shining in the moonlight. "They are ruthless. And will stop at nothing to protect their power and money. Which is why this situation is so perilous. I can't be dragged down for their wrongdoings, but that is exactly what they will make sure happens if we don't build a strong enough case against them."

I nod, believing all too well that the Elites will stop at nothing to protect their own asses. I would be scared too if I was in the Hendersons' position.

"Well, this has certainly been enlightening," I grunt as I stand from the shipping crate. "But I still don't see what any of this has to do with me. How am I supposed to help?"

Liam grows quiet in deep thought for a moment, leaning forward and running his palm to the back of his neck with what looks like remorse. Regret. He's sorry for something.

"Your father is sorry he hasn't been involved in your life," he offers as he stands, pacing in front of me. "But he wanted you to understand what was going on. So that maybe…you wouldn't feel so…helpless. He hoped the context would help."

His words suddenly sound more menacing. Something is about to happen, and the fear I was numb to before is creeping in full force. "Help with what?" I ask softly, taking a few steps back.

He answers with a silent smirk, nodding to Malcolm. "You can take her home now."

I pull away from Malcolm at first, wondering if he really plans to take me home or if something terrible is about to happen. I don't have a good feeling about any of this.

"But wait!" I shout, jerking away. "I still don't understand. What is it that I'm supposed to do!? If he doesn't do what they want, the Elites are going to kill me. They said they've sent him messages, but I don't know what they've said or what they're trying to do."

"They're likely telling him to back off," Liam deduces, tucking his hands into his suit jacket.

"Will he!?" My voice grows shrill with urgency. "Because like I said…they're going to kill me if he doesn't! Can you at least promise me that he'll respond? I mean…can't you all just work it out between yourselves without dragging me into it!?"

"All you need to know is that your father has a plan," he offers grimly, sparking more fear than reassurance. "Malcolm. That's all for now."

He steps toward me again, but I pull my arms back. I can't believe I'm getting shuffled off again without knowing what this all means for me.

"Come on, Ophelia," Malcolm says reassuringly. "I promise nothing's going to happen. I'm just going to take you back to your car."

My heart pounds as I follow along, convinced that at any step everything could change. He could turn on me. Someone could come after us. Liam was eluding to something. That much I'm certain of. But to go through all this trouble just to set me free again… something's not right about it.

My anxiety keeps me quiet on the ride home, my senses on hyper alert as I note every last turn the car takes. I'm ready to bolt the moment it goes any direction that is not toward the McDonald's I parked at.

But to my surprise, Malcolm keeps his word and drops me off at my car. Flashing me a sweet smile as I exit his vehicle.

"So, what now?" I turn back to ask him from the sidewalk, rubbing my arms as I look around cautiously.

"Go home," Malcolm answers dryly, not looking away from his steering wheel. "Like my father said, your dad has a plan. You just have to wait."

"What if there's no time for waiting!?" I shriek back. "What if the Elites kill me before he carries out his little plan?"

Malcolm is unmoved. "Go home and get some rest, Ophelia."

Without another word, his tires squeal and he's flying off down the street. I stand and watch as the obnoxious buzz of his car engine drifts further and further away, eventually vanishing altogether.

Not knowing what else to do, I turn to walk back to my car. It's easy for him to say. Wait. Rest. I can't do any of these things. Not with all of this hanging over my head.

My dad has it out for the Elites, and not surprisingly they have plenty of skeletons in their closet for him to play with. I've seen the rage of their entitlement. No one questions them or fucks with them in any way.

I'd be glad my dad is giving them a run for their money if it weren't for me getting dragged down into it all. And the fact that his motives are no different than theirs. He messed up, and he's mad at them for putting him in his place.

I wrap my arms around my chest, shielding myself from the night air chill as I climb back into my car. Everything around me is quiet to the point of being unsettling.

My car engine starts, and I drive back to my house as fast as I can. I'm in desperate need of some place that feels safe. With so many people watching me and keeping tabs on me, I'm not sure such a place exists anymore. But my room is the closest thing I have, so I'll take it.

All I want is to be curled up under my covers. Now I just have to hope that when I get there, dreams of Emmett don't come back to haunt me.

17

CHAPTER SEVENTEEN

My mind is on overdrive as I head home, but I'm relieved to finally understand what my father had to do with the Elites. And what all of it has to do with me now. But there is still a lingering fear that the Hendersons and my father aren't through with me yet. I'm able to push that further and further away as I get closer to home. At least for now.

I think about how badly I want to be able to ask my mom everything. I know my dad's side to the story, but I can't help but wonder what all of that must have been like for her. And I still have no clue what actually caused them to split up. Though I guess a gambling habit that ruined their lives would be reason enough.

As my car pulls into my driveway, I see movement behind the blinds. I consider marching in and asking my mom everything right away, but I'm too tired. I've taken in enough for the evening, and I just want to crawl back into my bed.

So, instead, I sneak past my mom and Brendan who are talking in the kitchen, bolting up the stairs into my room.

My heart plummets the moment I open my door. Emmett, Trey and Vincent are all standing right there in the middle of my bedroom, seething with anger.

"What the hell are you doing here?" I stammer nervously. "This is my house. How did you get in!? You can't be here. My parents are right downstairs. I'll scream."

"Where the hell have you been!?" Emmett growls, his nostrils flaring in anger. "We know you met with someone, but we couldn't track you after McDonalds."

"I just went for a run," I offered as innocently as possible. "It's not my fault you stabbed a faulty tracking device into my body."

"Bullshit," he fumes back, racing up to skillfully push me to the wall hard enough to hurt, but without making too loud of a sound.

I'm back to squirming beneath his violent grip and I want to spit at everything Malcolm tried to say. There is nothing good about Emmett. He's no different from the rest of them.

Unless…he's worried about me? Upset that he

didn't know where I was? But if that was the case, he wouldn't have needed to drag Trey and Vincent along with him.

"We've got to stop meeting like this," I quip defiantly, staring straight into his eyes from an angle that was becoming all too familiar.

"Oh, did you miss this?" he growls, his eyes taking me in with hunger. "Is that why you misbehaved? Just to get me here?"

"You wish," I roll my eyes, sparking a new rage behind his stare.

His hand jerks to the top of my head, gripping a fistful of what's hanging loose from my ponytail and pulling it back to raise my chin to him. The sting of it causes my eyes to water, and I have to blink away tears.

He pants over me, half with sexual desire, half with pure anger. I don't know whether to expect him to hit me or kiss me. All of my conflicted feelings are back in full force in only a matter of seconds of being in his presence.

"Let's see if you really know what it means to be a good little girl," he groans. "You broke the rules, so now you know we have to punish you."

Before I can even begin to guess what he's planning to do, he whips me around toward the door. I am shocked as he leads me out into the hall, Trey and Vincent following behind.

"I told you my parents are downstairs," I remind him, thinking surely he won't be so bold as to march me right out in front of them.

"Good," he retorts, unfazed. "I would like to meet your mom. I've already met your dad of course. Your real dad."

"Well, that makes one of us," I muster through a gulp as he practically pushes me down the stairs. I pray my mom comes around the corner and catches the way he's handling me, but he's too smart for that. He'd never let himself get caught.

"Ophelia!" she cries in innocent excitement as we round the corner of the kitchen. "I didn't even know you were home! Much less that you had company!"

Emmett's fingers pinch into my spine, just out of her sight. His fingernails sting the thin skin against my bone, causing me to wince. I am tempted to show how much it hurts. To jerk away from him and see what my mom actually does.

"Oh yeah," I play along, deciding to keep them out of this. If the Elites can take down millionaires and convince major universities to deny a potential student, it would be nothing for them to ruin everything my mom and Brendan have worked so hard for. I can't be the reason that happens. "I went out for a run. I just got back."

Her eyes look to the three guys expectantly, causing Emmett's fingers to twist even harder into my back.

"These are my friends!" I shout quickly, hoping he'll ease his pinch. "I ran into them while I was out."

"I remember you from the hospital," she shakes her head, looking like she feels foolish for not remembering sooner. "Emmett, right?"

I see Brendan's ears perk up from the kitchen at the mention of his name.

"And of course I know you two," she nods politely to Trey and Vincent, making my stomach turn.

"How are you, Mrs. Lopez?" they chime in almost comedic unison.

"Wonderful! How are you? And how is your mother!?"

My mom's small talk with them fades into the background as I look up to Emmett, searching his face for any clue of what's supposed to happen next. But he just smiles and plays along.

"It's kind of late for houseguests," Brendan finally jumps in, taking an authoritative stance behind my mom. His eyes are glued to Emmett. He still doesn't trust him after the accident.

"Yes, of course," Emmett agrees politely. "We were actually hoping we could take Ophelia out to a movie. If that would be alright with you?"

"Are you driving?" Brendan quips back, not missing a beat.

I smile up at Emmett in anticipation of his temper emerging, blowing their whole cover. But he's too smooth for that.

"Actually, no," he laughs. "Vincent is this time. I promise we'll take good care of her. And we'll have her home as soon as the movie is over."

"What are you going to see?" my mother asks sweetly, causing my heart to drop as I realize they're actually going to let them get away with this.

"There are a few things starting soon," Trey explains. "We were gonna decide when we get there."

My mom looks up to Brendan for final approval, but her eyes seem to be trying to convince him to say yes. I want him to look at me instead of her. To somehow telepathically read into my suppressed dread.

"I do have school early tomorrow…" I remind them gently, fully prepared for Emmett's responsive twist into my back. But Brendan seems to read it as some kind of reverse psychology, much to my disappointment.

"Well then…don't be out too late," he says finally, sparking an erupting of nervous sighs from the guys around me. "You haven't gotten out much with friends since you got here, Ophelia. You've been working too hard. It'll be good for you to have some fun.

Ha, I think. Fun. Somehow, I don't expect much fun to come out of this. At least not for me.

"Great, thanks so much," Emmett says sweetly. His façade of innocence and niceness making me sick. "We'll bring her home as soon as the movie is over."

I eye my mom desperately as they turn and push me toward the door, but she must be mistaking my fear for nerves or something else. Some other kind of normal teenage girl behavior. She responds with a wink and a wave before the two turn back for the kitchen.

They laugh victoriously as they shove me out to the car. We're all dead silent as we drive with me sandwiched in the backseat between Trey and Vincent. I catch Emmett glancing back at me every few seconds through the rearview, and I can't help but laugh about his blatant lie to Brendan about not being the one to drive tonight.

I hold my breath in anticipation of whatever happens next. Did this have something to do with what Liam seemed to be hinting at? Whatever it was he looked so sorry for? What my dad was worried I needed help with? But that can't be. The Hendersons and the Elites are working against each other now.

But to my amazement, they take me to the movie theater. I still expect it to be a front, even as they approach the counter and buy us tickets.

We file into the theater and find seats. I follow

along like a lost puppy, completely at their mercy. I know it's no use to try and get away. This whole town is full of their puppets, and no one would help me when they inevitably caught up to me.

Trey and Vincent even bought popcorn. They try to sit on either side of me the way we were arranged in the car, but Emmett snaps at them, demanding them to move aside so he can sit next to me.

"Move over, idiots," he hisses, pushing them out of the way and sitting down next to me. I search his face for some kind of emotion, but he's blank and avoiding eye contact.

The whole thing is chillingly normal. Just a group of teens going to the movies. I want to rest in that, but my nerves won't settle enough to let me. I know something is coming.

Vincent sits on the outside with Trey next to me. Once the movie starts, I can feel his gaze burning into me.

I almost laugh when I realize we're watching some old slasher horror flick. Of course that's the kind of thing they'd bring me to see. Forcing me to sit here and watch them get off on half naked girls running away terrified in the night, screaming in terror before they inevitably get slashed to bits.

I side-eye Trey as I realize he's still watching me instead of the movie. I try not to make eye contact, but his sneering lips are practically drooling as he grins at me.

"What?" I snap in a whisper, wishing he'd move the fuck over. But his arm inches further across the arm rest, taking up even more of my space.

He says nothing, and Emmett is distracted, looking straight ahead at the screen. A few seconds later, his arms inches even closer. His hand touches my knee and swiftly moves upward.

"Get off of me!" I hiss, trying to push his hand away.

"Come on," he whines. "I'm bored. Let me touch you. I'm tired of watching Emmett have all the fun."

His hand persists, trying to catch a handful of my breasts. I kick him away, the shuffle prompting a series of shushes from the back of the theater.

This catches Emmett's attention as he snaps to, looking over just in time to catch Trey's hand recoiling from my chest. Suddenly Emmett's hand darts out across me, catching Trey's hand in a tight grip. I can see their skin turning white and red from the force of his grasp.

"Don't fucking touch her," Emmett growls, his neck bulging with wide eyes as he stares Trey down.

Thinking back on one of my first encounters with them, and how Emmett seemed to even encourage other guys having their way with me…whatever it took to humiliate me, I am surprised at his sudden protectiveness.

Trey finally fights his hand free, glaring at Emmett with wrinkled brows as he rubs to self-soothe the bright red skin of his wrist. "Jeez, man," he yelps. "Chill out."

Emmett's eyes barely cross mine as he turns back to the big screen. I try to ignore how much it turns me on to feel protected by him in some way. Even if he's also my attacker at times, it's almost sweet in a sick and twisted way that he wants to be the only one bringing me harm.

Jesus Christ, Ophelia. He has really fucked you up in the head.

Even still, I can't help but glance up at him every so often, wishing this could be like a normal date with a guy I'm attracted to. That all the bad history between us and crazy events at play could just suspend in time temporarily. He could brush my hand over a shared bucket of popcorn. I could jump and scream when the killer in the movie pops out, sending his arms around me in protection with a comforting laugh. Maybe we'd even hold hands and kiss.

But that's not for Emmett and I. Or at least not for him. He's too fucked up, as Malcolm would say. And I'm just the idiot girl caught up in it all. Not knowing what's good for me enough to be able to stop these feelings.

The rest of the movie is uneventful, but I never feel at ease with them. I'm on high alert the entire time in anticipation of what comes next. It almost scares me more that we make it through the rest of it without incident. By the time the credits are rolling, I realize I've barely paid attention to a single second of the film. I was too caught up in a daze of uneasiness and dread. Expecting them to do something crazy at any minute.

But no. The credits roll and we stand to exit the theater. I realize whatever they're planning will probably happen now and my heart pounds so hard I can barely breathe as we approach the car again. I wish I could be back inside, not paying attention to another movie.

This time, Vincent drives and Trey sits in the passenger seat, leaving me alone in the back with Emmett. At least there's some distance between us.

As soon as I have the thought of gratitude, his arms wrap around me tightly, one hand wriggling down to unbuckle my seatbelt before he drags me into his lap.

"What the fuck are you doing!?" I shout, kicking and squirming to get away.

"We're gonna take a little drive," he explains in a hauntingly snide tone. "And I want you close to me."

All I can think of is the last time these fuckers took me for a drive, and the time after that when Emmett tried again to lure me away in his car. My hands and arms flail frantically for escape, but he quickly grips onto me in every direction. He holds me down long enough to secure his stretched seat belt over the both of us. With one arm held firmly across my chest, holding my arms down, a black cloth falls over my eyes.

"No!" I yell hopelessly, not wanting to be blindfolded. But the cloth ties tight across my vision, blocking out the outside world. "Emmett, please… don't do that!"

Vincent and Trey cackle. They love it when I'm struggling.

I finally give up and grow still, surprised by how quiet Emmett is beneath me. His hands move up my arms, making their way to either side of my head as he strokes my hair.

"Shhhh," he hisses into my ear like a snake, smoothing down both sides of my face in some twisted form of comfort.

I remain perfectly still, my pounding heart beating through both of us as I'm forcefully latched in his lap. Like a scared rabbit who finally gives up and goes limp in the arms of its captor.

The car drives off into the night, me bouncing around in Emmett's lap with every bump of the road. I can feel the stiffness in his pants against my thighs as he keeps his mouth close to my ears so that I can hear every deep, hot breath that burns against my skin.

I stay focused on trying to time how long we've been driving. I know it's an impossible task, but maybe even if I don't know where our final destination is, I can have some idea of how far it is from the theater in any direction. It's the only thing I know to do. But even that seems futile as Emmett's hands move over my skin in the dark.

"Hey man, let us have a go at her," Vincent blurts suddenly, sending chills down my spine. "We can pull over somewhere on the way."

Well, at least I know they would need to pull over on the way, meaning that's not the end goal when we get to wherever we're going. But I should know better anyway. The stakes are higher now as things are coming to a head with my father. Their fucked up sexual assault games are on the back burner now. Just a fun side perk for them as they hold me captive.

"Drive," Emmett demands coldly, stern enough to scare me. I can only hope it's as effective on his friends.

"Maybe we should just tell Vivian then," Trey taunts, staring us down threateningly in the rearview.

"She knows what I have to do," Emmett answers despondently. The threat doesn't stop his hands from creeping across me. He keeps my hands sandwiched at his sides, in between his chest and arms. Leaving me helpless as he runs his palms across my knees and up my thighs. He lingers too long at the tops of them, in between my legs.

In the darkness, knowing it would be undetectable to anyone but Emmett, I give in. I cave under his touch, leaning my head back against his chest in submission as he explores my body. Maybe it's because I don't have a choice anyway. Or because of all the tension that has been building since the first time we met. Or perhaps it has something to do with knowing I mean enough to him to stir up trouble with his girlfriend. Whatever it is, I decide not to fight it. He says nothing to acknowledge my sudden willingness. We both seem content to steal the time we have.

The muscles and folds between my legs swell with warm wetness as he clenches my inner thighs. I wish he'd move up higher, forgetting for a moment that we're not alone. But he moves up to my stomach, working his way under my shirt and sliding up across my abdomen. My hips buckle and my back arches, sending my tense abs further against his hands as his lips graze my neck and ear.

"Good girl," he whispers so soft that only I can hear it.

It almost kills it for me, causing me to recoil slightly. But as his hands move up to my ribs, I melt back into the touch. I'm putty in his hands. Just as his thumbs graze my bra across my hardened nipples, causing me to bite my lip to suppress a moan, his body straightens. He goes tense beneath my body and pulls his hands away. My shirt is swiftly tugged back down over my breasts, feeling cold in comparison to the warmth of his touch.

"We're here," he blurts coldly with a gentle smack to my thigh.

I am left unfulfilled and reeling. So much that I almost forget to be afraid of what happens next.

18

CHAPTER EIGHTEEN

I find my way down from whatever crazy plane of existence I was just on with Emmett as the car rolls to a stop, crunching across a driveway. I laugh once he slips the blindfold away.

They've brought me to Jameson Manor. Everyone knows where it is, meaning they never needed to blindfold me at all. It was just a fucking power move. Another scare tactic to mess with my head.

But if they hadn't done that, I wouldn't have just been felt up by Emmett. And judging by the dampness between my legs, I enjoyed it much more than I'd like to admit. Which only makes me hate myself. Especially as he yanks my arms behind my back and shoves me toward the door.

There's an ornate iron fence lining the property,

enclosing a large circular driveway in front of the main manor. A series of statues surround a huge fountain in the center of the drive, and there are several other smaller buildings in the back. Probably guesthouses and other quarters for their staff. I assume one of them is a pool house with the large bean-shaped swimming pool that peaks out from behind the house.

In the distance I can spot gazebos, a tennis court and putting greens for golf. Sprinklers are sputtering away as they mist the perfect green grass. I can only imagine what expensive cars must rest behind the garage doors. They really have it all.

The yard is huge and well-kept with big, perfectly trimmed trees. They lead me past brick walls covered in sprawling ivy and manicured hedges up to the thick white columns and large brick steps leading to the front door.

The manor towers above us as we approach the entrance, my neck craning to make out the multiple balconies and rooftop patios. I hope to god we aren't headed for one of those spots once we're inside. One drop down from any of them and I'd be a dead woman.

We enter into a foyer with high vaulted ceilings that are covered in ornate gold leaf patterns that match the crown molding. A large chandelier sparkles up above the wide spiral staircase. It's more classic than I expected, but I guess it makes sense since they are such old money. I imagine the Hendersons' mansion is more modern.

I am too taken in at the sight of it to say a single word as they lead me up the stairs and into a bedroom. Each door we pass on the way reveals another spacious room perfectly decorated with giant velvet curtains draped across tall windows. The hallway is lined with expensive-looking paintings and sculptures. I have never been in such a nice house before. Every room I've seen so far even has its own fireplace.

They say nothing as they file me into one of the bedrooms, before promptly leaving and locking me inside.

"Just wait here," Emmett calls out from behind the door. "I'll be back soon enough."

"Great," I grumble sarcastically. I'm still for a moment, in shock from the sheer size and decadence of the house. I quickly begin to look around the room, hoping to get some clue as to exactly where I am.

I recognize the backpack thrown on the floor in the corner, but I quietly look inside to confirm. The name scribbled across the notebooks and homework assignments tells me I was right. This is Emmett's backpack, meaning this is probably his room.

I scan the framed photos scattered across his dresser and nightstand, confirming once again that he's featured in each one alongside smiling friends and family. I even spot one of him and Malcolm together. They're younger. Probably close to the same age they were in the photos Malcolm kept in his glovebox. It tugs at my heart.

Why would Emmett keep this around after deciding he was too good to be close friends with him? What if what Malcolm said was true? Emmett's just as trapped as any of us are. That would at least make me feel better about the way I surrendered to his touch in the car, which I am still reeling from.

There's something intoxicating about being in his room, especially when he's not in here with me. I feel like I could learn so much about him and uncover so many of his truths, if only I knew where to look first. And if I wasn't terrified of them returning at any second and catching me.

His room is nothing like other teenage boys' rooms I've been in. It's missing the musty dirty sock and sweat smell, but that's probably just because they have maids. Even still, it's meticulously neat. In a way that seems impossible even with hired help cleaning once or twice a day. I speculate on what this could mean. Is he a sociopath? OCD?

Even his trashcan is spotless, only littered with one fresh apple core.

I realize I can't remember the last time I've eaten.

I'm kicking myself for not grabbing something from that McDonald's before heading home. That was the last chance I've had to eat since the Elites dragged me out of the lunchroom this afternoon. I've been running on nothing but adrenaline ever since.

The smells of popcorn and simmering dinner from home rush through my memory. I wonder how long they'll keep me here. Mom and Brendan will wonder where I am. I hate the thought of them worrying, but I can only hope that somehow saves me.

The door flings open again, sending me stumbling back innocently to the center of the room as the three of them re-enter with a pair of handcuffs in hand.

They're silent as Emmett walks over and handcuffs me to his bed, staring straight into my eyes the entire time. I wish more than anything that Trey and Vincent weren't standing right behind him.

The smell of his cologne fills my nose as I feel his hot breath bearing down on my neck. That smell is one that has haunted me. One that strikes both fear and arousal deep inside.

It's completely fucked up, but there's something incredibly erotic about him chaining me down in his room. It shouldn't be so fucked up. All sorts of regular couples do kinky shit like this, but Emmett's history of being rough with me makes it twisted. I can't help but admit that it somehow only makes it sexier to me. Maybe he has just completely worn me down.

"What are you doing?" I ask finally, reluctantly breaking the spell within our locked eyes. I imagine we're both thinking the same thing. I can see the desire glinting across his eyes.

"My father has put me in charge of watching you twenty-four-seven," he explains casually, as if it were the most normal thing in the world. "Your dad still hasn't responded to any of our messages, and his time is running out."

"How much time is left?" I try asking again, recalling that they refused to tell me when they first put me up to this and started tracking my every move.

They still don't answer. Probably just another power move, just like the blindfold. The only reason they could possibly have for not just coming right out with their deadline is to fuck with me.

"We're gonna go check in with the old man," Trey grumbles as he and Vincent turn to leave the room. "Don't do anything I wouldn't do," he winks disgustingly.

Emmett watches them leave with an excited but subtle grin, making a point to shut and lock the door behind them.

"This isn't necessary," I tell him as he turns back toward me. "You don't have to handcuff me. I'm not stupid enough to try and escape. I know you'd catch me."

"I have to do what my father tells me," he explains, not seeming too upset about it. Stirring up Malcom's words once again. I decide to try and play to this supposed good side he promised me is there.

"You always have a choice, Emmett," I beg. "You've done terrible things to me, but I know I've seen a glimpse of something good. Or at least I've wanted to, anyways. You don't have to do this. You could help me and they'd never know."

"It's getting late," he sighs, ignoring my pleas. "You want to sleep on the bed? You're already on it after all," he winks, eyeing my cuffed hands.

"You're sick," I bark back, my heart turning back over with hatred for him. I knew Malcolm was wrong about him. "I'd rather die than sleep anywhere you've slept." I let the sting of the words hang between us, wishing they sounded truer.

He pounces on me, pinning my cuffed hands beneath his hand as he towers over my body sprawled across the bed. His grip causes the cuffs to cut into my wrists against the hard bed frame.

"You're hurting me," I gasp with a squirm beneath his hold.

He's unconcerned. If anything, he's turned on. His nostrils flare as his eyes light up in anger and lust. His hand moves up to my neck, lifting my chin up to him. I blink and stare straight back, ready for whatever comes next.

All at once he takes my mouth to his, still fuming and breathing heavy as our lips crash together. I bite his lip defiantly, too hard, causing him to jerk back for an instant. But his hands quickly secure their grip again, jerking my head back to the center of his attention.

"You bitch," he growls, licking his bright red lip.

I soften under his stare, closing my eyes and leaning up again to invite him in for another kiss. He obliges, more gently this time, moaning into my mouth.

We melt into each other, losing ourselves as our tongues explore each other's mouths. This is all I've been able to think about since I ran from him in the classroom the other day. The drum of my heart picks up again, taking me back to all the fantasies I had of him in my bed. Everything that was stirred up again in the car ride here. Only this time, we're completely alone.

His hands trail down my arms that are chained behind my head, not breaking his mouth from mine as they travel down my chest. I groan as he gropes my breasts, unconsciously spreading my legs wider.

Suddenly, he stops himself. He pulls back in a frustrated gasp, looking at me helplessly. He looks just as powerless to this as I am. And for the first time, I realize if he is only obeying his father's orders, how much easier all of this would be for him if he wasn't so inexplicably drawn to me. I guess we could both say that.

He is pulled back down to me, perched next to me on the edge of the bed. His hand runs through my hair in shocking tenderness.

"Why are we so attracted to each other?" He asks breathlessly, his eyes lingering on my lips as I wonder if he'll give in and dive back down for more.

I can't answer him. I'm suspended in lust, wishing I could hate him as I know I should. If I can't have that, I just want him to take me. Just get it over with. But he's fighting it just as hard as I am.

In my silence, he moves back to the edge of the bed, collapsing his forehead to his hands in exasperation as he tries to collect himself. We sit like that for a long time. Unable to move, I am completely at the mercy of whatever he decides to do.

I swear I can feel his breath on my skin even though he's all the way at the other edge of the bed. I want more than anything for him to come to me. Take advantage of our situation. Have his way with me. I don't know what's stopping him. Maybe he only wants me when I'm resisting. I consider telling him I don't want him the way I have in the past. Maybe that would pique his interest again.

My thoughts halt as my stomach growls.

"Emmett, I'm really hungry," I finally speak up reluctantly, wondering if he'll exploit it to further my torture or if he'll actually try to help.

"It's late," he says again, running his hands back through his hair. His eyes are bloodshot, and I can see how tired he is.

"My lunch got interrupted, remember?" I remind him bitterly, crossing my legs, closing myself back off to him.

"I can't help," he insists bluntly, staring at the floor.

"Don't you have chefs or something?" I scoff. "You could just tell them you want a late-night snack. And bring it to me instead."

"And when I leave you alone," his brows raise, cutting his eyes back over to me, "what then? I'm not the only one in the house. You know that. Those other guys are like vultures. They'll be at my door the moment I leave your side, trying to get at you."

I'm quiet for a moment, taken aback with his concern. "I'm surprised you care," I hiss, jingling the cuffs behind my head. "You've watched those two try to feel me up before and did nothing to stop it."

"Shut up!" He snaps, jumping to his feet and hinting that I've struck a nerve.

I decide to continue trying to appeal to his nicer side. "I'm sorry," I lie. "I'm just hungry, like I said. Starving actually. It's making me cranky."

He looks over me again, looking hungry himself. But in a different way. "Maybe I can take your mind off of it," he suggests coyly.

I want to be intrigued, but it's no joke. "Emmett, if I don't eat something soon, I think I might pass out."

"Well, you won't go far," he jokes coldly, nodding to my position on the bed.

"You fucking asshole," I gripe, turning my head. No matter how hard I try, he never fails to remind me that there can't be another side to him. He is nothing beyond the guy who has tortured me. Who continues to torture me.

He sighs in exasperation. "Alright, hold on," he says with an irritated tone. He goes to his dresser and fumbles around in the second drawer, pulling out some sort of small electronic device. He opens the door and attaches it inside the lock and then moves a switch on a small remote around.

"What are you doing?" I ask, craning my neck to try and see.

"Making sure no one bothers you," he assures me, trying something on the lock a few more times. "I'll be right back."

I can't tell if I have physical symptoms of

emotional whiplash or if my neck is just aching from the suspension of my arms dangling from my hands. One minute he's as cold as ice. The next he's worried for my wellbeing. Or maybe it's just that he sees me as his property. He doesn't care what happens to me, as long as he's the one to do it.

Some boyfriend you've found yourself, Ophelia. And he's not even that. He's Vivian's boyfriend. He's just my kidnapper.

My eyes grow heavy as I wait for what seems like forever. I jump at the sound of the door, worried Emmett's contraption failed and someone else is coming in like he warned. But he appears with a tray of fruit in his hands.

"The cooks are gone for the night," he explains, taking a seat next to me. "This is all I could rustle up."

"I'm so hungry, I don't care. I'll eat anything," I state anxiously, moving my hands forward in anticipation. But he shows no signs of setting me free.

Instead, he takes a grape between his fingers and holds it to my lips.

"What are you doing?" my face twists in disbelief. "You're seriously not going to uncuff me long enough for me to eat?"

"It's more fun this way," he says mischievously, brushing the grape to my bottom lip, begging for me to open and let him feed me.

"This is ridiculous!" I protest, clenching my jaw shut tight.

But his eyes spark with that same strange tenderness. The one that keeps popping up suddenly out of nowhere and surprising me. A bead of moisture drips from the fruit across my lip and down my chin.

My stomach growls again, forcing me to give in. I part my lips slightly, letting my tongue brush the cold purple surface as he moves it closer into my mouth. The taste of it is too much to refuse. I unclench my teeth, letting him inch it in so I can take a bite. He watches intently, continuing to feed me slowly and sensually for what feels like hours. First grapes. Then strawberries.

I don't want to be turned on by it, but I am. Like everything with him. He stops every so often and runs his tongue along the edge of my mouth, collecting the juice of the fruit as it pools.

Once the tray is empty, things get awkward and silent. We're both breathing heavy, weighed down by all of the sexual tension and staring at each other with expectant "what now?" expressions. But we say nothing. Afraid to ruin it.

Finally, he stands and leaves the tray on the top of his dresser. He pulls some pajamas from the drawers and looks to me, as if he's about to say something. By the way he eyes my clothes, I think he might offer me something to sleep in. But he stops himself. I don't know why it's so hard for him to be kind and decent to me. Even offering me food has to be done on his fucked up terms.

"Well, we really should try and get some sleep," he grumbles half-heartedly. He knows that's going to be impossible. We're both too riled up and anxious about everything that's happening.

"How's this going to work?" I concede. "Where will you sleep?"

"The floor," he replies, pulling some spare blankets and pillows down from his closet.

I have to admit I'm disappointed that he plans to sleep on the floor. I've already come this far in surrendering to him. He might as well put me out of my misery and finish the job. But more than that, I'm afraid. I wish I was home. I don't know what kinds of fucked up things tomorrow has in store for us. I just want to be close to somebody…anybody for comfort.

"Emmett?" I call out softly after he's turned out the light and settled into his sleeping bag on the floor. He doesn't answer, so I try again. "Could you come to the bed?"

"That's not a good idea," he answers in an almost whine. For once, maybe I'm the one torturing him.

"Why not?" I persist. "I would just…I'd feel better."

"Ophelia," he says sternly into the darkness. My heart tightens with the way he says my name, so earnest and desperate. "If I come up there and lay next to you, I won't be able to control myself."

His words hang in the air, teasing me. Daring me. I want more than anything to tell him I don't care. That I'm counting on him giving in. But I take his restraint as an opportunity to remind myself what he's capable of. I'd hate myself for letting him fuck me. I'm chained to his bed for christ's sake. I'm his prisoner.

I don't answer him. Instead I try to settle down onto the pillow as far as I can, forcing myself to close my eyes. I'm exhausted, but nothing happens. Hours go by. I look over at him every so often and see that he's just as miserable as I am. His eyes wide and glaring at the ceiling. The room is pitch black, but the glossy whites catch the moonlight coming in through his window.

We both stay like that for the rest of the night, unable to fall asleep for more than a few seconds.

19

CHAPTER NINETEEN

I wake up with Emmett sleeping at the foot of the bed. I don't even remember him crawling up there or falling asleep at all. Last night was torture. The only sleep I did manage to get was when my body completely shut down for a few minutes at a time before I jerked awake again. Squirming with a need for Emmett. He must have finally had too much and thought being at my feet would be safe enough.

There's a strange beeping, which I quickly gather to be the alarm clock on his phone. I laugh as I watch him stir awake. It's time for him to go to school. Such a normal thing to be happening under such bizarre circumstances.

He sits up and rubs his eyes, avoiding eye contact with me.

"I guess you're off to WJ Prep?" I sing casually, still amused with the idea.

"Not today," he grumbles, checking for messages on his phone after he silences the alarm. "We've got something to take care of. Someone wants to meet you."

Fear falls over me again as I straighten up, my hands and arms filled with pins and needles from being handcuffed all night. "Are you coming with me?" I ask helplessly.

He smirks and nods, seeming pleased that I would want to keep him close. It surprises me too. But somehow, he has become a point of safety in all of this. At least when given the choice of all the Elites.

"But we have to get going now," he barks, jumping up to grab some clothes and straighten his appearance in his bedroom mirror.

"Can I at least take a shower first?" I ask, desperate for anything to postpone my meeting with whatever terrible thing comes next.

He shakes his head at first but looks around in consideration with his hand clenched into his hair. He is torn, grappling with another crossroads between being my tormentor and being attracted to me. If that's even what you call it. I've lost words for describing what's happening between us at this point.

I willingly grip his arm for support as he leads me,

my whole body feeling completely broken down. I don't see any chances of escaping on the short walk to the bathroom anyway.

"Okay, fine," he agrees reluctantly. "But it'll have to be fast." He comes over to unlock my handcuffs. My wrists burn and ache with the release, and I'm seriously concerned for what the extended loss of blood flow will mean for me later down the road. If I make it through this.

I bend my back and hunch my shoulders as he squeezes my elbow and leads me down the hall and into the bathroom. I walk stiffly, my limbs trembling. He's completely blank and unreadable as we go. Once we're inside, he follows me in and locks the door.

"I can't have any privacy?" I whine, hesitating to remove my clothes.

"Prisoners don't get privacy," he scoffs arrogantly, refusing to move from his spot in the corner of the bathroom. I see the Emmett I'm used to has returned with the light of day, which doesn't bode well for whatever we're preparing for.

I keep my arms wrapped around my body tight under his gaze, not wanting to undress right in front of him.

"Come on," he insists. "You were more than ready to take your clothes off for me last night."

His cockiness pisses me off, prompting me to stomp

into the shower fully clothed before undressing and throwing my clothes out onto the floor, not letting him see a thing. But I can see his silhouette watching me through the curtain.

I notice the way my body responds to him lingering on the other side of the curtain. My nipples harden and there's a warm swell deep in my core, rising with the yearn to feel him inside of me. I wish I could make it go away, but it's insatiable as I stand here completely naked and wet. His tense figure stalking me from outside.

I know he has to be feeling the same way, but I refuse to give into this. It's too fucked up. Last night my resolve was broken down, but if his cold heartlessness is back then my resistance will be too.

I go through the motions of lathering up with soap, carefully keeping my eyes pinned to the side at his shadow.

"Hurry up," he barks at me as I wash my hair.

"I'm going as fast as I can," I whine back, trying to hurry.

He huffs over, slinging back the curtain and reaching in to turn the faucets off.

"What are you doing!?" I cry, looking at him in shock. "I'm almost done. Just give me a minute."

"You're out of time, princess," he sneers, throwing a towel at me, but not until after he takes a good long slow look at my wet and naked body. I'm quick to cover up from his gaze, figuring if he can't even have the decency to give me a full five minutes in the shower, he doesn't get to see me naked.

Anger sparks in his eyes as I cover up, robbing him of his eye candy. His hand grips my elbow tightly as he yanks me out, banging my arm harshly against the sink countertop.

"Shit!" I shout, looking down to see fresh red blood pooling out into the beads of water still dripping across my skin. Just another reminder of who he really is, making me kick myself for every moment of weakness I had last night.

"We don't have time for all of this," he moans impatiently, snatching the towel and sloppily blotting down my skin himself. I cringe and recoil under his harsh touch. He seems completely unphased, wrapping the towel around my shoulders and leading me back into the hall with his hand gripping firmly to the base of my skull.

He takes me back to his bedroom and pulls out a dress in my size. "You have to look nice," he orders, ripping the garment from the hanger and throwing it in my direction.

"What's the occasion?" I quip back dryly as I reluctantly step into the dress. I'm frightened that he has something like this waiting for me. Whatever is about to happen, he's been prepared for it.

"You'll see soon enough," he spins me and quickly yanks the zipper, making me worry my skin would catch in the ferocity of it.

He pushes me out into the hall and back down the main stairs. He's tense and sweaty, his skin jerking every time it brushes up against my arm.

The more I take in of the decadent mansion, the more it disgusts me. What a waste for such beautiful things to house such ugly creatures. But really that sums the Elites up perfectly. Shiny and pretty on the outside, complete shit on the inside.

We walk into what looks like the parlor. Maybe some kind of office or study. His sneakers squeak across the glossy hardwood floors as we enter the sitting area arranged before a backdrop of thick velvet drapes across large French windows. The walls tower high above us, accented with crown molding that reflects the tiered crystal chandelier hanging in the center of the room.

It looks like a scene from the Godfather, decorated in dark mahoganies and olive greens and deep burgundies. There's a bar cart that mimics what you'd see in a Mad Men office, complete with a silver ice bucket and various bottles of scotch, brandy and bourbon. The room is dark and smells of cigars.

He leads me in, my hands pinned behind my back, to find a man sitting in a desk chair with his back turned to us. As the chair swivels around I see Mr. Thomas Jameson is the one waiting for us, instantly sparking fear in my heart.

I can already tell he is no different, not that I would have expected him to be. His lips snarl in a viciously sexual grin at the sight of me. I feel the slightest hesitation within Emmett's arms as he notices how he's looking at me, but he quickly pushes any reluctance back down dutifully and does nothing.

My guts churn as Thomas stands to walk over to me, forcing Emmett to hold his grip on me as he trails a finger across my cheek. Emmett forces my hand to his father's for a strong, businesslike handshake.

"I hear you've been quite the naughty little girl, Ophelia," he teases, his voice making me nauseous.

"Don't touch me," I whimper, jerking my arms away from Emmett.

He laughs at my protest, his nostrils snarling with gross heavy breaths. "I can see why you've been such a handful," he jokes, reaching out toward my breasts. I try to step backward, but Emmett blocks my way. I cringe under his touch, my face wincing and screaming silently as his hands move lower toward my stomach.

"Get your hands off of me you fucking old perv!" I

snap, unable to hold it in any longer. The words spill out over my fear.

My face is instantly socked with the bluntness of his knuckles. He laughs as I press my fingers to my cheek, my brow wrinkled in pain.

"You may be able to outwit my son and his little friends," he sneers with a crack of his knuckles, "but you're no match for me, you little cunt."

He steps away and pulls a handkerchief from his desk, wiping his hands down. Funny how someone so sexually interested in me can quickly turn violent enough to punch me in the face. Both acts apparently being repulsive to him, sparking the need to wash my germs from his hands.

"It's time to send a message to your beloved father," he explains mockingly as he paces before me, motioning to his cronies as they deliver a video camera and tripod to the center of the room. I watch him pace the room, his speech accelerating as he barks orders at everyone around. "We're going to record a little video."

I blink, processing his words, and focus on him intently. Clinging to any hint of what to expect.

Emmett pulls me from behind, pushing up a chair that I am quickly shoved into as he grabs my arms and ties them behind me. The rope burns into my wrists as he squeezes the knots securely, cutting off the circulation of my hands. My eyes narrow, peering into them as if I look hard enough all of this might start making sense.

"You're going to beg for your life," Mr. Jameson commands. "Let him know that if he doesn't stop, we have other ways to help make him." He speaks slowly and forcibly, trying to sound in control, but I can tell he's coming apart.

"I had never even heard a word from my father up until a few days ago," I protest. "I don't think I'm your best bet at getting him to do anything. He doesn't give a shit about me."

"Oh, I like a girl with daddy issues," he taunts, sweat gleaming on his face. "You let us worry about that and just do what we tell you."

Once the camera is in place, one of the men holds his finger over the red record button, waiting for his cue to start the video.

"Now, keep in mind, dear…the success of this message really is up to you," Thomas explains snidely. "Whether or not your father responds accordingly, allowing us to spare your life, will depend entirely on how convincing you are." He stops in front of me, leaning over to perch his hands across the arms of my chair. He winces, his face twisting into disapproval. "I don't know…you don't look afraid to me." He turns to Emmett.

"What do you think, son? Does she look afraid to you?"

I see Emmett turn away in the corner of my eye, refusing to answer. Suddenly my head whips around with a painful sting across my cheek. Thomas is laughing as he stands back, proudly admiring the redness of my face as I whimper in pain.

I rock back and forth in the chair, trying to control my heavy panting as I tell myself over and over that this will all be okay. It has to be. My back arches as I squirm in discomfort with deep, shuddering breaths that make me feel lightheaded.

Emmett doesn't make me feel the least bit safe anymore and with Thomas's looming presence, already having hit me twice just in the few short minutes I've been in the room, I feel like I'm having a panic attack.

Stop panicking, Ophelia.

Calm down, Ophelia.

I see starbursts behind my closed eyelids. I focus on keeping my breaths steady and normal, but my muscles are rigid, my tendons standing out on edge. My head still swimming from Thomas's blows.

A man walks over and places today's newspaper in my lap to show the date. This really is a full-blown hostage situation. Out of all the things I thought I'd experience in my life; this was not on my radar.

"Now you'll tell your father to stop. And that he

must answer to our ultimatum immediately. Or he'll never get the chance to meet his precious daughter," Thomas commands cavalierly.

"What if he doesn't care?" I propose, knowing all too well how possible that is. "Haven't you already sent him similar threats and got nothing? He's gone this long wanting nothing to do with me. Whatever he has against you seems to be more important to him than my life."

"Oh, don't be so cynical," he mocks condescendingly. "Even the most detached father wouldn't want to see certain things done to his baby girl. You see…I've put girls just like you in some pretty horrid conditions. There's good money in it. I doubt he'd want you to vanish into that kind of life."

I remember Liam's warnings about what the Jameson Automobile Company was fronting through the use of his software. Underage girls on the black market in sex trafficking rings. All this time I've been afraid of dying. It never occurred to me that my potential fate could be much worse. Maybe Emmett's sadistic sexual torture is just preparing me for what will happen if my father doesn't come through and meet their demands.

I look to Emmett again, desperately. He watches blankly. I want him to stand up for me. To say or do anything to intervene, but he cowers in the corner. Not lifting a single finger in my defense. Now I worry for how involved he might be in his father's business. Maybe he's just as sick and guilty of the same crimes.

"What do I have to say?" I ask finally, my voice cracking as I realize I have no choice but to give in. His scare tactics are working. Mostly because I know he's ruthless. Cold. Heartless. He doesn't make idle threats.

"Speak from your heart, my dear," he sneers. "I'm sure once we get started, you'll feel inspired." His menacing tone and grin frighten me even more as his men gather behind me.

I watch one of them press a button on the camera, causing a red light to flash. Thomas waves his hands through the air dramatically, like a maestro conducting an orchestra. His callous coldness is chilling. Enough to cause me to tear up in terror, but I hold back. Not giving them my tears is my last possible act of defiance. The only part of myself I can still hold onto.

"Dad," I begin, my voice already wavering more than I'd like. Even saying the title, addressing him directly, feels foreign and wrong. "You have to do what they say," I stammer, feeling at a loss for words. My mind is blank.

Still refusing to cry a single tear, one of Thomas's men crouches down behind me with a pair of pliers in hand, squeezing my knuckles in their grip tighter and tighter. I hope the lack of blood flow to my hands dulls the pain, but I can feel the cold metal cutting into me intensely. I still don't give in. My face winces in pain but I don't shed a tear.

"Dad!" I cry out louder. "Please…I don't know where you are or how far you're willing to go with this. But these people aren't fucking around," my sentiment sparks a maniacal, taunting laugh from Thomas. "You have to stop coming after them. Respond to their messages and let them know you'll stop. Please. They'll…they'll make sure I disappear forever if you don't." My throat tightens with even more building cries, threatening to forcibly erupt as I contemplate what could happen if this doesn't work.

"Are you sure you have nothing else to add? Nothing else to inspire your father to help you?" Thomas beckons, like a parent to a toddler. His tone soft and inviting in a chilling way, completely mismatched to his intentions.

I know he is encouraging me to cry, but I stay strong. Shaking my head. Liam promised me my father had a plan. And that I shouldn't feel so hopeless and powerless. It's all I have to cling to for now. I just have to hope he was right.

Thomas motions for the recording to be stopped and then nods to Emmett. He comes over and unties me, forcing me to my feet. He restrains me by the arms once again as Thomas approaches, coming too close.

"It was lovely meeting you, dear Ophelia," he groans with predatory eyes. "I'm sure we will meet again. Very soon. At least I hope it's soon…for your sake."

I want to spit in his face, but he hits harder than any of his younger Elite counterparts. I'm still weak, tired and panicked. I don't think I can withstand another blow. So instead I bite my tongue and turn my head, wishing Emmett would just hurry up and take me away.

Once we are to the top of the stairs, my tears flow like rain. I'm completely unable to hold them back a second longer now that it's just Emmett and I alone again.

"Thanks a lot," I sob, my throat tight with anger. "You really had my back in there."

"What do you want from me!?" he rumbles in a low, tired rage.

"Oh yeah…what could I possibly have wanted from you?" I fire back sarcastically. "What kind of guy lets his dad treat people that way?"

Suddenly I am thrown against the wall. Emmett's hands are digging into my shoulders, shaking me violently.

"Do you get it now, Ophelia!?" he shrieks in a hushed tone. "If you think my father was terrible just then…imagine the kinds of things I've…" He chokes, unable to say another word.

I bite back everything building up inside, feeling a new wave of pity for him. But he quickly pushes me along, both of us desperate to be back inside the privacy and safety of his room.

"Finish your sentence," I beg once we're hidden away behind his locked door. "What kinds of things…" I'm afraid to ask, but I need to know. It's his only chance at redemption. The possibility that he's just an abused fucked up kid who is too damaged to know how to treat people.

But he refuses to answer. He won't even look at me. He retreats back into his closed-off shell, staring despairingly out his window.

I'm certain Malcolm was right. There had to be something more to Emmett once. Something kind. But maybe as the years of his life went on in this fucked up house, in the world of the Elites, he was broken. My blood chills at the thought that he may never be restored. No matter what happens. Maybe he is fucked up beyond repair. And my biggest fear is that once he's through with me, I will be too.

20

CHAPTER TWENTY

"I have to cuff you up again," Emmett says finally, brushing a finger across his upper lip before reluctantly turning back to me from the window.

"Emmett, my arms are killing me from being cuffed up all night," I lament in exhaustion. "Can we just skip that part this time?"

"You saw him in there," he offers up dryly. "You know I have to do this."

I'm too tired to argue. I take my seat on the bed and offer my hands over freely. My mind racing as he secures the handcuffs once again.

I'm getting desperate for some way out of this. I know time is running out. If my dad doesn't give these people what they want, they're going to kill me. Or worse. Sell me off into some sex trafficking ring. And since I have never been able to count on him for anything, I'm not going to hang all of my hopes on him.

I study Emmett as he sits in the corner, listlessly tossing a ball up to the ceiling and catching it again. Out of everyone I've seen in this mansion, Emmett is my best shot at manipulating my way to freedom long enough to hunt down some shred of evidence.

I know there has to be something somewhere in this place. Something that my dad and the Hendersons can use in their case. It can't be spotless. Then maybe I would have something more than these ransom videos to count on.

"I gotta say…out of all the times I imagined being locked alone with you in your room…this is not exactly what I had pictured," I attempt to joke with him with a half-smile.

His eyes spark with interest. "So, you have fantasized about me?" he asks with a suggestive note to his voice.

"Don't be stupid, Emmett. You know I have. And you've fantasized about me too," I state plainly.

He catches the ball a final time and sits up to look at me. His eyes trail over my body longingly and then settle on the cuffs around my wrist with a tinge of pity. Blood is still dripping down my arm from where it banged against the bathroom counter this morning.

He raises to his feet at the sight of the blood and steps toward me. "How's your arm?"

"It's alright I guess," I sniffle. "After everything with Thomas…I guess I forgot about it."

Both of our eyes turn dark with the memory of Emmett being forced to stand there and hold me down while Thomas felt me up. I watch the memories roll around in his mind, sending him into a sudden manic pace across the room.

"It can't be easy to have a dad like that," I offer softly.

He turns but doesn't answer me. His face twists slightly with a flood of suppressed emotions.

"You don't know what you're talking about," he mumbles half-heartedly. "You don't know anything about us."

I kick myself for having crossed a line, closing him off. But his voice is blank. He's lying to protect himself, and he's not even that adamant about it. I can tell he's tired and worn down from everything. Maybe just as much as I am.

Without another word, he leaves the room. His feet march toward the bathroom down the hall before returning a few minutes later with first aid supplies in hand. Taking a seat near me on the edge of the bed, he leans forward to clean my wound.

"I didn't mean for you to get hurt," he says softly, gently blotting a cold, damp cotton ball to the cut.

"I know you didn't," I lie, looking deep into his eyes.

His head raises with my words before he kneels back down to put a band-aid over the cut. "What's got you playing nice all of a sudden?"

"I'm just done playing games," I explain. "I'm tired and scared. And you're the only person I care about in any of this."

He laughs mockingly. "Care about?"

"You know I care for you, Emmett," I soften my voice. "And you care for me too."

"What makes you so sure of that?" he scoffs through a thin veil. I can see everything stirring up inside of him.

I strategically uncross my legs, revealing a slight view from where my dress is riding up my thighs, and move closer so that we are touching. His eyes drink in the sight of my hiked skirt and everything peeking out from underneath. Putting us right back in the tempting spot we were the night before.

"You made me sure of it," I explain, lifting my leg to rub against his, sinking beneath my hands that are chained behind my head. "All the times you knew you were supposed to beat the shit out of me, but you were too turned on to really hurt me. The classroom after I slapped Vivian. And again, when she was standing there watching us. I could tell how badly you wanted me by the way you looked into my eyes. It took everything in you not to take me last night."

He shifts uncomfortably, trying to look away but unable to.

"You didn't have to kiss me when you tracked me down at that meet…before I came to WJ Prep," I continue, wearing down on his defenses. "You know I'm not so gullible that I'd melt for any boy who kissed me. You did it because you couldn't help yourself. And I fell for you because I couldn't help myself. You can't deny that there's something between us."

My throat hitches as I realize everything I'm saying is true, even if I am only trying to butter him up. All of the tension between us amplifies with every word I speak. My lips part as I rest my eyes firmly on him, my suspended hands growing moist. "I didn't know what to say when you asked last night…but I feel it too. We are so attracted to each other."

His fingers trail across my arm too slowly as he tends to the wound, his legs spread, opening slightly wider as mine do. He leans forward, continuing to bandage my cut. Not saying a word. But I can see a million things going on in his head.

"What are you thinking?" my tone is soft and low. I

relax into my captive state, turning my chest straight toward him.

His eyes soften and gloss over with desire. "You don't want to know what I'm thinking."

"Don't be so sure," I dart my tongue across my lips, loosening the tension in my muscles. "I don't have the energy to fight this anymore."

He shifts uneasily, clenching his hands briefly before tugging at his ear. I feel the skin on my chest grow flush as I swallow hard with a slow smile that builds. "How long do you think it will be before they want me again?" I ask as I lift my chin, holding my breath. "Can you let me go? Just for a little bit?"

He eyes me suspiciously before tensing up again, moving away as if he's trying to break the spell. "It's not a good idea," he insists. "My father will kill both of us if we don't do what we're supposed to."

"He'll never know," I protest, pulling at the cuffs eagerly. "Emmett, I won't try anything. I just want to be able to talk to you without being all chained up."

He scoffs with a dismissive smirk. "Fuck off, Ophelia. I know you too well. You may be attracted to me, but you also hate me. This is just a game so you can pull some kind of shit over on me. Which wouldn't be good for either of us."

I back off, shifting to make myself uncomfortable as I resign to being handcuffed longer. I wrack my brain for anything I can say to sway him as I feel the building intensity of time running out.

"Do you remember when we first met?" I try again. "I thought you were so hot. But then again I also thought you were normal."

I catch a faint smirk on his lips. "So, I'm not normal?" he teases.

I answer with my brow raised sharply, letting him figure that one out for himself. "The way you kissed my hand," I laughed. "And then you demanded that I let you kiss my lips."

He plops into a chair in the corner as his leg starts bobbing up and down. He presses his palm to his mouth and looks anxiously around the room, fighting hard not to let my words affect him.

"I can't believe I let you," I mused. "Something about the way you commanded me…I just couldn't refuse. I guess you still have that power over me somehow."

"I wasn't expecting to feel like that when I kissed you," he responds with a surprising tenderness.

His recollection of it makes sense. The way he seemed confused and tormented as he grabbed at my body with an almost punishing touch. He hated me for the feelings I stirred up inside of him. He was just doing what he was told, scoping me out and luring me to WJ Prep. He never meant to feel anything for me.

"I still never expect to feel that way when I kiss you," he added in a disappointed mutter.

"But you do," I offer optimistically, thinking maybe I've found my way into him. "And I do too. There's something between us, Emmett. Enough that…surely you can trust me to let me go for just a little bit. My arms are still sore from sleeping like this all night."

He eyes my red wrists in concern, rapidly already turning white and red with numb tingles that hurt much more than the first time around.

Springing to his feet like he might actually let me loose, he stops again. Eyeing me suspiciously.

"Come on, Emmett," I encourage him, sounding as innocent as I can. "Part of what made that first kiss so fucking delicious was the freedom of my hands. Do you remember how I explored your body? Trailed my fingers through your hair?"

He turns with a growl, growing more frustrated. "You drive me crazy, Ophelia. Just stop it!" he snaps finally. "When this is all over…"

He stops himself, and I'm surprised at his subtle implication. He's hinting at an end to this. One in which I'm maybe still alive. Does he know something I don't?

"I think a lot about those first couple of times we met," I carry on, mostly out of bored resignation at this point. "The way I saw you before I started piecing everything together. Before I knew about the Elites…or that you were one of them."

"Oh yeah?" he mumbles, doing a poor job of hiding his interest.

I part my legs again, spreading the tight black dress as my head falls back in a nostalgic moan. "I wish things didn't have to be so complicated."

He's started throwing his ball again without saying a single word in response. Just a frustrated sigh and quick glance in my direction.

"Do you remember the other day in the classroom? The things you did to me against that wall," my voice trails off into an almost whisper.

He coldly pushes back, "Ophelia, stop it. Everything's different now."

I grow still, feeling embarrassed. And also afraid, worried about what's happened since then that's changed everything so much. I have to remember he has the upper hand. He knows more than he's telling me.

I have to stop thinking about him like this anyway. It makes no sense. There are much bigger things going on. My life is in danger. I shouldn't be pining for some boy…especially when that boy is one of the people tormenting me.

He hangs his head in exasperation and heaves a sigh, "I don't know what you want from me. I just want this all to be over with. I have to be careful or…"

"Or what?" I try again, needing him to look at me – to want me the way he used to. The way he did just last night. I need a distraction from everything that just happened with his father. The fear of the unknown and what happens next. "I know you're keeping something from me. Just tell me."

"I can't do this right now. Why can't you understand that? You don't listen to me," he grumbles. It's a relief to see him angry but calm. To know he's capable of less than the extremes I've seen up until now.

"Where's Vivian been this whole time?" I ask finally. I'm curious, but also seeing how many different nerves I can strike. Hoping one of them will make him spill whatever it is he's hiding.

He shakes his head, not answering me.

"Did you two break up?" I ask lightly, trying to sound indifferent.

"Oh, just because she's not around for your kidnapping you assume we broke up?" he snaps back with an arrogant grin, his brows raised. "What's it to you anyway, Ophelia?"

Now I grow silent, angry that he even needs to ask why I care with everything I've said to him. He thinks it's all just an act. I wish it was. Mostly I just wish I didn't say anything at all.

"I need to go to school," he finally relents, giving up on his fight against me. Needing to retreat somewhere far away from me and this whole mess. I know he doesn't need to go to school right now. He's just looking for an escape.

"Take me with you," I beg urgently, cringing at the thought of being left alone in the same building as his father. "Don't leave me here alone."

"I can't," he insists sternly. "There's no way that's going to happen."

"Then at least let me loose," I cry sincerely, feeling unable to bear another few hours of my arms being suspended this way. "Please, Emmett. My arms are killing me. I won't leave your room."

"I know you won't," he huffs as he marches over, pulling the key from his pocket and unlatching the cuffs. "This door locks from the outside, and I'm the only one who can unlock it." He holds up the small remote from last night. He clicks the button a few times, prompting the latch of the door to move to and from.

After demonstrating the lock, he finally unlocks my handcuffs again. My arms shake as I groan with their release, wringing the soreness of my wrists.

He gathers his things, refusing to look at me, stopping once before he reaches for the door with a subtle glance over his shoulder. I pray for him to turn around and do whatever is going through his mind, but with another exasperated grunt he carries on his path. The door is swiftly shut and locked from the outside.

I'm relieved to be alone again as he leaves for school, but I would still give anything to be able to go with him. Though I know in reality I am no safer out there than in here, the illusion of freedom, even only for a brief afternoon, would restore me. Give me the strength I need to maybe gain a new perspective. Some new idea of what to do next.

My hands and arms still ache, and I wonder if I can use this time to sleep it off. I am exhausted. Being left alone finally, I try to make the best of it and rest in a way I couldn't when Emmett was just a foot away. But a strange longing for him lingers. I am once again left with frazzled senses, not knowing if I want to run to him or away from him.

I lay down, relishing in the relief of tension in my body. Time passes slowly as I'm unable to fall asleep. I'm too afraid of what might happen while he's gone. I know Thomas is lurking out there somewhere, and I can only hope he is too distracted to realize I'm up here all alone. Maybe my dad has responded to him. Maybe he's finally giving up and giving them what they want. But I know better.

The clock on his bedside table says it's close to noon. Every time I close my eyes, I swear I see someone moving in the corner of the room, jerking me back awake. Great, I think. Now I'm hallucinating.

I try to stay perfectly still, thinking maybe if I don't make any noise, Thomas will forget I'm up here all alone. But I can't lay on the bed anymore. I'm too anxious to stay still.

I pace the room in dreaded anticipation of what happens next. My skin is crawling from the memories of Thomas's hands on my body, and I swear I can still feel him touching me. I shake it all away, trying to bring myself back to reality. I am alone and safe. For the moment.

But then footsteps thud down the hallway, sending me back into panic.

Anyone would want to run if they were in this position, but being a runner at heart, it's that much more painful to be so trapped. My legs moving as fast as they can, the wind brushing against me as I leave everything behind, is the only thing that could make me feel better right now.

I just want to go home, far away from this hellhole. I wonder if my mom and Brendan have started looking for me yet. I never came home after the guys convinced them to let us go to the movies together. Surely, they would have contacted the police by now. I figure the Elites must have warned the authorities that they'd be up to something and not to look for me.

They'd do whatever they asked. They could literally get away with murder.

The footsteps draw closer and suddenly there's a knock on the door that causes me to jump.

"Ophelia?" Thomas' voice calls out from behind the door, sending chills down my spine.

I'm too afraid to move. I stand there hopelessly, thinking maybe if I'm quiet he'll just go away. I know all about his preference for underage girls.

"Let me in, sweetheart," he croons, his voice making me sick. "I only want to talk to you."

"Go away," I answer softly, my voice cracking. "I don't want to see anyone right now."

"Now, is that any way to treat your host?" he taunts me, jiggling the door handle. "Emmett doesn't have to know we've seen each other. And I can make you much more comfortable…if you'd only let me."

"No…no thank you!" I stammer out. "I'm fine in here alone."

"Suit yourself," he jests finally. "But I'll be seeing you soon." I hear him cackle as he turns down the hall. The moment I hear his footsteps starting down the stairs, I race for my phone and open it up to Emmett's number.

Thomas is trying to get into the room. Please help.

I sit on the edge of the bed and wait anxiously, but there's no response.

Suddenly I hear the lock on the bedroom door click. My heart pounds as I think it must be Thomas. He's returned with a key. But the hallway is silent. I peek out and see no one. I quickly dart across the hall and lock myself inside the bathroom, only for that lock to click open a few minutes later.

A scream rests on the tip of my tongue as the handle turns and the door slowly creaks open, but I'm relieved to see Emmett on the other side.

His hair is disheveled, and he looks distressed.

"Are you okay?" he growls, fuming with anger. "I can't believe my dad tried to get at you again. I can't take this. You're *mine*."

"Please let me go to school with you, Emmett," I plead again. "The moment you leave, he'll be back. And I don't think he'll give up so easily next time." I can see him considering it as he grazes his palm across the back of his neck.

"Convince me," he demands, for his own sake just as much as mine.

I step closer, leaning into his chest. "I'll stay by your side at all times," I argue. "For better or worse."

My head lifts, my eyes meeting his. They furrow narrowly, reading my face and body, before he blinks and leans back into my stance. My eyes are glued to his lips, begging him to make a move.

"Oh god, Emmett…please. Just fuck me," the words spill from my mouth in a breathless stream, surprising both of us.

He tenses, a faint smile turning up the corners of his lips as his fingers skate across his jaw. A faint jumble of syllables escapes his lips, but quickly trail off as he clears his throat.

My head tilts and my lips part as I slowly breathe faster under his gaze across my body. He moves even closer, as if he has no choice. We're both at the mercy of the magnetic pull between us.

My heart rate quickens as my body heat rises. I can't stand it anymore. I dig my fingers into his forearm, pulling him closer. The tension melts away with each touch, giving us release. We've kissed so many times before, but we know this time is different. Once we start, we won't stop.

I swallow hard, alert and waiting for what he will do next. My muscles tense as I note the sweat beading across his brow. It's taking every muscle in his body to resist me right now.

Finally, he gives in, sliding his hand across my thigh under my skirt, gripping my ass as he lifts me up onto the bathroom counter. His hips push in between my legs, pressing the strain in his pants against the warm wetness between my legs. I can feel the stiffness through my panties.

His hand tugs at the back of my hair, pulling my head back and my mouth wider for his kiss. His tongue fills my mouth in slow steady waves, groaning so deep that it vibrates through my throat.

He pins my hands to the counter, frantically plunging his tongue in and out of my mouth. We kiss so hard and quick, drinking each other in so desperately that we accidentally scrape our teeth together a few times. Kissing each other with such urgency it's as if our lives depend on it. His tan fingers grab at my breasts, rubbing my nipples in tiny circles every so often – just enough to make them hard and send shooting signals down to my clit. I'm so caught up in lust, and wetter than I thought possible, enough to soak my underwear, which are now completely exposed from my skirt that Emmett has hiked up over my thighs.

I lift my arms, begging him to slip the dress over my head. He does slowly…too slowly. Torturing me with his soft touch and the hotness of his breath meeting my exposed skin.

His hands pull at the clasp of my bra, releasing my breasts into the open air as he kisses me harder. His palm stretches over one of them, squeezing it firmly before his fingers trails across my nipple. The curls of his hair brush my cheek as he drops to my neck, biting and kissing ferociously, working his way down to my breasts.

I moan as his tongue darts across my nipples, and I consider pushing him away as memories of the abuse I've suffered at his hands come back to haunt me. But the sensation of his warm mouth shoots straight to my core.

"Stop," I offer weakly, but the desire dripping from my tone betrays me. I'm unable to resist any further.

His fingers move my folds in circles, almost too roughly, but the force is just right. The burn of it only pushes me closer as he pushes the sharp zipper of his pants against his grip. He pushes my panties aside and slides his fingers inside of me. The roughness of his skin gliding into me is like nothing I've ever felt before.

I'm no virgin, and I've certainly been fingered before, but no guy's touch has ever felt like this. My eyes roll to the back of my head with a deep moan as I brace my arms against the counter.

He steps back to unzip his pants, staring me straight in the eyes, pulling out the most gorgeous long, hard cock I've ever seen. I lick my lips and can't stop myself from breathlessly exclaiming, "Oh, Emmett." He keeps staring me straight in the eye as he reaches down and begins stroking himself. "What is it, baby? Is it this?" he rasps in a deep sexy voice, "Is this what you want?"

"Oh god, Emmett, yes. Please, give it to me now. Fuck me."

He drops his pants and inches closer. Once he quickly manages to pull on a condom from the bathroom drawer, I grab his hips and pull him back toward me. He slams me back up against the bathroom mirror in a wave of excitement. I frantically remove my underwear.

As his big strong arms hoist my hips up in such a perfect way that his dick slides perfectly into me from just the right angle. I'm so overtaken by his strength and how good those first few deep thrusts are, sliding his hard cock inside of me. He fits into me perfectly. Big enough to hit all of the right spots without hurting me. Every thrust of his hips puts him deeper inside of me than the one before. He's large and the size stretches me, but I'm so wet that he goes right in. My muscles tense in pleasure around him as he growls into my ear. His rhythm speeds, his fingernails digging into my ass. Any brief sharp pain he causes me now isn't from hatred. He's just as overcome with passion as I am.

I cry out, "Oh Emmett! Emmett, fuck yes!"

He grips his arms under my legs, reaching around and tightly squeezing my ass, as his long dick slides in and out of me. He thrusts hard and deep but pulls out so slowly each time – sending ripples of sensation through my entire body.

Everything about it makes me more wet – the smell of his cologne, the sweat dripping from his tan gleaming chest, the way the muscles in his neck tighten and bulge as he moans with each thrust into me. His voice is smooth like honey, and it excites me to know that I can bring sounds like that out of him. The stretch of skin and muscle just above his dick is sweaty and smooth and gliding across my clit pushing me close to climax.

"Emmett," I whimper against his neck as he moves faster, pushing me closer to the edge.

His eyes meet mine, burning straight into me as he moves faster. His breath quickens and catches with the rhythm as sweat beads across his upper lip, dampening the strands of hair hanging in his eyes.

I almost don't hear him at all as I cry out in pleasure, but the softness of his voice catches my attention. He whimpers tenderly, in a way I've never heard from him before. We're suspended for a moment, frozen with our bodies pressed together. He slowly pulls back, his eyes studying me as his face turns.

"That's it, baby. Come for me. I want to feel you come. God, I'm so close…I'm going to come too. Are you ready?"

I'm so overwhelmed with the strange feelings surging inside of me, I can barely answer him, "I...I think…fuck, that's so good…" I cry out as I realize how close I am to coming.

His hand spreads over my mouth to muffle my cries.

"Fuck, yes, I'm going to come…don't stop…right there…that's it!" I manage to say, muffled against his hand.

His groans in my ear grow deeper and entangled with a slight growl as he slams into me harder and faster over and over… He hisses through clenched teeth against my ear. He lets out a few manly grunts and final thrusts before vanishing, as if he disappeared into a cloud of smoke, vanishing to some other forgotten part of my brain.

We both lose ourselves, crashing over the edge in ecstasy. My head drops to his shoulder, both of us damp with sweat.

But suddenly, he pulls away, tossing my hands off of him and back down to the counter. Like a switch, I see the old familiar Emmett return almost instantly as he turns cold. I'm left alone and frustrated. My body feeling completely void of the desire I felt only moments ago.

He shakes his head, his lips ruffling like a horse. As if he's trying to shake me away. His shoulders roll with a crack of his jaw. I'm waiting for him to kiss me, to turn back to the way he was before. But his eyes turn distant and cold.

I suddenly feel vulnerable and ashamed, my naked body perched on full display in front of him on the bathroom counter. He pulls the full condom from his dick and tosses it into the trashcan, wiping himself down with a towel before tossing it to me callously. I jump back as it slaps against my arms.

"So…that's it then?" I ask in bewilderment, shocked that such an intense encounter could fade off into such ordinary awkward teenage behavior.

"What do you mean?" he asks as if everything is normal, but his refusal to look at me tells me what I need to know. He's hiding from me. Hiding from this.

"Is something wrong?" I try again.

"Ophelia, I don't know what you're talking about," he smirks with a perplexed grin that implies I am crazy. "We fucked. We're done. And now I need to go."

"Bullshit!" I cry out, clutching the towel around me to cover myself up. "You're acting weird. What's going on with you? How can you just shut off like that?"

"Maybe you've forgotten why we're here," he growls. "You're our hostage. My father is waiting downstairs right now, trying to decide when he's going to kill you or sell you off into his sex trafficking rings. It's not exactly a romantic time."

"Then why did we do it?" I huff, wishing I could take it back.

"You begged," he replies arrogantly.

I want to slap him across the face, but I'm afraid of what he would do in response. Instead, I curl into myself, making my body small. Wishing I could just disappear. I thought giving myself over to Emmett would make me feel better about the chaos and danger around us, but his quick withdrawal of feeling is only making it worse. I feel even more alone than before.

I stare with empty eyes at my feet dangling from the counter, turning the same shades of red and white that my hands and arms have been up until now. I wonder how long it will be before I'm chained up again. And how long after that before they finally kill me.

That's it, I think. He's gone. Everything I thought was between us was just his urge to get what he wanted. And now that I've given it to him, I have no more power over him. Not only am I disgusted with myself for caving in, I've endangered my life. He's the only one who's given me any hope of maybe helping me. At feeling something for me enough that I might be able to get out of this. But now I've lost that.

But it isn't a conclusion I'm prepared to come to yet – I don't have the energy. I let out an exasperated sigh and tuck away all of my thoughts to some other part of my brain, as I've grown so used to doing.

"Well...thanks. I guess," I grumble awkwardly in the face of his sudden cold detachment as he fumbles to put his pants back on, refusing eye contact.

"I really do need to go to school," he replies dryly. "I never made it before. I had to come back when you texted."

"Emmett...please, please let me come with you," I try begging again, forgetting about the rest of what just happened for a moment. "You know as soon as you leave that your dad will come for me again."

He nods knowingly, his eyes deep in thought. "You're right," he resigns. "But it's too risky."

"You told me to convince you!" I cry out, losing my composure. "And I gave myself over to you. Which I realize now was a fucking stupid thing to do. But the least you could do is have the decency to take me with you now that I gave you what you wanted."

"You think that was a mistake?" he asks, almost looking hurt.

I am stunned and silent. Does he not think it was a mistake? Could have fooled me with the way he immediately pulled away. Unable to look at me. All I can do is shake my head in exasperation.

"Alright," he mutters. "I'll take you."

My heart surges with renewed hope. I know it

means nothing and that we'll end up right back here afterward. My fate being no more certain than before. But at least I can have a few brief hours of escape. And outside of these walls, the possibilities of being saved or helped in some way are a million times stronger.

I awkwardly put my clothes back on, too tired to think about this thing with Emmett anymore. All I care about right now is getting the hell out of this house.

21

CHAPTER TWENTY-ONE

As Emmett's car pulls up to WJ Prep, the sight of the kids gathered in front of the school in between periods gives me hope. Though my situation may be completely fucked, there is still a normal world carrying on without me. And maybe, if I play my cards right, I can find some way to rejoin it all soon.

It's strange to be back at school, pretending that everything is fine. No one knows that I'm being held hostage. If this school wasn't so fucked up, I'd try to ask for help, but I know all too well how futile that would be.

I try to convince myself my life *is* normal for a moment. I think back on Emmett's and my encounter in his bathroom as I watch him kick a few pebbles around on the ground on our walk to the front of the building. I want us to just be normal teenagers. A guy and a girl who like each other, who've just had sex with each other for the first time. We should be giddy and all over each other, but instead we're caught in our parents' traps. He's too damaged to ever truly feel anything for me, which he made obvious by his behavior when he was finished with me.

I have to remind myself of everything Emmett has done. He is not so innocent, and I'd be dumb to forget that. I feel dumb enough for the times I've forgotten it up until now. But it's tempting. That's how desperate I am for things to feel ordinary.

Emmett escorts me to my next class, refusing to leave me as he takes a seat next to mine. The teacher eyes him questioningly.

"You're not even in this class," I hiss into his ear.

"I'm not letting you out of my sight," he barks. "They're not going to do anything."

I shouldn't be surprised when the teacher starts the lesson as normal, ignoring Emmett's unexplained presence. Neither of us can focus on the lecture. This is just a way to kill time and keep up appearances until everything comes to a head.

After class, we meet Bernadette out in the school yard. We all stand in a silent daze. We only made it in time for the final period, and it's time to go home now. But I can only assume Bernadette and Emmett are just as eager for an escape as I am, avoiding going home. At least that's one thing I can take comfort in. They're all just as stressed as me, just for different reasons.

Emmett's phone dings, and whatever he receives causes his features to twist. "I'll be right back," he announces suddenly, prompting me to shake my head in protest. But he ignores me, turning to Bernadette. "Don't let her out of your sight," he tells her sternly.

"Where are you going?" I ask desperately, afraid to be left alone without him. But he ignores me and disappears around the corner of the building.

Bernadette and I are left alone in awkward silence as she scrolls around on her phone. As much as I hate her, it feels strangely good to be around anyone who understand what our lives really are right now.

Anxious and unsure of what else to do, I pull out my own phone, thinking surely my parents have called and messaged me a hundred times asking where I am. I'm surprised they're not at the school looking for me. But of course, my phone is dead. Leaving me completely detached from anything outside the bubble of the Elites.

"My parents are going to be looking for me," I say without thinking to Bernadette, wondering how she'll respond with no one else around.

"We've taken care of that," she states plainly without looking up.

"How?" I gape, shaking my head. "What could you possibly have done to make them okay with me just vanishing and not coming home?"

"The principal talked to them," she smiles with creepy confidence. "You don't have to worry about them. In fact, that should be the last of your worries. You need to be more concerned with your biological father and whatever he decides to do next."

I look back down to my phone and then around the schoolyard at the other students and teachers. Everyone is decidedly ignoring me once again, even though I know my appearance must be rough. They've got everyone playing along with their game, and I guess it makes sense. Everyone seems to be tied into Jameson Automobile Company to some extent, and if it goes down…the whole town goes down with it.

Before I can muster a response, I hear Emmett's voice from around the corner. He sounds upset, but I can't make out the words. I know Bernadette won't let me out of her sight, so I try inching far enough away without looking suspicious…just enough to get a better view of him.

I step a few feet away casually, looking around at random things in the parking lot before darting my eyes to the side of the school. I see Emmett's arms flailing. He's talking to someone. As he moves to the side,

I'm able to make out Vivian standing next to him. They're having some kind of argument.

I assume she must be in the loop. Steering clear this whole time to let Emmett do what he has to do, by orders of his father. If she only knew just how well he was doing it. How serious he took his orders to look after me. I bite my lip with the memories of him taking me over the bathroom sink. The sounds of his moans and hot breaths as he came.

I look back to Bernadette to see if she's alarmed by my distance, but she doesn't seem concerned. She's too wrapped up in her phone, but she glances up every so often to make sure I'm still within her sights. I should be trying to run away, even though I probably wouldn't get very far. But instead, I'm drawn to Emmett's conversation with Vivian like a moth to a flame.

As I boldly wander just a few steps further, hoping to get close enough to hear them, Vivian's eyes bolt toward me, sparking the moment they meet mine. She looks furious. Without another word to Emmett she pushes past him and barrels toward me furiously.

"You!" she growls. "Don't fucking move."

Emmett rolls his eyes and follows slowly behind as she marches forward. I do as she asks, not moving, trying to hide the curious grin sparking across my face. I don't know what I expected, but of course Vivian parades right up to me and punches me square in the face. I buckle over from her blow, trying to straighten and hit her back, but she grips my hand in midair.

"You have some balls, you little whore," she hisses at me, full of hatred. "You're lucky I don't kill you right here."

"Vivian," Emmett groans, doing nothing to step in and make her loosen her hold on me. "I told you she has nothing to do with this."

"You think you can come in and steal my boyfriend?" her fist shakes, twisting my arm around. "If you survive this shitshow with your dad, I'm going to make you wish you never even looked at him."

I have no idea what's going on, but I can only assume Emmett has told her about us. Maybe he broke up with her. The thought makes me happier than it should.

"Enough, Vivian!" Emmett barks, coming over and ripping her hands away from me. "You're being paranoid. I told you I don't want anything to do with her. I love you."

My heart plummets. How stupid I was to think, even if only for a second, that he would actually leave her for me. Of course, he wouldn't. I'm just his hostage. Everything in me screams as I watch him try to pull her in for a reassuring kiss. I have to stop myself from going over and socking him in the face.

Emmett is sick. Just a couple of hours ago he was

fucking me in his bathroom. And now here he is telling Vivian he loves her right in front of me.

"Get it together, Vivian," Bernadette chimes in, looking around in embarrassment. "What the hell are you thinking?"

Vivian huffs over to her. "What am I thinking!?" she scoffs. "What is your stupid fucking brother thinking!? He hasn't answered my calls or texts. I've had no idea what was going on. My parents won't tell me anything. I can only assume this little bitch has been whoring herself out to Emmett."

I press my hand to my cheek, still sore from Thomas and now even worse off thanks to Vivian. I ache with disappointment, having thought Emmett might have told her something. Broken it off. But no. She just jumped to conclusions in a frenzy of feeling left out of the loop. And he's doing nothing to let on that her suspicions are true.

"Emmett doesn't want anything to do with her," Bernadette defends half-heartedly. "He's just looking after her for Daddy. You're making a fool of yourself."

Vivian turns back toward me, her arms crossed in shame now that her friend isn't backing her up. It's strange to see her slip from her pedestal. Humbled into being worried about her own position in things. They're all acting on edge, and it's making me nervous.

I'm used to seeing them calm and in control. Always one step ahead of the game.

I should be comforted that my dad's threats have them so afraid, but it only makes my position less certain. They could get tired of waiting at any moment and follow through on their own threats.

"Bernadette's right," I offer dejectedly. "Emmett doesn't want anything to do with me. And I sure as shit don't want anything to do with him."

I don't know why I say it. Maybe as some last desperate attempt to hurt Emmett back. It looks like it might have worked as his eyes glint over to me in subtle surprise.

"I don't need you to placate me," she barks back. "Soon this will all be over, and you'll go back to whatever little white trash hole you crawled out of." Her voice wavers with doubt. "Emmett, take a walk with me."

"You know I can't," he walks over to her, keeping his voice down while cutting his eyes over to me. "I can't let her out of my sight. I'll call you later, okay?"

She looks to him with an almost comedic pout, but her phone rings, pulling her attention away. "Hello?" she picks up, pressing a finger to her ear. "Daddy?" I watch her face wrinkle as she steps away. She's quickly distracted with her call, leaving Emmett and I in a stand-off.

I lift my chin and straighten my shoulders in resolve. I don't know what I expected him to do with Vivian, but at least now his intentions are clear. I was just a convenient fuck while he has me as his prisoner. And I'd say as much to him if Bernadette wasn't standing right there. If I make it out of this, I don't need Vivian's jealous wrath to worry about afterward.

Suddenly a black car whips around in the parking lot, screeching to a halt right in front of us. The back window rolls down as Thomas hangs his head out in a seething rage.

"Get in the car! Now!" His voice bellows with sharp command, and we're all too afraid to hesitate to obey him. I'm not supposed to be outside of the manor, and Emmett looks terrified of the consequences. We quickly file inside.

I start to follow into the back seat behind Emmett, hoping he'll protect me in whatever way he can. But Thomas suddenly appears behind me, clenching his hand around my wrist and yanking me to the front seat. Emmett and Bernadette comply, but I can feel Emmett's rage that he can't be near me.

Regardless of whatever he told Vivian, or whatever he feels for me, he still has a sense of ownership over me. He thinks I belong to him.

"Daddy, what's going on?" Bernadette asks from the backseat.

"The Whitworths tipped me off," he growls, his eyes darting over to me in disdain. "It appears the Hendersons are working with your father now.

I tense up in fear that they somehow know about my meeting with the Hendersons. I don't want to know what the repercussions for that will be.

"The feds are closing in," he continues. "My guy on the inside says I have less than twenty-four hours to leave the country."

Vivian's phone call makes sense now. Her parents must have been catching her up to speed with this new development. I can't help but smile slightly at my father's jump on the deadline. "Well then maybe that's what you should be doing," I offer coyly. "Instead of wasting your time with us."

He slams on the brakes so suddenly my forehead shoots straight toward the dash, but I'm saved with a searing pain to my scalp as he violently yanks back my hair. His lips snarl as he looks over to me.

"Watch your mouth," he sneers. "We told your father our terms. If I have to leave this country, you're coming with me and you'll never be back."

After glaring into me for a few moments, his nostrils flaring with hot and angry breaths, he finally lets me go and returns to driving the car. We screech around every turn as he flies down the streets back to the manor. I bring my knees to my chest, making my body small as I press my forehead to the window.

He doesn't take it any easier on me once we're back to the manor. Before I can pull the handle to get out of the car, he is yanking the door out of my hand and reaching in to pull me out by my hair. I clasp my hands to his grip, trying to lessen the pull to my scalp, but he's moving too fast for me to keep up. My eyes water with pain as he marches me back into the parlor and flings me back down into the chair.

He takes long and smooth cavalier strides over to this desk, his sudden calmness frightening me. With a tug of a drawer, his hand grips something and pulls it up into the light. My heart plummets at the sight of his pistol. He grins as he holds it up and cocks it before marching back over to me with purpose.

With another yank of my hair, he puts the gun to my head. "We warned you," he growls into my ear. "We told you if he didn't stop, we'd kill you."

"I told you I don't know him," I plead. "I didn't think he'd listen to me! He doesn't care about me! This is a waste of your time!"

"He'll listen," Thomas barks. "At least you better hope he does. Now…what do you say we try again? Maybe this time with more feeling now that you understand we're not fucking around?"

"It's no use!" I argue with clenched fists, my voice trembling.

I look to Emmett hopelessly. He cowers, refusing to look up from his feet. His jaw is tight and clamped.

My teeth clench and grind as I grab at the finger marks on my arms. "Emmett, please! Do something!" I cry, but he just turns away and does nothing. I'm getting reacclimated to his indifference now. It was silly for me to think he would ever be some kind of savior. He's just his dad's puppet.

Thomas's angry eyes turn to Emmett. He looks completely disgusted with him. "What's this, son?" he calls out in a chilling tone. "Why is it that she's turning to you for help?"

"I have no fucking idea," Emmett lies in a low grumbling tone, shifting uncomfortably.

"You sure about that?" he continues, looking at his son with such hatred. "You haven't been sampling the goods have you, my boy?"

"No, Dad!" Emmett defends with a nervous shriek. "I swear! I haven't touched her! I just did what you said!"

"Well then, maybe you'd like to come over here and prove it?" Thomas calls his bluff.

Emmett's fists clench, his lips snarling as he glares at me. Ready to pounce and do whatever his father says. He doesn't even look like himself anymore. He's running on fear. Whatever his father would do to him is enough to put him back in his place.

My breaths are so quick and shallow, I'm certain I'm hyperventilating as his grip in my hair tightens. I shudder to think what Thomas might make Emmett do to prove his loyalty. It shouldn't matter right now, but I realize this is how he maintains control. Calling anyone out the moment they question him or go against his wishes.

I squeeze my eyes shut as the cold metal barrel pushes into my temple, Emmett's stand-off with his father quickly being filed away for later. Thomas clicks the pistol with what I can only assume is the removal of the safety.

"Wait" I cry, desperate to do anything to get out from under the barrel of his gun. "I'll do the video! Please! I'll do it!"

He throws me back to the chair, nodding for his men to come and hold me down as the video camera is brought out again. I'm overwhelmed with sudden dread as I calculate the likelihood that I will die in this mansion. I try to think of anything else to calm myself, but it's no use.

"He has two hours to respond," Thomas barks. "He puts a stop to this or you're dead."

I rub against the bulging veins in my neck as I try to steady my voice. He leans against the edge of his desk, adjusting his cufflinks calmly. He's too confident. Whimpers escape my lips in between each breath.

My trembling fingers dig into the seat of the chair as I straighten my spine and brace myself, my leg bouncing uncontrollably with adrenaline and panic. I note my flushed, sweating skin on the screen as I gasp to control my breathing.

One of his men pushes the red button and flails his hand at me to start talking. I jump from my seat, desperate to wipe the tears from my face as I step backward, wanting to feel a wall behind me for security, but they quickly barrel toward me and fling me back to the chair as I cry hysterically.

I want to call for help, but I know that no one here will save me. My eyes dart around the room in desperation for anything that could inspire an idea for how to get out of this.

I gulp down acceptance. I have no other choice but try to plead for my father to save me once again. Feeling even more hopeless now than I did the first time.

"Dad, please," my pitch spikes and cracks as I sob. "We don't know each other, but I'm your daughter. And they *will* kill me. Just do what they ask."

"Is that all you got!?" Thomas bellows from behind the camera. "This is your life on the line, Ophelia! Better make this one better than the last!"

"Please!" I scream out again at the top of my lungs. "Please, dad, I'm begging you! Stop all of this and let the Jamesons be! He's not going to go down without taking me with him."

I scream and cry every plea I can think of until they're finally satisfied, taking the camera away again. As the recording stops, my muscles twitch and there's a cold silence. All there is to do now is wait.

My heart races in palpitations as adrenaline shoots through my body, and I think I might choke on my breaths…short and out of control. I can't get enough oxygen and my limbs are tingling. My fingers and toes going numb. I think I might pass out as spots dance across my line of sight.

Thomas wipes down his pistol but doesn't return it to the drawer. He keeps it close to his side. His eyes are glued to Emmett, and I can see him contemplating bringing up the issue of our involvement again. Emmett has braced himself against the wall, blowing sharp breaths from his cheeks.

"We'll come back to you later, son," he announces grimly. "I can't have you making friends with the enemy. You know that."

"Dad, I promise…," Emmett tries to defend weakly, his voice trembling. "I didn't…"

With one swift raise of Thomas' hand, Emmett stops cold. Not bothering to say another word. No wonder he is so afraid to step in and help me. Why he never even tries to defend me. He wasn't kidding. His father would kill him or make him do something terrible to me to prove himself.

Thomas has him completely under his thumb, and he's too afraid to question him or go against him in anyway. For a second, I almost feel guilty for tempting Emmett. For putting him directly in the line of his father's wrath. But remembering all of his inappropriate touches from before, I wonder if it even would have mattered how willing I was.

Thankfully, Thomas seems to let it rest again. Huddling with his cronies as they discuss what happens next, leaving me to try and control my crying. I hate that I let my last ounce of control slip. They saw me break down on camera. The composure I clung to the last time completely vanished this time, solidifying that when it comes down to it, they really can make me do whatever they want me to.

If time could just slow down somehow, or if I could just go back to a different time when I felt safe. But now, life feels like a broken hourglass in my hands, with the sand slipping through my fingers and blowing off in the wind. Time is running out. All I can do is hope my pleas appeal to something in my father.

22

CHAPTER TWENTY-TWO

The room stills as my cries slowly quiet, trailing off into nothing. I notice Bernadette perched in the corner of the room, looking bored. She pops her gum as her pastel pink nails flip across the screen of her phone. As fucked up as Emmett may be, at least he is feeling something in the middle of all of this. She looks completely apathetic and indifferent.

Thomas turns to his cronies and whispers instructions in hushed tones. They look to me with evil grins, nodding as he tells them what to do. I know he's preparing them for the time to kill me. A time which I know is quickly approaching. I can feel the desperation in the air.

"Let's hope this last performance inspires more than your last one," Thomas announces to me coldly.

"Makes no difference to me. I'm getting out of this one way or the other. It's just a matter of how hard it will be on everyone else."

He probably does have back-up plans galore. Anything to save his own ass, but I see the subtle panic in Thomas's eyes. His life is just as much on the line as mine. If my father succeeds, he'll be in prison. And for underage sex trafficking at that. An offense that I imagine all the other cons don't take kindly to, with their own troubled daughters waiting for them on the outside.

I want to believe this video could save me, but given my father's lack of response so far, I'm not hopeful. The most frustrating part about their entire plan is that it hinges on my father giving a shit about me enough to stop in order to save my life. He had to have known the risk he was taking by continuing, even after Vivian and the other Elites made sure he knew I had been uprooted to WJ Prep. If he hasn't stopped before now, I have no reason to believe he'll have a change of heart in time.

The room is tense, filled with impatience. I worry Thomas will grow restless and just shoot me before fleeing. I look to Emmett once more, but he's still and silent. Doing nothing to intervene.

With a father like Thomas, I know his life has probably been fucked up in more ways than I could ever understand. But I have even less sympathy now that I have learned my father isn't so different. Maybe he did me a favor by not being around.

I remind myself I'm not so above it all. Not now that I've given myself over to Emmett willingly. Even with my life hanging on the line, resting in my father's hands, the haunting memory of his touch still plagues me. The torture and the pleasure all blurs together. The times he inflicted violence on me didn't seem so different from when he was moving inside of me. Our movements and noises were almost the same.

I meant everything I had said when I was trying to convince him to release me. There was an undeniable connection between us, but it obviously wasn't strong enough to inspire him to save me. I watch him shift uncomfortably, his hands in his pockets, looking almost as dejected as his sister on the other side of the room.

What a strange world these people live in where torture and hostages and death threats are so normal. No wonder Lily tried to warn me and was so scared shitless of these people. Seeing how cold and cavalier Thomas can be with a young girl's life on the line, I'm not surprised his kids and friends' kids are so sadistic.

My disgusted gaze drifts from Emmett, who is decidedly avoiding me. And I realize all at once that no one is within a few feet of me. They're each distracted and dispersed into their own corners of the room. It's now or never. If he's not going to do anything to help me, and my dad's intervening isn't guaranteed by a long shot, I might as well try to make a run for it.

My eyes are bright and feverish as they dart around the room, noting everyone's position one last time. No one is paying attention to me, probably assuming I'm surrounded enough not to try anything. My fingers twitch against the edge of my chair, and my heart drops knowing if I don't do something right now, I won't have another chance.

I leap out of the chair and bolt toward the door, my heart plummeting to my stomach. I instantly hear Thomas shout behind me followed by feet pounding in my direction, but I don't stop. My throat chokes as I race for the front door faster than I have ever ran in my life.

I feel a surge of hope as my hand grips the handle, flinging it open so fast I almost hit myself in the head as I waver with the surge of adrenaline and panic. I come to a dead halt at the front doormat. A figure is blocking my way, and I look up expecting to see an unfamiliar guard or house staff member ready to snatch me up and return me to my captor. I scream, thinking I've been caught. I know the reprimand for an attempted escape will be brutal.

But instead I see a familiar face. One that I know but am unable to fully comprehend. I am almost too panicked to fully take in the features, but my brain slowly pieces it together.

Standing before me is the man responsible for all of this. My father. Theodore Nickelson.

There's a quiet rage burning behind his eyes. He's alone with only a gun in hand for protection.

"Ophelia," he announces in an unreadable tone.

I never expected to meet my father. I had no intentions of ever trying to find him. But if I ever did have some kind of fantasy about us meeting for the first time, this was definitely not one of the scenarios I pictured. Not by a long shot.

"Theodore..." I blurt. "Or I guess...Dad..." I am overcome with anger, wanting to lash out at him for never being around. For being such a shit loser that he started all of this mess and nearly got me killed over his pathetic gambling habit and need for vengeance.

I never noticed in pictures, but now that he's standing here in front of me, I can see the resemblance between him and I. Though I certainly favor my mother, our eyes are the same shape. And the curve of his lips is the same as what I've studied in my own reflection every day. It stirs a strange tenderness in me, but it's squashed by the threat lurking behind me. And the fact that he is the reason I am here in the first place. Any ounce of curiosity or kindness I could feel for him quickly fades back to anger and resentment.

"I'm surprised to see you here," I gulp. But I quickly remember my life is still in danger. There's no time for any of that now.

His eyes dart to something over my shoulder as the army of marching feet rapidly approach. His hand brushes my shoulder, pushing me aside.

"Kill him!" Thomas's voice shouts from behind me suddenly.

I am barely shoved aside just enough to gauge how far away Thomas is from me when a deafening crack shoots through my ear drums, following by an incessant ringing. I can hear nothing else as I look to my father's hand, raised and on the trigger, smoke trailing from the barrel of his gun.

My eyes dart over in Thomas's direction, but everything is moving in slow motion. I see him falling to the ground. Blood instantly pools around his head. I take a couple of steps back from my father, my eyes bulging as I look back and forth between my dad's gun and Thomas's body. I am deaf and speechless, my eyes blinking rapidly as I try to process the scene before me.

Thomas is dead. My dad shot him. My brows raise as my mouth falls open, my palm shooting up to cover it. I step back again, searching for something behind me to steady against, but there's nothing there. My gaze wanders around as my brain struggles to settle on my next move.

I feel suddenly heavy as my muscles get weak, my head feeling dizzy with a tight feeling in my chest. I replay it in my mind over and over, what bit of it I actually saw. My father's hand raising, the crack of the gun, Thomas falling to the ground.

This is definitely not the first in-person impression I wanted of my father. But at least if he was going to kill a man right in front of me within seconds of us meeting, it was a terrible man who was going to kill me first if he had the chance.

I look to Emmett who is standing in the parlor doorway, keeping a safe distance from his father. But his wide eyes are glued to the lifeless body laying there. The rest of his cronies and the staff stand there frozen, just as shocked as everyone else.

I study Emmett further, waiting for him to fall apart the way Bernadette is in the corner of my eye. I think I hear her scream, but my ears are still ringing so it's hard to tell.

Emmett is strangely calm. Shocked, but not upset. I assume it has to be the shock that is keeping him so collected, but then I catch a subtle nod between him and my father. Did Emmett know this was going to happen?

23

CHAPTER TWENTY-THREE

We all stand there completely clueless as to what we should do next. Thomas is dead. I'm dumbfounded and have no clue what the fuck is going on. Emmett doesn't look the least bit bothered that his own father was just shot right before his eyes, but Bernadette's screams and cries grow more vivid as the ringing in my ears fades.

"Come with us," my father states suddenly, causing me to jump as he takes me by the arm and leads me to an adjacent room. Emmett follows behind.

"What's going on?" I ask, plopping into the nearest seat, taken aback by how comfortable the two of them seem.

They hesitate and look to each other for a moment, not saying a word.

"Someone better start explaining things real quick!" I snap. "Do you two know each other!?" My features twist with an impending sense of betrayal.

"Your father approached me three weeks ago," Emmett starts. "His terms were simple enough. I grant him access to the manor grounds when he asked, and I wouldn't lose Jameson Automobile Company. He'd no longer hurt you, and my mom and sister would be safe."

I'm frozen under his explanation for a moment, my face contorted in shock. I quickly shake it away. "Wait, so you've been working with my father!? You son of a bitch!"

"Ophelia, please," he begs. "I was so desperate to get out from my father's thumb, I was happy to do whatever he asked. You don't know Thomas like I do. Even with what you saw…you have no idea what kind of monster he was."

"So you think mine is any better!?" I fire back, ignoring my father standing in the corner.

"I was trying to help you," he defends desperately, kneeling at the foot of my chair. "That night you met with Malcolm and Liam, your father planned to kidnap you. We barely got you in time before his guys showed up to take you away. I convinced him you'd be safer with me."

"Liam's warning," I mutter under my breath. Now

it all makes sense. The ominous threat dripping from Liam's words. That his explanation of things, by order of my father, would somehow make things easier on me when I was taken captive by him. "What would you have done with me?" I ask him timidly, afraid of the answer. "If Emmett hadn't intervened…what were you going to do when you had me as your prisoner?

"The Elites thought they had too much bargaining power with you around," he defends weakly. "I just needed to remove you from the game. So they no longer had you to hold over my head."

"Take me out of the game how?" I ask, my voice trembling. "As in keep me somewhere safe until this was all over? Until *you* decided it was over? Or take me out as in…kill me?"

My mind freezes, unsure if I was better off with Emmett, right in the hands of danger and so close to his father. Or if I would have been more screwed in my own father's possession.

"None of it matters now," Theo says dismissively. "It all worked out. Thomas is dead. I'll make sure his death is labeled as a suicide," The flippance of his voice chills me. "The investigation into the extortion rings, child prostitution circles and illegal arms dealings will continue on the Whitworth and Blackwater families. But now the Jameson family is free. As promised."

"I can't believe anything you're saying." My fingers

rub into my temples as Emmett stays at my feet, looking to me desperately for approval or forgiveness. We exchange a knowing look. My father isn't denying that he would have killed me if it came down to it. Maybe I was better off with Emmett. Especially if he knew the entire time we had my father to fall back on, hoping he would come in and take care of Thomas.

"You both seem like lying snakes to me," I snap. "I can't trust either of you. Your solution to learning my own father wanted to kidnap me…was to just do it yourself instead?" I muse in disbelief to Emmett. "You've got to be kidding me," is all I can manage to say, as my hands rub absently against my arms. "You're like a bunch of children fighting over candy. But you don't even care that real human lives are at stake." I step to the other side of the room, needing to be as far away from them as possible.

"We would have never let you get hurt," my father protests dryly. His calmness makes me sick. As if this whole thing was just some minor blip.

"I did get hurt!" I scream, jumping to my feet. "I have done nothing but get hurt from the day I got here! And you're both to blame!"

"I did what I had to, Ophelia," my father responds coldly.

"We both did," Emmett adds.

My mouth slacks as my eyes widen. I have to look

away from them. I can't stand the sight of either of them. I rub my eyes, trying not to see them, and am at a loss for words.

"You didn't have to do any of this!" I scream back to my father. "You're the one who fucked up when you gambled away all of that money! You could have just accepted your fate and left things alone. You had plenty of money. You didn't have to come back here and…," I turn away and cover my mouth. My face blanches, turning white, as I shake my head.

"But the lives that matter the most made it out unscathed," Emmett offers with a startling indifference to the death of his own father, leaving me to wonder how I'd feel if my own monster of a dad had just been shot right in front of me.

I pivot on my heel, my brow raised as I tilt my head. "I am hardly unscathed," I scream. "You've both caused irreparable damage. I'm not just some toy or game piece for you to toss around. I'm a human being! Your daughter!" I turn to my father with tears in my eyes, and then back to Emmett. "And I'm your…" I stop myself, unsure of how to finish the sentence, but his eyes look to me hopefully. My eyes blink rapidly and unfocus as I my hands carve back through my hair before my arms drop limply to my sides. "Someone that you should care about, but then again…I guess that makes me sound stupid. You've done nothing from day one to indicate you care about me at all."

"That's why you're here, Ophelia," he argues back. "Because I do care about you."

My chest tingles as my stomach hardens. I feel lightheaded. I try not to excuse any of Emmett's behavior, but knowing he was intercepting my father the night he kidnapped me almost makes his actions more tolerable. I shudder to think what my father had planned if he had been the one to kidnap me instead.

"What the hell is wrong with you, Emmett!?" I ask, shaking my head. "I may not care for my father…but I don't know if I ever could have willingly assisted in his murder."

"You don't get it, Ophelia," Emmett fumes. "Thomas Jameson was enough of a monster to justify me being an accomplice in his murder. We're all better off. You'll just have to trust me on that one."

"So, what now?" I blurt without thinking, frightening myself with my own question as it hangs in the air. No one answers, but my mind skips across the possibilities.

I can't imagine ever having any kind of relationship with Emmett. If that's even something he would want. Everything up until now was a product of force. And now that I know he's been working with my father for weeks; I can never trust him again.

Now that I am not being stalked by a pedophilic murderer and he's not perched on a doorstep with a gun in hand, I am finally able to study his features more carefully. My father is a handsome man. His dark brown hair is wavy, similar to my mother's and my own. But with touches of blonde, giving him a more Caucasian shade. He's tall and slender, and his words are sharp. Intimidating. But I could see him turning that over in a second, becoming a complete charmer.

My mother always said I had a mischievous smile, and I wondered why when she said it, she sounded sad. Angry at times. I can see now it's because that smile came from my father. He has the same devilish spark to him. I can picture them as teenagers, both young and attractive. Falling in love with each other. But then I remind myself they were in Jameson surrounded by the Elites, and I can only hope my mother's experience wasn't anything like mine.

There is nothing to be salvaged between my father and I. Knowing what I know now, I would have been fine never meeting him. And now that I see firsthand what having him around brings, I am eager to put him back out of my life. But while I'm here, I think I might as well try and get some answers.

"What happened with you and my mother?" I ask him suddenly in desperation. "Tell me everything. I deserve to know after everything you've put me through."

He takes a seat with an exasperated sigh, running his hand across the top of his hair. I study his hesitance, but finally his lips part as he braces himself. "We went out west after the Elites took everything from us," he explains. "Lala started a bakery and you were born, while I worked trying to rebuild my fortune. But then I found out your mother was cheating on me. I did things I'm not proud of. I flew into a rage. I beat her. That's when she took you and left."

"My mother would never do something like that," I defend.

"She didn't cheat on you," Emmett blurts suddenly, shocking both of us. "That was my father and his friends. They set her up. They weren't going to stop coming after you because of all the money you squandered." His head hangs sheepishly in fear of my father's reaction. The words spilled out faster than he meant, sounding too accusatory.

I see the dots connecting in my father's eyes, but any regret is quickly shrugged away. "She went back to her maiden name, Lopez, after that," my father finishes, looking as if he's fighting away the new information.

"So it turns out you laid your hands on my mother for no reason, forcing her to leave," I gaff at the whole idea. “The Elites strike again. Stopping at nothing to destroy anyone who crosses them, even if children’s lives are destroyed in the process. Though I can’t really say we were so bad off without you around. Brendan is ten times more honorable than I think you could ever be.”

“Yes…Brendan. Your stepfather,” he concedes with a knowing nod. “I looked into him when he and your mother got engaged. He is a good man. That’s why I never intervened.”

“You’ve got some nerve,” I shriek. “So you’ve been keeping tabs on us this whole time!? And what do you mean…that’s why you didn’t intervene!? What makes you think you’d ever have any right to try and influence her life after everything? And my life too.”

“She belonged to me before anybody else!” he roars back in a sudden show of emotion. More than he’s shown this entire time, even after having just killed a man. “I promised to take care of her.”

Funny, I think. Girls really do go for men just like their fathers. Apparently even if they don’t know their fathers. I could imagine Emmett saying the exact same bit about me belonging to him. He has several times. Always pointing out that I am his.

“So, you were taking care of her when you beat her?” I square up to him, too pissed to back down, even though he towers above me in height.

"I don't expect you to understand any of it," he resigns, turning to calm himself. "I loved your mother. I was furious when I thought she had betrayed me and been with another man. And it was right after everything that happened with the Jamesons and Whitworths. I was humiliated. Desperate."

"I wonder if your family and their friends were pleased with themselves, Emmett," I channel my anger back to him. "They had already ran my father out of town. He was completely broke. You'd think they could have just let him be. But no…you just had to come and put one last nail in his coffin."

I am angry about it, but I'm glad in a way that things happened as they did. I can't imagine what my life would have been like if my father had stuck around. I want to say as much, but I can see he is already reeling from Emmett's confession about their responsibility in breaking up my parents' marriage.

"I'm going to give you two a moment alone," Emmett responds, his eyes hopeful and desperate.

"I don't have anything else to say to you," I bark as he exits the room.

"I'm going to do everything in my power to make sure you don't leave without seeing me again," he states calmly before turning to shut the door.

It almost makes me want to crawl out of the window just to prove him wrong, but I'm left alone with my father who is coldly staring off into the corner.

"So…do you have anything else to say for yourself?" I sneer, crossing my arms expectantly.

"I can leave you alone now, if that's what you want," he offers sympathetically. I can't tell if the softness of his voice is out of respect, or just a manipulation tactic. "I can walk away from all of this now that Thomas Jameson and the rest of them will be going away."

"And what about Emmett?" I ask, my voice wavering. "What makes you trust him so much more than the rest? How do you know he won't come after you for revenge?"

"I could tell Emmett was scared shitless of his father from the moment I first met him," he explains. "His father would have dangled the company over his head for the rest of his life, threatening to snatch everything away any time he didn't comply with his whims. Thomas would have made his son do terrible things. Turned him into a monster just like his dad. Emmett could see it coming and wanted no part of it. Now he'll walk away with his father's fortune. Free to call the shots without the Elites pushing him around."

I roll his explanation around in my mind, wanting it to be true. But I don't know who I can trust. "How do you know he's not already just as fucked up as

Thomas Jameson?" I propose. "He sure has put me through hell. Something I'd think my own father would take issue with."

"Things are different around here," he answers flippantly. "You're dealing with generations of ruthless entitlement. Emmett is salvageable though. I can tell you that much." He stands and begins to button his coat.

I study his movements in confusion. "You're leaving!?" I belt out unexpectedly. Moments ago, I was praying for him to just go. Now I'm offended that he would just walk off. "You're just going to leave things like this? What about me? What do I do?"

"You and Emmett will tell the police you ditched school and came back to the house to fool around and found Thomas Jameson dead. I'll take care of the rest. After that, you're free to go."

Free. I don't even know what that word means to me anymore. Now that it's so close, it's almost frightening.

"Talk to the police and go home, Ophelia," he orders me, turning for the door. "I won't be bothering you again."

"It doesn't make any sense," I mutter, my eyes darting to connect the dots. "You said you loved my mother. But what about me? Does finally meeting me mean nothing to you?"

I see him shake his head with his back turned, but he won't look at me. "I know I've done too much damage," he answers with quiet resolve. "You and your mom are better off with Brendan. Without me. I've been working your whole life toward what transpired today. And now that it's over…it's time for me to go."

"What will you do?" I ask, fighting back bewildered tears. I don't want to care, but some primal part of me still does.

"You don't need to concern yourself with that," he reaches for the door handle, pausing one last time to glance over his shoulder, his eyes still not meeting mine. "I'm going to make sure you're taken care of, Ophelia. You'll go back to WJ Prep on scholarship, and if you need anything after that for college…I'll see that it gets taken care of."

"What do I tell Mom?" I suggest, wondering if she has any idea he's been lingering around Jameson this whole time. But he doesn't answer. Just like that, he's gone again.

I liked it better before when I never thought twice about him. Now I'll always be afraid of when he might pop up again, and what kind of havoc it might wreak on my life.

My mind jolts back to action mode. I am ready to go home, but first I have to talk to the police. Which means talking to Emmett. I pull myself up from my chair and head for the door, not surprised to see him waiting for me just outside.

I'm just about to fly right past him when he yanks me back, pushing me against the wall. His icy gray eyes burning into me intensely.

I try to look anywhere else. I'm too raw to look him in the eyes right now. But he desperately bobs his head to force himself in my way. I still can't deny how handsome he is, even after everything. Even though he is a sweaty, disheveled mess just like me.

"Kiss me," he pleads harshly, pressing his face to mine. His breath is hot and frantic. "Please, Ophelia. Before we go back out there. I need to feel close to you again."

"You're fucking crazy!" I cry and squirm in his arms. "I'd rather die."

He leans into me anyway, the strain in his pants giving away how much he wants me. I see it burning him from the inside out, and I feel the same way. Whatever this thing is between us will eat us both alive if I don't put a stop to it. Especially now with no outside forces standing in our way.

Is he angry because he can't have me? Because I'm not giving in to him as easily as he is probably used to? The moment he had me before, he turned cold again. Without my resistance, he's uninterested. I still and search his face, exasperated with how much I still don't understand about him.

"I'm begging you," he murmurs softly. "Please, just one more taste of you. Before we have to face everything out there."

His words draw me in. I can't deny how nice it would be to give in to him one last time before we walk out into whatever happens next. When I intend to fully put him out of my life altogether. Nothing about my feelings for him have changed. Still just as wanton and helpless as day one. I need him and am repulsed by him all at once. He scares me, but I want to give myself over to him completely.

My heart stings with an afterthought. I want to torture him the way he's tortured me. And that desire rises quickly above everything else. "You'll never taste me again," I growl sternly, looking straight at him in pure coldness. His brows raise to my quivering voice. "You'll never have any part of me again."

He raises a hand, and I don't know if he'll hit me or force me into his kiss anyway. But instead his forehead drops to the wall above my shoulder. Like he's completely broken.

"Never say never, Ophelia," he whispers into my neck before pulling away. "There's too much between us for you just to walk away from."

"Is there?" I question defiantly, steadying my voice. "There's nothing between us. You've tormented me, Emmett. Your family and friends did too, and you're no better than them. I see that now. I don't care what anyone else says. I've looked into your eyes and have seen nothing. The same cold, empty, blank stare of your father."

"That's not true," he snivels, shaking his head to block out my words. "You know it's not true. Everything I've done up until now…none of that was the real me. Just the small moments we shared when we both gave in…when everything else fell away. That's all you really know of me. And I can show you so much more."

His words instantly slice through my resolve, pulling me in as his lips brush my cheek. I want so badly to make him hurt, and I can't seem to convince myself that what he's feeling now is hurt enough. It can't be if he's still insisting he's entitled to me somehow. A truly sorry man would just walk away and let me be, just like my father did.

His lips melt to mine as I surrender one last time. Everything inside of me screaming to push him away, but I'm paralyzed. Finally I hear sirens wailing outside, and I'm surprised it's taken this long. "We have to go soon, Emmett," I remind him, thankful for the escape as our lips part. "Do you know what we're supposed to say?"

"I want to talk to you after," he insists again.

"Emmett, no!" I beg against his persistence. "Please…why can't you just let me go…"

"I don't know," he rasps. "But I can't. Not like this."

I see the red and blue flashing lights reflecting through the front windows and know we're out of time. My fingers pull to the wet circles under my eyes, and I try to smooth back my hair. It's no use. I'm a mess. We both are.

"I'll explain everything," he maintains, pulling back to straighten his shirt and put on a composed face. "You'll see. You have to listen to me."

Without another word, he walks confidently out into the foyer. I want to remind him he'd do well not to act so put together this time. He did just see his father die. A fact that will make the police suspicious if he's not distraught enough, even if it's fake. But I quickly remember he doesn't have to worry about things like that. Not really. Whatever his own personal sway and power doesn't take care of, my father's influence will.

I am left alone in shock once again. Still amazed that I'm so intertwined with this world of powerful and ruthless men. It's too much to take in. All I can do for now is prepare myself to give a statement, putting myself that much closer to freedom at last. It will all be over soon.

24

CHAPTER TWENTY-FOUR

I follow behind Emmett to face the sirens wailing outside of the manor. Bernadette is still hunkered over his body, crying in mourning. It's a relief to see her feel something, even if Emmett would argue it's misplaced. The room goes dark as the sun's rays disappear from the windows behind cloud cover.

The police don't waste any time explaining they'll need to take us into the station to give our statements. I don't feel too nervous about it, knowing our story will be backed up with whatever contact my father has in their department. Plus, I have Emmett on my side for this one. They assure us it won't take long.

The police escort us from the manor as the sun starts to go down. On our way to the station, a thick fog falls over everything and I can hear thunder rumbling in the distance.

The wind howls around us as we approach the front of the building. Buzzing doors and jingling keys echo out through the sparse waiting room of the station as we are both led through long winding back halls of officers speaking to each other in hushed tones, tucked away into different corners.

We are, of course, separated. I'm taken into an interview room that is gray and plain with one small table scattered with pens and notepads. I note the handcuff rings implanted in the surface, wringing my wrists that still ache from my own time in cuffs.

My stomach is uneasy as I rub my arms, nervously giving my statement to the police. I stick to the story made up about ditching school and coming back to this house to hook up. That's where we claimed to have found his body dead on the ground. Anyone can see plain as day that he was shot directly in the forehead from the direction of the front door, but my father will make good on his promise. He has contacts who will still by some miracle get this written off as a suicide.

Even though I don't give two shits about whether it's coined as suicide or murder, I must admit there is something satisfying about my own father having his sway over this town. Maybe for his sake some of that will be restored with Thomas Jameson out of the way.

But I still have every intention of staying as far away from him as possible.

"So, you and Emmett Jameson returned to his residence around four o'clock in the afternoon. Is that right?" The officer asks me again after he's collected my statement and asked me to repeat it.

"That's right," I say as confidently as possible.

The officer scribbles a few more notes, scratching his head, and then whispers a few things to his partner. "Thank you, Miss Lopez," he states, dropping his pen to the pad of paper. "We won't be too much longer here."

I try to hide a sigh of relief that they're buying everything. Either that or they've already been bribed and aren't even going to bother with a real interrogation. I've been warned countless times that the cops around here can't be trusted.

"You haven't been attending Weis-Jameson Preparatory Academy long, have you, Miss Lopez?" he stands to pace the room, changing his tone.

"Just started this semester," I reply glumly, feeling weighed down by everything that's happened in such a short amount of time. "I'm attending on a track scholarship."

He nods, biting at his lip. "And you live with your mom and dad?"

"My mom and step-dad, Brendan. Why?" I am

starting to grow nervous with how personal the questions are becoming. What does any of that have to do with Thomas Jameson's supposed suicide?

"What about your biological father..." he proposes timidly. "Do you know him?"

"No." I blurt too curtly, causing his brow to furrow suspiciously.

The room is suddenly cold. My heart starts to race. No one told me I should be prepared for questions about Theo. I don't know whether to deny everything, or if they already know he's been poking around in the Elite's business recently. What if I incriminate myself by lying about something they already know?

"You don't know him at all?" he asks again, his tone peaked.

"No, not at all," I confirm nervously. As long as he keeps phrasing it that way, I'm fine. Because I can honestly say I don't know my father. But if he gets any more specific...I'm going to freeze up.

"You seem nervous," he observes, towering above me with his hands rested on the table. "Does it make you uncomfortable to talk about your father?"

"I just don't know him. Like I said." I bite my lip and stare to my hands, falling into a snowball effect. The more I know I look and sound nervous, the more nervous I get.

He concedes with huff of breath, taking a seat

once again. "Miss Lopez, I don't want to be the one to have to tell you some of these things," he continues gently, "or maybe you already know some of them and just don't want to say... That's fine too. I understand. But...your father is a pretty dangerous man."

"How so?" I try to plea ignorantly, the image of him shooting Thomas fresh on my mind. But that's the last thing I need to be thinking about right now.

"He's been investigated by the FBI for quite a few hefty crimes," his fingers clasp and open as he speaks. "Insider trading. Money laundering. Extortion. Blackmail. The list goes on and on."

"Oh, I had no idea," I mutter truthfully. I thought my father's only crime was his relentless pursuit of the Elites, and whatever gambling trouble he had from before. I guess I should have figured there was more to it than that.

But as the two officers stare me down, the weight of all the warnings I've been given about the local police looming right above them, I wonder if I can trust anything they're saying. My father just took out the central figure of the Jameson Automobile Company...the town's livelihood. Leaving everything in the hands of Emmett...a teenage boy.

If they have any inkling at all that he's responsible for Thomas's death, they might be eager to take him down. I know my father has contacts in the police, but I'm clueless as to how far his reach extends.

"Do you know where your father is right now?" they ask bluntly.

"I have no idea," I reply, once again grateful that I am telling the truth.

"I understand," he says again, only this time he seems to know there is more that I'm not saying. "Listen, you've had a hard day, I'm sure. We don't want to keep you any longer. But could you do us a favor and let us know if your father tries to contact you?"

"Why?" I protest, not wanting to commit to that position. "You said he was investigated for those crimes. But that doesn't mean he's guilty, right? Is he wanted for arrest or anything?"

"Nothing quite like that," he answers with a cocky grin. "We just want to let you know…if he pops up again…you can come to us. It might be in your best interest to keep us informed of any communication. To protect yourself."

"So…we're done here?" I ask, already posed to exit. I feel like I'm lost in a minefield. One wrong word and the whole thing will blow up in my face. This was supposed to be a simple statement. Not an interrogation about my father, and I have no idea who to trust.

"For now," he leans back smugly, pressing a button that sparks a buzz and shoots my escape door open.

"Thanks," I huff as I bolt for the door. I start marching through the winding halls back out into the lobby. I need to be outside and free. My heart is still pounding in my chest, and I desperately need to run far away from here.

I walk down the sidewalk away from the police station, trying to add everything up in my head. The police can't be trusted. I don't know who is on my father's side and who isn't. I don't know who is playing for the old gang of Elites and who is rooting for whatever is on the horizon for Jameson Automobiles. I definitely don't know where Emmett stands in all of this.

My walk turns into a sprint the moment I'm back in a residential area. I decide to run home. I need it. I don't even care that it's starting to rain.

I haven't been running for long when I hear footsteps plodding up from behind. I glance over my shoulder to see Emmett racing behind me.

"Ophelia!" he calls out breathlessly. "Can I talk to you? Please!?"

I don't answer. He is the last person I want to talk to. But with him following behind, I don't want to go home. I don't ever want him in my house again. So instead I keep running.

He keeps stride with me, holding back by just a few feet. His stalking presence makes me feel like I am being held against my will, hitting the nerves of trauma from everything I experienced when I was being held hostage. All that his father did to me.

Every sudden movement startles me, my brain jumping back to the abuse I endured at the hands of the Elites, Emmett and his father. It just makes me run harder as the rain pours down around us.

We run like that for miles before finally stopping in a parking lot. I buckle over, resting my palms to my knees as I catch my breath.

I notice clumps of feathers scattered across the ground nearby, sticking to what remains of a dead bird. I have to laugh to myself, thinking it's a fitting representation of my life right now. Pieces of me still sticking around but maimed beyond recognition. All I can do now is try to reassemble the pieces, and I can't do that with Emmett around.

"Ophelia, please," he pleads between gasps for breath. "Can't you see now? I'm one of the good guys. I'm on your side."

"Are you fucking kidding me!?" I fire back with an angry laugh. "Is that why you beat me? Threatened me? Humiliated me? What was your excuse for all of that!? That was long before you supposedly started working with my father."

"I had to," he defends softly, his eyes glinting with regret. "I had no choice. As far as I could see, my father was going to get away with everything and be fine. I couldn't go against him or the other Elites."

"And you and Vivian?" I shoot back, still unconvinced of a single word and rapidly piling on more offenses in my memory. "What was all that about?"

"At first I didn't know any better," he defends adamantly. "I mean, it'd make sense for Vivian and me to be together. It's practically an arranged marriage with the way our families are. But then I met you..."

"You met me, and you continued seeing her... flaunting it in my face," I argue, still somewhat in disbelief that I'm even worried about his relationship status with everything else he's done.

"Vivian knew I had a thing for you," he explained, flailing his arms in the air. "If I had broken up with her she would have told everyone it was because of you. I would have been blacklisted. If my own father didn't kill me for thinking I was in cahoots with you and your father, I definitely wouldn't have been able to help your dad. We'd probably both be dead right now."

"I'll never be able to forget the ways you've treated me," I continue, unmoved. Shaking my head at the memories flashing through my mind. "Then you sided with my father to get what you wanted. For all I know, you're still working for him. It's unforgivable."

"I had to, Ophelia," he continues pleading. "If you

just give it some time…I think you'll understand that I had to. I had no choice."

Maybe he's right. Maybe small parts of his behavior will seem better once I've had some time to think. But there's too much of it staring me right in the face. The way he roughed me up with the other Elites. Sexually humiliated me. Acted like Vivian's little puppet and did nothing to stop my torture.

"Please let me try and make it up to you," he asks softly with a painful sincerity.

"What will you do now that your friends' families will fall and yours won't?" I ask bitterly, figuring he must think he's hot shit right now. The Elites have been upgraded to a one man show. The rest of them are going down and he gets to walk away with everything. "I can't help but think your motivations weren't as centered on my safety and well-being as you claim. I mean, you ended up with a pretty sweet deal out of all this."

He moves closer in slow cautious steps, his eyes trained to me. "Not if you won't talk to me," he protests. "I don't care about the money and all that other shit. The Elites can kiss my ass. I've always hated the whole fucked up game. None of it means anything if I don't get you in the end. Please, Ophelia. You're *mine*."

I want to scream. I don't belong to anyone. Especially not him, but I can't deny the way my heart warms and swells at the thought of it. What he used to always say…his little pet. I'm tempted to give in to it. Curl up right in his arms. Submit and give myself over to him the way I did in his bathroom. It felt so good to stop fighting it for once.

He can sense my hesitation and takes it as an opportunity to inch even closer, placing his hand to my cheek. My lips part beyond my control and everything in me yearns to feel his lips against mine again. I am so close to giving into him. My eyes close and I want to melt against his body, but I force myself to pull away.

"I can't, Emmett," I whimper as my voice cracks, taking a few steps back and looking off into the distance. "I don't see how I can ever trust you."

Maybe if I just try to forget any of this ever happened, I can move forward. It's too painful to face straight on.

It's not just about Emmett. I don't know how I can ever trust anyone ever again now that I know the kinds of things my father is capable of. My own father. His greed and maliciousness could be hereditary. Maybe it's in my blood. Either way, even my own father would kill me to serve his own desires.

I don't let myself feel certain of anything anymore. I've learned my lesson well enough to know I'm not in control of what can happen. I have to trust my gut now. And I can't shake the feelings of unease that plague me when I look into Emmett's eyes, no matter what other feelings I have for him.

But his moans of pleasure haunt me. The way his face wrinkled in ecstasy. I want to go back to that place with him, where I was able to let go as my body did the talking. Responding to him without hesitation. Surrendering to the sensations of how he felt inside. The touch of his hands. I half consider begging him to take me somewhere so we can have sex again. That made sense to me. But I know when it's over, it would only confuse me more and leave me worse off than I am now.

"I know you deserve better than me, Ophelia. You deserve better than your father too," he insists, speaking to my hesitation.

"I have better, Emmett," I remind him bitterly. "I have a whole life outside of this shitstorm you're wrapped up in. I have a mom and stepdad that love me. I had a promising running career ahead of me, if that hasn't been ruined by everything that's happened. I was just fine before you, and I'll be just fine after you. If you'll just leave me alone."

"But that's just the thing," he rasps. "I can't. I knew this whole thing was fucked from the moment I first saw you. I knew I'd never be able to do the things I was expected to do. I feel too much for you."

"It sure didn't stop you in the beginning," I sneer.

"Come on…you know you want this just as bad as I do," he pushes toward me again, his touch begging me to melt into him. "Give me a chance to make all of that up to you. We're both fucked up. But…maybe we can find some way to make each other better. Look, Ophelia, I'm sorry. Just please try to understand – I'm not perfect. Neither are you, okay? I'm not going to stand here and lie…"

"For once." I cut him off. "I didn't do anything wrong, Emmett. That's the difference," I growl, resenting that he could even begin to suggest I am as fucked up as he is.

"I'm not going to stand here and pretend like I have all my shit figured out or that I knew what I was doing this whole time," he carries on, rain dripping down his face. "I just…I just didn't think and got in over my head and…and I really didn't mean to ever hurt you. I was selfish, I know that. I did it all wrong. But I'm lost too, okay? That's why you and I get along…because we're both just lost and fucked up and trying to figure it out."

"I wasn't fucked up until I met you," I hiss, making him recoil finally. He looks genuinely sorry. I want more than anything to tell him it's all okay and we could keep trying to figure it all out together. But then my father resurfaces in my mind, and I just know this can never work.

"So…what now?" He looks at me eagerly.

"It just…it has to be over now. That's it. It's ruined. I can barely look at you now, knowing what you were doing this whole time…working with my father behind my back," my words trail off into the sounds of the rain, my head shaking in exasperation.

He hangs his head and I think I see a tear streaming down his cheek, surprising me. But the downpour makes it too hard to tell. "I'd take it all back if I could." His voice is cracking.

But knowing so many lies have been told by this point, I don't know whether to believe his tears or not. It is still so hard to walk away. Half of me wants to run away and never look back. The other half of me would let him take me again right here, right now.

"Emmett…" I walk over to him and touch his cheek, as we both sob uncontrollably. This is the only time in my life I have ever cried so openly with another person. "I wish you didn't do all of those terrible things, but…maybe this just wasn't meant to be."

He leans his forehead against mine and we're both paralyzed in the pain for a moment. I realize if I don't leave now, I might lose the strength. I pull away and start walking down the sidewalk.

"Ophelia…" I stop and face him, afraid of what

he's about to say. Afraid I won't stick to my resolve. "Do you think…maybe after some time has gone by… maybe you could give me another chance?"

"I think it's better if we just let it go. Just let me go," I turn to run away before he can say anything else. Before I can change my mind.

I run through the dark streets, my wet cheeks freezing in the wet wind. I don't stop until I'm home. The heat in the house burns my face when I walk in, and I find mom sitting at the kitchen table leaned over with her head in her hands.

"Mom?"

She jerks up, her eyes bloodshot. "Ophelia, sweetie…hey. I'm glad you're finally home." She notices my face and looks concerned. "Are you okay? You're soaking wet!"

"No, not really. Are you okay?" I respond breathlessly, still confused as to how she is so calm about how long I've been missing. I join her at the table. "We have to talk, Mom."

"I know we do," she nods, wringing a tissue in her hands. And yet, we sit in silence for what feels like forever.

"I'll start." She says with a heavy sigh, "Ophelia, there are some things I need to tell you about your father."

I blink, my eyes wide and blank. Out of all the times for her to bring this up…

I have no idea what lies the Elites have fed to her or how. "Wait, Mom…" I stop her. "Before you start talking about him…about me being gone…"

"Oh sweetie, don't worry about that," she waves her hand with a sniffle. "The principal called and told me Coach Granger had been keeping you late for practice and that he saw you leaving every day with that Emmett boy. I tried to call and tell you to come home, but your phone was dead. Then the police called and told me what happened at Emmett's house. Are you alright, honey? That's a terrible thing to go through. That's part of what I wanted to talk to you about."

A sarcastic grin eases across my face, out of my control, and I look down to my hands, shaking my head. I don't know if I'm more surprised that they went to such lengths to keep her from interfering or that she actually bought all of that so easily.

"You weren't mad?" I gaff, peering into her. "You didn't try to come find me?"

"I wanted to, but Brendan said we should give you some space," she explains. "You've always been so responsible and well behaved. You were bound to get a wild streak at some point. When the police called…I felt terrible for not coming to find you. Maybe if I had…"

If she had. Suddenly I'm relieved she didn't try to find me. If she had tried to, the Elites may have taken care of her just to get her out of the way.

"That wasn't your fault, Mom," I clasp my hand to hers, unsure of what else to say.

"When the police said Thomas Jameson was dead, I…well…this will sound terrible, but I thought your father had done it," she confesses through sobs. "But then they said it was a suicide, and I just felt so guilty. I felt bad for not telling you more about your dad in case he ever did try to come back into our lives. For not protecting you from the possibility of something like that."

I have to bite my tongue to keep from screaming out that she's right. My father did kill Thomas Jameson, and if she had warned me about what kind of person my father was…it might not have done any good or changed anything. But maybe I would have made different decisions along the way. I could have had somewhat of an upper hand.

"Mom, I know all about my real dad," I blurt out finally, searching her face to see how she'll respond. She looks completely shocked, her bottom lip trembling. "The kids around here…they know the story of his family and everything that he did. They told me."

"You should have come to talk to me!" she shrieks. "Ophelia, you never should have had to learn about all of that on your own!"

"I guess that's why I was gone for a bit," I murmur, knowing she'd never understand what that really means.

"I understand," she nods, blotting the tears from her eyes, squeezing my hand tight. "So then you know he had it out for the Jamesons. That's why when I heard about Thomas…I just jumped to conclusions."

I look at the regret and sadness in my mom and wish I could take it all away for her. She deserved better than my father, and so did I. The thought stings as I think back to what Emmett said earlier. Even he admits I deserve better. Part of me wants to see if he can be better for me, but I'm not going to let myself go there.

If I meant what I said about wanting him to let me go, I needed to do the same and let him go. I'm eager to find my way back to the person I was before I ever met him. Before enduring all the torture of the Elites. But I don't know if I will ever shake this feeling of unsteady ground beneath my feet. Now that I've seen firsthand just how wrong it can go and how fast, I will always be worried that around any corner…everything could go to shit again.

I'm quiet, afraid if I say too much else everything

will spew out of me. "Mom, should we be afraid?" I ask timidly. "Of Dad I mean. In case he ever came back around. I…I heard he had hurt you once. When the Elites framed you for that affair. Do you think he'd ever do anything like that again?"

"No, sweetie," she replies confidently. "I don't think he ever meant to hurt me. But…who are the Elites?"

"Oh," I stammer, pinching the bridge of my nose. "That's what they call them. The Jamesons. The Whitworths. The Blackwaters. They're called the Elites. They didn't call them that back in the day?"

"Ah. Well…I don't think so. But I don't really know. I stayed out of all the high school cliques as much as I could. Which is how your father preferred it. He said it was all too cutthroat for someone like me. As long as I was with him, no one messed with me. Other than that, I mostly stayed to myself," she explains, her eyes drifting to distant memories.

"But Trey and Vincent's mom…," I puzzle out loud. "You seemed so friendly with them at the hospital. You had said their mom and you were friends. I thought…"

"We were friendly with each other in school," she twists her lips glibly. "Like I said, no one had the nerve to be unkind to me when I was with your father."

If only it could have been like that for me. The only perk that came with Emmett being attracted to me was being tortured, kidnapped, beaten and having my life threatened. And my dad sure didn't do anything to help me. I still wasn't even entirely sure he wouldn't have killed me if it came down to it.

But I guess the kind of protection my mom was talking about was reserved for Vivian in my case. The real girlfriend. I'm suddenly overwhelmed, unable to swallow away the hardness in my throat.

"I'm tired," I whisper. "I'm going to get some rest."

"I understand, sweetie," my mom says sweetly, standing to hug me goodnight. I head for the stairs. "Ophelia," she adds as I walk away. "Don't disappear like that on me again, okay?"

"Come hunt me down if I do, Mom," I smirk, trying to pass it off as a joke. But I mean it with every fiber of my being.

My father and I aren't so different in some ways, I think as I shuffle to my bedroom. He refused to bend to the Elites' intimidation when they ran him out of town. They stripped him of his shares in their business, cast him out into society and made my mother leave him, taking me with her. He never stopped trying to jail them for all their crimes, and then he came charging back after all this time to make them pay.

I may not be able to do much of anything to make the Elites pay for what they've done to me. I guess he took care of that for me in a weird way. But I didn't let them break me. And I only fully realize that now. I may have been afraid and had moments of weakness as anyone would in my position, but I stayed strong. I never let them fully break me.

Except for Emmett. I don't feel strong when it comes to him. He got to me more than anyone, and now I have to walk around haunted with the memory of him being inside of me.

My shoes are still squishing from the rain across the carpet of my bedroom. I would collapse on my bed right now if I wasn't soaking wet. I peel the heavy wet clothes from my body, tossing them into the bathtub with a plop. My fingers trail across the bathroom counter, and I wonder if I'll ever look at one of these the same again.

I try to push it down. I'll never sleep if I start thinking about Emmett, and I'm in desperate need of rest. But his words haunt me anyway. My stomach turns to remember the way he suggested over and over that he had no choice in all of this. For all that I've been through, it never made me do horrible things to the people around me. The only horrible thing I've done is fall for him. One thing that I'm certain of is that I never have and never will be as messed up as he is.

I slide on some clean underwear and an oversized shirt, blotting my hair with a towel. I probably need a shower, but I'm too tired. Now that I'm dry, I instantly collapse into bed

It's an intense feeling to return home when you never thought you would again. Everything feels different. The sheets feel softer. My mom's cooking wafting from downstairs smells stronger and more inviting than ever before. I'm free. Something that I worried I would never feel again.

I relish in the feeling of my own bed. I am certain that once I fall asleep, I will sleep for a million years. But neighborhood dogs are barking, prompting me to shove my pillow around my ears to block it out. They sound louder than they should, giving me a headache.

The police station. Emmett. My mom. My dad. It all swirls through my head, making me nauseous. I can't shake the feeling of dread that this isn't over yet. Emmett won't give up so easily. It seems my father may not either. Everything between my mom and I will be different now. Especially as I try to recover from this nightmare.

I feel like my chest is caving in from the weight of it all, but thankfully I am so exhausted that my body takes over and goes into autopilot. At some point, I finally drift into a deep and heavy sleep.

25

CHAPTER TWENTY-FIVE

Things have almost gone back to some semblance of normal. Coach Granger is back and working me harder than ever. I'm happy to have running back as a form of distraction and therapy as I'm still reeling from everything that's happened.

Brendan and my mom bought into my story, writing off my disappearance as reckless abandonment. I just got so swept up in my feelings for Emmett that we ran off together. They're of course not happy that I would be so careless, but my mom mostly just seems relieved.

But I think she suspects my father may have reemerged and is somehow responsible for the Elites' demise. No matter what the police say. I see her frequently reminding herself to write it off as paranoia. She's just so happy he doesn't appear to have got to me, that she's welcomed me back with open arms, just asking that I never do it again.

I still desperately want to ask her more about her side of the story. Especially now that I know they tried to accuse her of adultery to ruin my parents' marriage. My mom is the most loyal person on the planet, so I have no doubt that it was a set-up. And even if it had been true, it wouldn't have excused my father's behavior. She had to be so afraid and alone. Punished for something she didn't do and then left on her own to raise me.

But I know it's too soon to start digging things up with her. She's already suspicious and on high alert, and I could use a little more time to process what I already do know.

I wish my lies were true. I wish this has all just been normal teenage misbehavior. And that my father really hadn't got to me. If she only knew just how much he did…or how close she came to losing me, I don't know what she'd do. I have to convince myself my alibi is the true story sometimes, just to make it through the day.

It's been a few days since the news started spreading about the investigation into all of the Elites' dirty dealings. Emmett and Bernadette coming out on top, completely unscathed as promised. But word is that Bernadette is so distraught from the loss of her father that she's completely hysterical and inconsolable. She obviously didn't know her father the way Emmett did.

My heart hurts for Bernadette in a way. To see her own father be murdered. I remind myself that she'll have it out for me. After all, it was my father who killed him. But maybe Emmett will protect me. I have no idea how he feels about me now that I've refused to give in and give him a chance at redemption.

I've heard nothing from my father, thankfully. I know he never really cared about me. I was just as much a pawn to him as I was to the Elites. Emmett claims I was more to him, but I haven't heard from him either ever since I asked him to leave me alone. I told him only space and time would determine if I could ever find some way to forgive him. It was a fib I threw out to get him to leave me alone, thinking I would never really be able to trust him again.

But secretly, I did wonder if I could bring myself to open up to him. I am still fiercely attracted to him, and there aren't many parts of the day when he isn't taking up at least some portion of my brain. I worry it might be some kind of Stockholm syndrome, so I am grateful for the space to sort it out.

I fire through track practice, leaving all the other girls in the dust. Though the nightmare I've been through took up a lot of time, putting me out of practice, I have a new fuel out on the track. Now running is a mission to escape everything I have been through. I tell myself if I run fast enough, maybe it will all be so far behind me that I won't see it at all anymore.

Every slam of my foot to the ground is the crushing of another memory. Each mile behind me puts me further into the future. Every pained breath in my lungs washes out more of Emmett. I am taking it one day at a time, but at this rate…everything will be behind me in no time.

The other girls can't even touch me now. No matter what hell they've seen in their lives, I doubt any of it holds a candle to what I've experienced. Emmett and I are connected in that way now. The strange isolated privileged life of wealth he's known makes him so different from everyone else around him. And now I feel different too.

As I'm finishing up, I can't help but think how happy I am that Coach Granger is back. I don't pry into his personal life to ask what pulled him away, but I suspect the Elites had something to do with it. Maybe he was the only person they couldn't sway, so they caused some kind of trouble in his life that forced him to be away.

"Good work out there today, kid," Coach Granger beams, patting me on the shoulder.

"It's good to have you back," I tell him, swinging a

towel over my shoulder as I head for the locker room. "Is everything okay? You were out for a pretty long time."

His stare grows distant and stern. "Just some trouble at home," he answers lightly, with a strange unease about him. "It's funny," he remarks in a way that doesn't sound amused at all, "I had just mentioned to some people I know how worried I was about you right before everything happened."

"Before what happened?" I ask cluelessly.

"I heard you were absent for a bit yourself while I was gone," he continues. "According to the other girls on our team. If I didn't know any better...I'd think someone wanted me out of the way for something." He lets the idea hang there, studying me carefully.

"I wondered the same thing myself," I reply gingerly.

We exchange a knowing nod before he walks away. I think we both know better than to say too much more about it right now. But that brief conversation told me everything I needed to know. He was the only person in the school who would have my back over the Elites. And that's exactly why they made sure he was gone during the final stages of their plan. They knew I would go to him in desperation.

But what I really want to know is...could he have helped? Is that why they needed to make sure I couldn't confide in him when I needed it the most? I don't want to know what they did to make sure he'd be gone. I'm just glad those days are over. And that now I know he's a safe haven for anything that may come up in the future. Hopefully none of us ever have to be so careful again.

I walk across the black, cracked pavement navigating around cars that are coming and going from the painted white spaces. I have started parking closer to the building now, despite the assigned parking. No one seems to care now that the Elites are out of the way.

Much like my home has become more comforting to me than ever before, long walks like this are more precious. I close my eyes and lean my head back, feeling the warm sun on my face. Relishing in the freedom to come and go as I please without worrying who is waiting for me around the corner.

It's well into fall now and I have to wear a hoodie when I'm not running. I curl into the warmth and comfort of it around my skin. All of these small things have become so big after wondering if I would ever live to see another day.

Suddenly, I think I catch a glimpse of Lily in the distance, but she disappears around the corner before I can even think about catching up to her. I hope when the time is right, things will be easier to mend with her now. But I'm giving her the same space I requested of Emmett.

I wonder when Emmett will come back to school. And when he does, if he'll be different. He has to be. Everything is different now.

A few days later, I see Lily sitting alone in the lunchroom. The social dynamics of school have changed completely now. All of the Elites have still been absent, including Emmett.

Still dealing with the aftermath of all their families have been implicated in and Thomas' death. At least for a little while, none of us have to worry about being seen talking to the wrong person. Everyone is much more relaxed. The laughter echoing through the rooms sounds less menacing. Kids seems to be talking about normal things again now that they're not terrified and wrapped up in the game of the Elites.

I take the opportunity to approach Lily's table, thinking maybe things will be different between us now. I stand there for a moment, my tray in my hands, trying to read her receptiveness. "Mind if I sit?" I ask finally, after she tries to ignore my presence.

"Go ahead," she answers, not looking up from her sandwich as she takes another bite.

I slide in across from her and start picking at the food on my tray, cutting my eyes up to her every few seconds. "I guess you've heard about everything that's happened?" I question her carefully.

"Thomas Jameson is dead," she replies curtly.

I nod, hoping she'll say more from there. "I'm surprised you didn't come talk to me when you found out. It's big news after all." But we fall back to silence. "So, did it help your situation at all?"

A smile curls across her lips, giving me hope. "Actually…I got a call from Julliard a few days after it happened," she gushes, still holding back from being too warm with me. "I've been accepted on full scholarship. They claimed the rescinded interest was a mistake."

"Lily, that's amazing!" I shriek, wishing things would go back to the way they were before between us. "And the other schools? Did you hear from any of them?"

"That's what's funny about it," she continues, turning cold again. "Julliard was the only one to call."

"I guess that is a little funny," I nod cluelessly. "But good…because that's the only one you cared about, right?"

She looks back down to her tray, spitting out a bite of food in disgust before going quiet yet again. I am completely lost as to why she still hates me or why she's being weird about the school calling.

"Come on, Lily…the Elites are gone. There's no reason to be angry with me anymore. It's not like they can punish you for being friendly to me now. We're free," my eyes light up optimistically, but she seems unconvinced.

"The only person left who has the kind of sway to turn things around with Julliard like that is Emmett," she proposes in an accusatory tone. "And the only person who knew Julliard was my top choice was you."

"What are you getting at?" I cut my eyes upwards and shake my head. Refusing to believe that Emmett would do anything nice for anyone. Especially after the way he has tried to keep Lily and I apart.

"What happened with you and Emmett?" she sneers. "You two must have got awfully close for him to want to do something like that for me."

"There's nothing going on with us," I defend bitterly. "I didn't even know about any of this until you told me. I had nothing to do with it, I swear."

"Well…that's hard to believe, but I sure hope it's true," she bites back. "Emmett is a monster. I would hate for the Elites to get taken down just so you can become the new Vivian."

"Don't be ridiculous!" I snap, the tremor in my voice sounding too defensive. "I could never be like her! I can't believe you'd even suggest something like that." I watch her tear away pieces of a roll only to throw them down again, forming a tiny pile of torn crumbs. "A lot has happened, Lily. I wish I had you to talk to during some of it. You probably could have helped."

"I doubt it," she murmurs. "I don't want to help anyone but myself from now on. I've learned my lesson."

"I don't understand why you're still being this way!" I force myself to lower my head and speak in a hushed pitch, to avoid screaming so loud the entire cafeteria hears me. "The Elites are gone! Sure, maybe Emmett will still be around, but he hasn't been at school since his dad died. And if you do think he took care of the Julliard thing…don't you think that proves maybe he's different than the rest of them?"

I think to myself that it's a good sign that he would do something like that for Lily even while I'm not giving him what he wants. Maybe he does stand some chance at being redeemed. But I don't dare try to argue that to Lily right now.

"I knew it," her eyes cut into me. "I knew you were going soft for him. He got to you, didn't he? Buttered you all up to make you think he wasn't like his dad and sister? Don't fall for it, Ophelia. You're only going to get hurt."

"I've already been hurt plenty," I quip back. "You have no idea." I study her to see if there is any hope of this conversation turning with a positive spin, but she seems dead set on keeping me as her enemy for some reason. "Look, if that's how you want to be…I'll leave you alone. But I hope you come around someday. I'm not with Emmett. We don't even speak anymore. And even if I do ever get 'buttered up' as you say…I could never be like Vivian."

"You keep telling yourself that, sweetheart," she answers coldly. "I know all about who your father is."

My blood runs cold. "What the hell do you know about my father?"

"I know he was one of them, and I heard he's back," she thunders.

The words of the police officers ring through my ears. If my father is still around, I don't want to know anything about it. I don't want to be held responsible for not reporting it or being faced with the choice of what to do with that information. As much as I want to pry into what exactly Lily knows, I want even more to protect myself and stay blissfully ignorant for as long as I can.

"I have to go," I quake, rushing up from seat without bothering to grab my tray. "Take care of yourself, Lily," I offer sincerely as I bolt from the cafeteria.

"You too, Ophelia," she calls out menacingly as I flee.

My chest burns as I race through the halls, looking over my shoulders in paranoia. Lily's words echoing through my brain with each step. He's back. What did that mean…he's back? What could possibly be left for him in Jameson? Surely, he was smart enough to know it'd never be safe here for him. He got his revenge and took out Thomas Jameson. Why wasn't that enough?

Unless…with Emmett's rise to power as the new alpha of Jameson…he latched on to work his way back up the top, taking back everything he lost and then some. Could they still be working together?

Why would Emmett do that for Lilly? Was that some sort of peace offering? An attempt to show me he's changed now that he's free from his father?

Lily's accusations rest sour in my gut. How could she ever think I would be anything like Vivian? I think back to what they did to her freshman year. How they took her in, treated her like a friend. All so they could humiliate her at the homecoming dance.

That was the same Emmett. Not too different from the way he declared his love for her in the schoolyard right after we had sex. Lily once had the hots for him too and even considered Vivian a friend. Was it just history repeating itself with me? Only the torture tactics intensified with age?

But maybe Emmett really was just always doing what he thought he had to. Looking tough and cool in front of his friends, because if he didn't they'd destroy him. And make sure his father made his life more of a living hell than he already did.

Emmett said I would understand more if I gave him a chance. If I knew more about what his life had been like. But opening myself up to his side of things only opened me up to more manipulation. More risk of harm. And I just don't think I can do it again.

I make my way down the mostly empty halls, trying to keep my breathing under control. I go to get my things for my next class out of my locker. I stop for a moment, smoothing my thumb across the metal of my lock. I want everything to be open like that. To have all the answers so I can be free from worrying and not knowing who to trust. The moment I was freed from the Jameson's, I was thrown into the crashing waves of the mind fuck that lingers after.

I shrug my shoulders and slam the door shut, jumping at a figure that appears suddenly behind it.

It's Emmett. He has dark circles under his eyes and his hair looks damp from sweat.

"What the hell are you doing here?" I gasp, feeling uneasy with his disheveled appearance.

"Come with me," he barks, not bothering to

explain before taking me by the hand and leading me into a janitor's closet.

I try to pull away, but he's too strong.

We shuffle in between shelves filled with chemicals and boxes of supplies. A cascade of mops and brooms clatter in the corner as we accidentally bump into them. He quickly turns me around, placing his hands across my shoulders in urgency.

I start to squirm to pull away, but I sense an urgency in him. He's looking over his shoulder in fear as footsteps echo beyond the door, but he seems to breathe more easily when he hears the unrecognizable voices of two girls laughing and talking about normal things.

"What's going on?" I shriek as he pushes me into the closet, locking the door behind us.

"Shhhhh, please," he's panicked, looking around with his palms suspended midair as he tries to quiet me. "Keep it down. I know I'm being watched."

I have never seen him so vulnerable and afraid. I don't want to buy into it, but a big part of me also just wants to take him into my arms like a scared little child.

Emmett's grown up in a life of privilege. He's never had to want for anything. He's intelligent, selfish and dangerous. He harbors a caged-in resentment toward everyone, and I am all too familiar with the violence he can inflict when he's angry. He's nothing like an innocent little child. But for some reason, as I look at him now, all I can see is a lost little boy. And I want to hold him.

"By who?" I answer in a more hushed tone to appease him.

"I don't know, but I need your help," he explains in terror. "Bernadette is missing."

"What do you mean she's missing?" I respond with a bored and dismissive sigh. "She's probably just hiding out somewhere. She doesn't have her precious Elite gang to back her up anymore and she can't stand to be on her own."

"No, she hasn't been home," he insists frantically. "I'm worried someone's taken her."

"Who!? Who's taken her?" I put my hands to his shoulders trying to calm him down. But I quickly stop myself from getting roped in. "Why are you coming to me with this? I told you I don't want to see you, and I definitely don't want to get dragged into another mess like before."

His muscular arms are tense beneath my touch. I realize this is the first time I've seen him in at least a week. It catches me off-guard instantly. Erasing all the work I've done to run him away. To sweat him out of my system.

Strands of his dark wavy hair hangs in his eyes,

damp with sweat. His magnetic gray eyes burn into me, pulling me back into my undeniable attraction for him. I bite my lip, wishing it would go away. I thought I was past this.

Thankfully, his mind is nowhere near any of that. He is completely lost in panic, saving me from my desires.

"You're the only one I can trust," he heaves. "Will you please come with me? Can we go back to your place? I'll explain everything."

I look into his eyes, paralyzed with uncertainty. I don't know if I should believe he really needs my help or if this is some kind of trick. It's funny that he thinks I'm the only one he can trust, while he is the last person on earth I feel like I can trust.

"Okay," I sigh, against my better judgment. "You can come with me to my house, but my mom and Brendan are home, and they're not going to be so easily charmed by you after what happened last time. You try anything and they'll kick you out."

He nods urgently, desperate to agree to whatever I ask if it means he finds some kind of sanctuary. He clings to my hand as we walk. He's afraid in a way I've never seen before, and I'm terrified to hear about what has him so shaken.

Thank you for reading RECKLESS RULES. Don't miss BROKEN RULES, book 2 in Emmett and Ophelia's love story, and be sure to join my SMS list below to don't miss any of my future books!

Want to read an exclusive FREE novella from Emmett's point of view? Check out book 1.5: RELENTLESS

Get an SMS alert when Rebel releases a new book:

Text REBEL to 77948

If you want to support me, consider leaving a review on Amazon. I'd love it!

ABOUT THE AUTHOR

Rebel Hart is an author of Contemporary and Dark Romance novels. Check out her debut series Diamond In The Rough.

NEVER MISS A NEW RELEASE:

Follow Rebel on Amazon

Follow Rebel on Bookbub

Text REBEL to 77948 to don't miss any of her books (US only) or sign up at www.RebelHart.net to get an email alert when her next book is out.

autorrebelhart@gmail.com

CONNECT WITH REBEL HART:

ALSO BY REBEL HART

Click for a full list of my books:

www.RebelHart.net

Made in the
USA
Columbia, SC

82034913R00248